P9-CET-046

"LOVE AND MADNESS ON THE FRONTIER
. . . totally involving from its very first words . . .
a dangerous journey into the soul, an exploration
of the relationships of men and women to each
other, to their environments and—ultimately and
most devastatingly—to themselves . . . impressive
. . . shattering . . . convincing . . . nothing less than
a study of the human spirit."
—*Los Angeles Times Book Review*

"A FINELY CRAFTED NOVEL . . . told with
smooth economy . . . re-creates a seamless and
accurate territorial Nebraska . . . with characters so
real the reader resents it when one dies."
—*The Kansas City Star*

"GLENDON SWARTHOUT HAS DONE IT
AGAIN . . . A novel of real people, real places,
real emotion, real conflict. As real as feeling the
gritty dust on the hat brim after a long day's ride
across the American frontier." —Douglas C. Jones

"GLENDON SWARTHOUT IS A MASTER
STORYTELLER . . . *THE HOMESMAN* IS ONE
HELL OF A RIDE." —*Los Angeles Daily News*

"CAPTURES BOTH THE ADVENTUROUS
SPIRIT AND REALITIES OF FRONTIER LIFE."
—*Booklist*

"MOVING . . . AN EXCELLENT NOVEL!"
—*Needham Times*

UNTAMED ACTION ON
THE WESTERN FRONTIER

☐ **THE TERREL BRAND by E.Z. Woods.** Owen Terrel came back from the Civil War looking for peace. He and his brother carved out a cattle kingdon in West Texas, but then a beautiful woman in danger arrived, thrusting Owen into a war against an army of bloodthirsty outlaws. He would need every bullet he had to cut them down.... (158113—$3.50)

☐ **CONFESSIONS OF JOHNNY RINGO by Geoff Aggeler.** It was a showdown for a legend: Johnny Ringo. Men spoke his name in the same hushed breath as Jesse and Frank James, the Youngers, Billy the Kid. But those other legendary outlaws were gone. Only he was left, and on his trail was the most deadly lawman in the West. (159888—$4.50)

☐ **SALT LAKE CITY by A.R. Riefe.** Mormon settlers and U.S. soldiers are on the brink of catastrophic conflict—in a Western epic of challenge and triumph. (163265—$4.50)

☐ **CHEYENNE FORTUNES 2 by A.R. Riefe.** As the Civil War ended, cattlemen, sheepherders and farmers in Wyoming vied for the land against the fierce Cheyenne and Sioux. Dedicated officer Lincoln Rhilander had to defy his superiors to rout the redskins ... and had to choose between duty and desire in the arms of a beautiful woman. Stunning adventure! (157516—$4.50)

☐ **A LAND REMEMBERED by Patrick D. Smith.** Tobias MacIvey started with a gun, a whip, a horse and a dream of taming a wilderness that gave no quarter to the weak. He was the first of an unforgettable family who rose to fortune from the blazing guns of the Civil War, to the glitter and greed of the Florida Gold Coast today. (158970—$4.95)

☐ **THE HOMESMAN by Glendon Swarthout.** A spinster, an army deserter, and four women who have gone out of their minds and out of control on a trek through the wildest west that turns into the ultimate test for them all. A Spur Award winner. "As good as novels get."—Cleveland Plain Dealer. (164296—$4.95)

Prices slightly higher in Canada

Buy them at your local bookstore or use this convenient coupon for ordering.

NEW AMERICAN LIBRARY
P.O. Box 999, Bergenfield, New Jersey 07621

Please send me the books I have checked above. I am enclosing $_____
(please add $1.00 to this order to cover postage and handling). Send check or money order—no cash or C.O.D.'s. Prices and numbers are subject to change without notice.

Name_____

Address_____

City _____ State _____ Zip Code _____
Allow 4-6 weeks for delivery.
This offer is subject to withdrawal without notice.

THE
HOMESMAN

Glendon Swarthout

A SIGNET BOOK

NEW AMERICAN LIBRARY

A DIVISION OF PENGUIN BOOKS USA INC.

PUBLISHER'S NOTE

This book is a work of fiction. Names, characters, places, and incidents either are the product of the author's imagination or are used fictitiously, and any resemblance to actual persons, living or dead, events, or locales is entirely coincidental.

NAL BOOKS ARE AVAILABLE AT QUANTITY DISCOUNTS WHEN USED TO PROMOTE PRODUCTS OR SERVICES. FOR INFORMATION PLEASE WRITE TO PREMIUM MARKETING DIVISION, NEW AMERICAN LIBRARY, 1633 BROADWAY, NEW YORK, NEW YORK 10019.

Copyright © 1988 by Glendon Swarthout

All rights reserved. No reproduction of this book in whole or in part or in any form may be made without written authorization of the copyright owner. For information address Weidenfeld & Nicholson, A Division of Wheatland Corporation, 841 Broadway, New York, New York 10003.

This is an authorized reprint of a hardcover edition published by Weidenfeld & Nicholson, and simultaneously in Canada by General Publishing Company, Ltd.

The lyrics from the song "Weevily Wheat" are from *The Penguin Book of American Folk Songs,* edited by Alan Lomax, © 1966 by Viking Penguin Inc. Reprinted by permission of the publisher.

 SIGNET TRADEMARK REG. U.S. PAT. OFF. AND FOREIGN COUNTRIES
REGISTERED TRADEMARK—MARCA REGISTRADA
HECHO EN DRESDEN, TN, U.S.A.

SIGNET, SIGNET CLASSIC, MENTOR, ONYX, ROC, PLUME, MERIDIAN and NAL BOOKS are published by New American Library, a division of Penguin Books USA Inc., 1633 Broadway, New York, New York 10019

First Signet Printing, March, 1990

1 2 3 4 5 6 7 8 9

PRINTED IN THE UNITED STATES OF AMERICA

Kate: then, now, ever

THE
GATHER

S.*E. 2, Section 10, Township 8, Range 4E.*

In late summer Line told him she was two months along. Another mouth to feed. And besides, she said, forty-three was too old. She said it would be a melon-head or all crippled up or have a harelip because God must be angry with them because look what had already happened this year.

In the spring they lost all but one cow and her calf to blackleg.

At that time also Virgil, their only son, sixteen, a real go-ahead boy, up and ran away to scratch for fool's gold in California.

Hail in July flattened their wheat, and in August, as the corn was heading out, two weeks of winds right out of Hell burned up so much of it that come fall they snapped the pitiful small ears and shelled them by hand rather than bothering them to the mill. Twenty acres of wheat gone and thirty of corn. Cash crops. God made the weather, Vester said.

It was March now, and Line went on reciting their woes like a child a poem, and he heard her out because she seldom spoke these days and maybe it would help whatever ailed her.

Then, before the first snow, when they knew it would be nip and tuck to feed themselves through the winter, they sent Loney, their eldest girl, fourteen miles away to drudge for a family far better off. For a third of a bed and keep, the poor child.

Then one of their oxen got the warbles, worms under the skin. You could cut open the swelling and douse the worms with coal oil to kill them if you had any coal oil. Let be, the worms would suck the very soul out of the ox, Line was sure, and come spring, yoked up, it would fall down dead in the field, the poor creature.

Then this winter of damnation. How had they sinned? It was so cold they were out of wood and corncobs by the end of January and had to heat and cook with hay cats. Twice when it must have been forty below they brought the two pigs into the house for the night to save them from freezing, but another night they failed to and a pack of wolves ate them down to the bones. The blizzards were so fierce you were blind three feet from the door. They had to run a taut rope from the door to the stable and a second rope from there to the outhouse or lose their way. Reverend Dowd stopped by in January during a short thaw, and likewise Mary Bee came from her claim in February to bring them food; but except for these two, the circuit rider and their nearest neighbor, the family had set eyes on no other human in five months. The school-church was snowed in, no one ever hollered greeting, and they ached for the sweet sound of a bow put to a fiddle. Father, mother, and the three girls shivered and were sickly and drank from the same dipper.

And now a baby, Line concluded.

Vester was forty-four. He put a hand on her belly and said a baby was not his fault. A man had his needs, he said, and the Almighty had provided woman for those needs.

She pushed his hand away.

Ever since she told him last summer she was two months along he had watched her change. She would go hours speechless. Some days in clear weather he would come in from the field to meet her outdoors standing staring over the prairie as though there were something to see. She slept restless. She was cranky. She picked at her plate. She had headaches. Proud of her hair once, black once, cut and washed and brushed like clockwork, she let it grow long and gray and dirty. The girls said some days she would sweep the house out three times, letting in the cold, but other days he would enter to find her hindside on a chair throwing her eyes around. She fretted him. He studied her and was minded of warbles. A worm under her skin, inside her, was sucking out the strong, cheerful, loving wife she had been, and there was no coal oil for that. A worm? The baby?

Vester and Theoline Belknap lay beside each other

in bed on the hay tick, listening. It was night in
early March, and that afternoon the wind had
switched to blow warm from the south, warm enough
to let the fire go out in the stove after supper. It
was raining heavy. The sod and hay and pole and
dirt roof of a sod house wouldn't turn much water.
Small streams of muddy water poured down into
the four buckets they had placed before retiring.
Rain was a tussle between sleep and mud. Unless
the buckets were emptied out the door often, in the
morning the dirt floor was a bog. They listened. Far
off, the coyotes yapped. Nearby, on the other side
of the quilt behind them, hung up to partition a
third of the house for a back bedroom, one of the
girls spoke in her sleep. There were three girls left
at home after they had to send Loney away. Junia
was eight, Aggie six, and Vernelle four. The house
was built of sod blocks three feet long and a foot
wide, turned up out of virgin prairie sod by a breaking plow behind the oxen and laid side by side to
form a wall three feet thick. Measured on the inside
the house was eighteen feet long and fifteen wide.
It had one wooden door on rope hinges which would
not close tight and one glass window, framed, through
which they couldn't see because it was so wavery.
Behind the quilt was the girls' bed and before it was
what they called the "front room," where they all
lived. At meals they sat around a sawhorse table,
father and mother in the two chairs nearest the
stove, one girl on a cracker box, and two girls on
the side of their parents' bed. Line's other furnish-

ings were few. She had two shelves pegged into the sod wall for cutlery, cooking utensils, and dishpan, and a small, cloth-fronted cupboard for salt and saleratus and rye coffee and such. Finally there was the trunk she had brought when they came out west three years ago containing her valuables: a hat she had never worn, a dress of real silk she was saving for her daughters' weddings, a Bible, daguerreo-types of her dear mother and father back in Kentucky, in Heaven now, a tortoise-shell comb, her sewing basket, a looking glass into which she couldn't bear to look, letters from home, her wedding ring, and the seven dollars she had earned sewing for Mary Bee.

"When're you due?" he asked. She moved, trying to make herself comfortable. She was big and the hay tick was lumpy. "Two weeks," she said.

They lay in the dark listening to the buckets and the warm wind blow over the world. By and by Vester said he had made up his mind. This was the third thaw, and this being March he believed it would hold. They had her seven dollars to their name. They must have food or go hungry, seed for a crop or go broke. He said he intended to ride to Loup early in the morning and sign a chattel mort-gage at the bank, take the money and buy food, order and pay in advance for seed, pick up their mail at the store, and be home by dark or there-abouts. She lay silent a spell, worrying about a chattel mortgage he reckoned, the homesteader's plague, and he was dozing off when she spoke, sud-denly, rousing him.

"You leave me and the baby'll come."

"Line, I have to go."

"It'll be cursed."

Come daylight Vester got up and dressed and went to the stable to feed the stock and saddle his horse. Line got up and dressed and started a fire in the stove and went to the outhouse. On return she emptied the buckets and waked the girls and standing in mud made corn dodgers. All she had left was cornmeal, which she mixed with water until it was too thick to run, then fried. She made extra, enough for herself and the girls later. Vester came in and she used the last of her sorghum molasses on his dodgers and the last of her coffee, which was rye parched brown, for two cups for him. He guaranteed again he'd be home by dark. Loup was sixteen miles north and east of their claim. He tried to kiss her on the cheek, but she turned her face from him.

After she fed the girls she put them to twisting hay cats and piling them against the wall. They brought in hay, prairie grass, from the stack under the snow outside and twisted it tight into rolls a foot long. Hay burned hot but fast, and the stove needed steady tending.

Midmorning the wind veered around from south to north and blew biting cold.

In the afternoon it commenced to snow. Then she knew Vester wouldn't be home before morning and she would have the baby. It was snowing too hard to risk sending Junia the two miles to fetch Mary

Bee for help. She would have to help herself, however she could. God made the weather, Vester said.

Just before dark she went to the stable and fed the oxen and cow and calf. She laid a hand on the flank of the ox with warbles, right on a swelling, and was sure she could feel the worm move. Then she returned to the house, bringing with her two picket ropes.

She sent the girls to use the outhouse. While they were gone she tied a rope to each of the bedposts at the foot of the bed.

When the girls were back she gave them a cold dodger apiece and told them to get into bed with their clothes on and to stay there and not come past the quilt, into the front room, no matter what.

It was pitch dark now. She lit a candle. In the trunk she found her thin gold wedding ring, dropped it in water, and set it on the stove to boil. On the bed she placed scissors, thread, and the dishpan where they would be handy.

She took the pan from the stove, let the water cool a bit, drank it from the pan, and replaced her wedding band in the trunk. Since she was a girl she'd heard that wedding-ring tea would comfort a body and ease your labor pains.

She stuffed the stove with twists, pulled the cracker box next to the bed, set the candle on it, took off her boots and trousers and feedsack drawers, settled herself in bed with both pillows at her back, closed eyes, and waited.

She heard the girls whispering.

In an hour or so she felt squeezings inside, and presently her water broke, wetting the bed. In a few minutes the labor pains commenced. They went on a good hour, she reckoned, coming closer and closer together. She tried not to make a sound, but soon the pain was so fierce she groaned and cried out so loud that the girls, scared to death themselves, began to cry like a choir of cats.

The fire in the stove died. The house was cold, but she was wringing wet with sweat.

Suddenly the pain was steady, and she knew her time had come. She sat up and threw the covers aside and raised her knees and drew her wampus, the long hickory shirt worn over trousers, up to her breasts. Reaching, she took hold of the two ropes tied to the bedposts, one in each hand, and pulled on them as she pushed with her lower parts, pulling and pushing and screaming now and her girls screaming.

The baby presented itself head-first.

She let go of the ropes and freed herself of it and saw that it was perfect and a girl.

She lifted it by its slippery legs and shook it until it began to cry.

She laid it between her legs and ran a forefinger around inside of its mouth to rid it of mucus and to make sure its tongue was straight forward, not back, so it would not strangle. Finding scissors and thread, she tied the umbilical cord and cut it. Then she wiped the tiny thing off tenderly with bedding, nestled it beside her, placed the dishpan between her legs, and fell back against the pillows, dead tired.

The girls were silent now, but she thought she could almost hear hearts beating behind the quilt.

In another minute or two she received the afterbirth in the dishpan, but she continued to bleed, so she rubbed her abdomen to stanch the flow.

As soon as she was strong enough, she got out of bed and by the light of the candle took the baby up and cradled it in her arms. Wearing only shirt and wampus, she crossed the muddy floor and went outdoors. It was still deep dark, but it had stopped snowing and there was no need to find her way by the ropes.

She went barefoot by the path to the outhouse, opened the door, stepped inside, and pushed the naked baby down the hole head-first.

Vester Belknap reached home before noon. He saw blood on the snow. He dismounted directly, left the horse, and entered the house.

Theoline Belknap lay in bed throwing her eyes around the room. He saw blood on the bed and the guttered candle and the bloody dishpan tipped over on the floor. There was no sign of the girls.

"Line, what's happened?" he asked.

At the sound of his voice, the girls behind the quilt began to bawl.

"Pa! Oh, Pa!" they bawled.

"What's the matter?" he cried at them.

"She had the baby!"

"Where is it?" he cried. He looked at his wife. "Line, where's the baby?"

"Tha," she said.

He stared at her. "Where's it at!" he demanded.

"Tha," she said. "Tha, tha, tha, tha, tha, tha, tha, tha."

On a thought he roared at the quilt. "Junia, did she leave the house?"

"Yesss!"

"Christ Lord!" he cried, and rushed outdoors.

It was as though a great grave had been opened and light, blinding light, let in. From a sky of blue the sun blessed what was below. The body of the plains, cold, silent, white, vast, was laid bare at last. Men and women and children, long buried there by winter, came out of the dirt like creatures to see what the months of darkness, storm, and death had done to one another. Some despaired. Some thought on spring. Some gave thanks to God.

His representative, the Reverend Alfred Dowd, rode out on his nag in the early morning. A ragged woollen muffler was wound around his neck and nose and ears and tied on top to hold his hat on. For food and shelter he depended on his flock. For the wages of sin and the IOU's of salvation, for marrying and burying and carrying the news, they depended on him. Alfred Dowd was a circuit rider. Methodist by denomination, he had six appointments, or churches, or what passed for churches, on his circuit; and if the weather was fair enough and the trails passable enough, and if he rode hard enough and preached fast enough three times every Sunday, he could bring the Word to each congregation every two weeks. Given these if's, Dowd did. Between the fire and brimstone he attempted also to visit every family in his charge once or twice a season, breakfasting at one place, dining at a second, supping and sleeping at a third. It was a matter of speculation which covered the more miles on the back of a horse, the minister or the doctor. Dowd was generally acknowledged the winner, but he had the lighter load, the Good Book and a change of socks, while the doctor, Jessup by name, was slowed by a black bag, a whiskey bottle, and an ability to sleep in the saddle which permitted his mount to poke. Dowd was probably the more useful to his people, too. He sat up with the sick. He advised the troubled. He consoled the bereaved. He restored to harmony the discord between husband and wife. He bucked up couples close to foreclosure. "There's more in the man than there is in the land," he would say to them. He was not too holy to roll up his sleeves when needed, and pitch in with a fork or an ax or a plow. He had been known to wash dishes. His cash income last year had been twenty-eight dollars, but as he sowed he reaped a harvest of chickens, hogs, calves, eggs, garden truck, and wood for his stove. He had two small children and a wife twenty years younger and worshipful. His only expletive was "Bosh." He was respected for long rides and esteemed for short prayers and sermons.

He stepped lively. He was welcomed everywhere. Alfred Dowd was beloved.

It was custom in the Territory to ride up and wait some rods before a sod house until someone came out and you were recognized before you rode near and dismounted. On this faultless March day Vester Belknap burst out of his house to meet the minister, trying simultaneously to run and haul on his coat.

"Oh, Reveren', Reveren', you ain't come a minute too soon!"

Dowd couldn't tell whether the man's eyes watered with sun or with tears.

"It's Line! She's gone crazy on me!"

"Come now."

"Day before yestiddy! I come home from Loup an' she'd had the baby an' killed it!"

Dowd was dismounting. "You can't mean it."

"She did so! Crazier'n a bedbug!"

"Calm yourself, Vester," said Dowd, boots on the snow. "Tell me."

The homesteader was built like a barrel, and it was as though the bung had been pulled. A horrified Alfred Dowd listened, untying and unwinding his muffler to bare his face, feeling the palms of his hands perspire. Belknap finished. "Her own babe, her own babe. Kin you b'lieve it?"

The minister shook his head, then asked, irrelevantly, "What have you done with the child?"

"Put 'er in the stable, high up. Wolves. She'll keep till I kin get in the ground."

"We must have a service."

"If you say so."

"In the meantime our concern must be for your poor wife." Dowd glanced at the house and saw in the wavery window what seemed to be the faces of three young girls peering at him. "I'll go in and see her."

"Oh, no." Belknap set his belly between them. "Nope, I don't want no one t'see 'er. Not like she is."

"Are you ashamed of her?"

The man colored. He knew what he wanted to say, and on the other hand, what he should say. "Course I'm not! She's my wife!" he cried. Line wasn't herself, though, not by a long shot, he insisted. When she talked you couldn't make sense of it, just noises. He had to feed her by hand, like a baby, or she'd starve. He had to carry her to the outhouse and pull up her clothes and set her down or she'd bust her bladder. "Does that sound like a wife?" he demanded, convinced he had made his case. "Is that like a human bein' atall? You tell me, Reveren'!"

Dowd nodded. "I understand. Still, someone had better see her. Let me pass, Vester." He smiled. "Remember, when I go in, the Lord goes with me."

Belknap stared at him a moment, then subsided and moved, and the minister stepped lively for the door, removing his hat.

He was inside the house only a short while, and when he came out he walked slowly, almost unsteadily to his nag, hat in hand, and laid his forehead against the animal's neck and closed his eyes.

He thought of his own wife. When he raised his head, squinting into the sun, Belknap was nowhere to be seen. Just as he was about to call, Vester emerged from the outhouse, buckling his trousers, and came to him.

"Let us pray," Dowd said.

They bowed heads.

"Dear Lord, restore this woman to Thy grace. And comfort her husband in his time of trial. We ask Thee in the name of all those afflicted in mind and spirit, and those who love them. Amen."

The minister put on his hat. "Vester, I am truly sorry," he said.

Vester was vindicated. "Told you so, Reveren'. But sorry don't help. What in hell—I mean, what'll I do? I cain't live like this. She cain't cook or clean or nothin'. She's no use to anyone, leastwise herself."

Dowd was rewinding his muffler. "I've been thinking. It may not be good for the girls to be with her long. Why can't you send them over to Mary Bee's? She'll take them in."

"Oh, no." Belknap was stubborn as before. "I won't be alone with 'er. Gives me the shakes. Think some more."

The minister sighed. "Well, what did you intend to do?"

"Me? What kin I do? I figgered you'd come by or I'd get word to you someways."

Dowd sighed again. He tied the muffler on top. He asked where Theoline hailed from originally, and Belknap replied from Kentucky, little town in a hollow called Slade's Dell, same place he did, and she still had folks there, sister and a brother.

"That's where she must go, then," said Dowd.

"How?"

Dowd said they'd have to have a homesman. He'd heard of two other wives in the same pitiful state, one up northeast of Loup named Petzke, and one over east, a Mrs. Svendsen, which, with Theoline, made three, the same number as last year. "We can manage it soon, I predict." He squinted at the sky. "This day is a sign. We'll have spring before we know it." He took up his reins. If he had hoped for dinner at the Belknap place, he had hoped in vain. "I will pray for her, Vester."

"Pray for me. Reveren'. She's past it."

Dowd frowned. "You'll hear from me in a week or so."

Belknap frowned. "I better. I cain't put up with this for long."

The minister hopped on his nag and looked off over a world glazed a pure, almost a divine, white. "This winter," he said through his muffler, as though to himself. "Oh, this damnable winter."

Belknap shoved hands into coat pockets and snuffled. "Why'd she do it, Dowd?" he pleaded, pulling a long and sorrowful face. "You're a parson, Why in hell'd she do this t'me?"

Alfred Dowd rode away from him.

Charley Linens picked up John Cox at his place and the two men rode south and west. In the scabbard by his saddle each carried a rifle, loaded.

In the late fall, just before the first snow of that winter, a young bachelor named Andy Giffen had left his claim and gone home to Pennsylvania. On the door of his dugout he posted a sign: GONE BACK EAST TO GET A WIFE.

This was not unusual. If they were able, homesteaders often took advantage of a winter to cross the Missouri and return to their roots for sundry reasons: to visit family, to enjoy civilization, to scratch and claw in court over inheritances, to borrow money from prosperous in-laws, or, in Andy's instance, to find a girl, paint her a rosy picture of life on the frontier, wed her and bed her and knock her up, and escort his darling and her belly back with him come spring. Brides-to-be were scarcer than oysters in the Territory, where men outnumbered women eight to one. Andy had staked a claim to a hundred sixty choice acres near the Kettle River and lived on it two years and taken two crops from it. He had built a snug home by digging into the side of a ravine, fronting the hole with sod blocks, installing a door and a window of wood that swung open and shut, and running his stovepipe upward through the earth to clear prairie level by several feet to allow for snow. Andy Giffen was twenty-nine and ripe. He had a house and a fine team of horses and a good milch cow and plenty of tools and implements and seed for spring. All he lacked to be sitting pretty were a wife and children.

So he thought. He also lacked registration papers for his claim. He had complied with two provisions of the Preemption Act by living on his land and improving it, but he had not yet got around to appearing at the nearest land office, in Wamego, seventy miles away, to file and to pay the $1.25 an acre appraised value. Andy calculated to kill two birds with one stone—to bring his brand-new bride home by way of Wamego, to sign papers and pay up and show her off at the same time. It was a small matter. Several of his neighbors were in the same fix and seemed unconcerned. Technically they, too, were "squatters," with appurtenant "squatter's rights," and possession was nine points of the law. But what he did not reckon with was the fact that where there were squatters, there were bound to be claim-jumpers, and sure enough, soon after he left on his matrimonial mission, one such individual tore down his gone-east-wife sign and moved into his house.

Charley Linens and John Cox added Martin Polhemus and his rifle and the three rode on together toward Andy Giffen's place, straight of face, speaking little. The day was dark. The thaw continued. The snow was crusted. Under the snow they could hear water running now and then, and the pull of a hoof from the snow made a sucking sound.

No one knew a particle about the jumper. Some had heard his name was "Briggs," others "Moore." He could be a loner, working his game on his own. He could be in cahoots with a lawyer in Wamego, which, it was said, had more lawyers than human residents. In either case, claim-jumpers were as hard to get rid of as fleas, and Mr. and Mrs. Giffen would soon have one hell of a homecoming. If the jumper offered to sell, it would be at a price Andy could never afford. If he took the matter to court in Wamego, the lawyers would bleed him white. If he got fighting mad, he might face a gun. No two ways about it, his friends agreed, come spring, before Andy returned, the varmint would have to high-tail it or have his hide nailed to a wall. It was spring now, or looked to be, and time to get down to business. Andy would have done as much for them.

So they rode on through the snow and darkening day, Linens, Cox, and Polhemus, until they spotted smoke rising out of Andy's stovepipe. Then they rode to the north of it a few rods and down into the ravine. They passed Andy's stable, and there was nothing in it but the rear end of an ugly horse. They reined up about thirty feet in front of the dugout door. Charley Linens slipped his rifle from its scabbard and balanced it across the pommel of his saddle, in plain sight, and the other two did likewise.

"Hullo in there!" called Charley.

Taking his sweet time, a man opened the door and stepped out and stood facing them. They noticed two things. He wore no coat, just trousers and the top of his longjohns, which meant he was keeping himself mighty comfortable burning Andy's wood. And sticking out of his belt was the handle of a big repeater.

"Your name Briggs?" Charley inquired.

"Might be."

"Moore?" asked John Cox.

"Might be."

He was a cool customer. In his jaw he had a chew, and he let it rest.

"Now you know," said Charley, "this here is Andy Giffen's place. He's a friend of ours. He's gone back east to get him a wife, but he'll be back any day now. What d'you propose to do about that?"

"I propose to stay."

This riled Martin Polhemus. He was a poor man. To keep his feet from freezing through the holes in his boots, he wound them with strips of meal sack. "Shit," snapped Martin Polhemus. "You're a damn jumper."

"Where's his papers?" Briggs asked.

"Where's yours?" countered John Cox.

"Possession nine points of the law," said Briggs.

This shut them up for a minute. The jumper looked them over and spat some juice.

"Where's his team?" inquired Charley Linens.

"Sold 'em."

"Where's his cow?" Cox asked. John Cox was the most peaceable of the three. "Andy had a right good cow."

"Ate it."

"You sonvabitch," said Martin Polhemus, and laid a hand on the stock of his rifle.

Briggs did a sudden, peculiar thing. He had a snake for a right arm, and he snaked that pistol out of his belt and raised arm and fired straight up in the air. The report ricocheted between the banks of the ravine like whipcracks. Briggs put away the repeater. The three visitors sat their horses like stone men. They figured the gun was a Navy Colt's.

After a time Charley Linens said, "All right you listen, Mister. We aim to have your thievin' ass off this place before Andy shows up. We'll do it however we have to. So our advice is, hop to it."

Briggs or Moore or whoever he was took a long steady look at Charley, then the others. Then he unbuttoned his trousers, took out his pecker, and pissed in the snow. It steamed. Then he buttoned up, turned his back on them, and stepped into the dugout and shut the door as though it was time for supper.

He saw Mary Bee Cuddy from a mile away, a dot of black on white near her house. Riding, he reflected. He had heard from neighbors that she often stood so when the weather was clement, staring out over the spaces in hopes of seeing—what? A buffalo? A rider? A wagon train? Or a miracle, a tree growing, just one tree to remind her of home? He wondered if there was a way to measure loneliness.

When he came within half a mile he waved and she waved back, and both were reassured. They had neither seen nor heard of each other for two months, since the January thaw. The minister knew Mary Bee Cuddy almost as well, perhaps, as did the Lord. Three years ago she had journeyed alone by train and steamboat and stagecoach from upper York

State to take a school south of Wamego. She taught a year, then resigned abruptly and bought this claim from a new widow who was going back east because her husband had been caught unarmed in a field and killed and mutilated by Pawnees. Mary Bee had evidently come into some money. She paid six hundred dollars cash for the claim and hired men to build her a new sod house and stable and even an outhouse of sod, the marvel of the neighborhood because no wind could blow it down. Several other old maids in his congregations were trying to prove claims up by themselves, but none made a go of it as successfully as Mary Bee. She taught herself how to hang on to a horse and use a rifle like a dragoon. She could cook and sew and keep house and track of her neighbors from the start, but she soon learned how to plow, plant, cut, bind, shuck, and get her grain to a grist mill, and to know when her stock needed doctoring. She set a fine table and her door and heart were always open. It was she who raised enough cain to help him get a church-school constructed, and gave a hundred dollars to the cause. It was her gifts of food, Dowd knew for a fact, which had seen the Belknaps, her nearest neighbors, through a good part of the winter. She rode her own generous circuit, cheering the dejected, nursing the sick, and playing auntie to the little ones. Oh, she was a pillar. She was educated, she appreciated the finer things, she was gritty as all get-out. In his opinion, Mary Bee Cuddy was an altogether admirable human being. He wondered if there was a way to measure character.

Notwithstanding, he worried as his nag whuffed up the rise toward her. She had to be on the shady side of thirty by now. He had hoped, as everyone had, that she and Andy Giffen might make a match, but Andy had gone back east for a wife. In good weather a lone lady might be busy, visit and be visited, but how had she survived a winter like this, eating solitary food, talking to knife and fork, going to bed at night with the wind? If others fell by the wayside, dear women and strong, loved by men, how had she, single and unloved, kept her sanity? He wished he bore her glad tidings now, but he had none. He wondered how to tell her about Theoline Belknap.

Dowd reached her. He dropped reins, hopped out of his saddle, she came to him, and they clasped hands, both hands. Hers were bigger than his, and she was much taller than he.

"Spring!" she said.

"Spring!" said Alfred Dowd.

They grinned at each other while a wind blew over them, a warm wind. She let go and took his reins and asked him to guess what they'd be having for dinner, he couldn't, and she said antelope. Yesterday afternoon she'd spotted one below the house being chased by wolves. Running for her rifle, she shot the lead wolf, which was closing in, and dropped the buck with a clean shoulder shot at three hundred yards—some shooting, eh? She dragged it in, dressed it out, and they'd have antelope steak for their main course, she'd started dinner as soon as she saw him coming. Did he approve?

Dowd smiled approval, then put on a serious face. "I have bad news. Do you want it now or later?"

"Now."

He told her about Theoline Belknap. In the telling she turned away from him, slowly.

"Dear God," she said.

"Yes."

"Was it a boy or a girl?"

"A girl."

"How is Vester taking it?"

"As you'd expect. He blames Theoline."

"As you'd expect. Why, oh, why didn't he send the girls to me?"

"He claims he can't be alone with her."

Mary Bee stood a moment more, then led his horse toward her stable. "You have a wash," she said, "and go on in. I'll be along." She wanted to be by herself.

Dowd brought basin, soap, and a towel outside the house, washed, emptied the basin, went inside, inspected the antelope frying, had a sniff, and a second sniff, then removed his coat and sat down at the table. Mary Bee came in and set the table and worked at the big Premium stove, and words passed between them only once.

"Guess what I'm ordering," she said.

"I couldn't."

"A melodeon."

He knew she loved music. "You aren't."

"Yup. I don't trust freighting a piano, so as soon

as I can get into Loup I'll order a Mason & Hamlin." She spoke almost defiantly. "Back home I used to play the piano by the hour. I can't live without real music much longer."

"You'll have the first melodeon in the Territory," said the minister.

Waiting, hungry, he admired her home again. For the time and place it was grand. The floor was laid of cottonwood planks, and on it were several rag rugs. Her sod walls were plastered and whitewashed, which thwarted the bedbugs. She had real chairs, including a Boston rocker, and a table and a chest of drawers over which were hung two tintypes, framed, one of her father, he assumed, a glum, bearded man, and one of her sister Dorothy perhaps. On another wall was a large, colorful print of what appeared to be Niagara Falls. Her bedroom, which he had never seen, was in back, divided by an interior wall from this room, and he had heard she slept on a feather bed. From this living-dining-room–kitchen a carpentered ladder ran up to a loft, used for storage but also as a spare bedroom for guests. Everything was neat as a pin.

Then she served them a feast—antelope steaks, fried potatoes, corn bread and molasses, dried-apple pie, and Arbuckle's Ariosa coffee, which his wife had informed him went for thirty-five cents the pound. When she sat down, he bowed his head. Mary Bee bowed hers.

"Lord," he improvised, "bless this lady and her table. Let me dine here as long as I'm able. Amen."

When he looked up his eyes twinkled, and she thanked him with the stoutest smile she could muster. They ate and talked about the weather and winter and neighbors and lack of mail and spring and coming summer, but no matter their effort to be cheery, to enjoy the meal and each other and their privacy, Theoline Belknap ate with them, and there were silences.

"She's not the worst of it," said Dowd after one such.

"No?"

"No. There are two others. One up north of Loup named Petzke, and one west named Svendsen. Both in the same sad state. I don't know the circumstances yet."

A silence.

"Then there are four," said Mary Bee.

"Four?"

"The last thaw, Harriet Linens came by and told me. There's a family near them named Sours, both of them very young, with small children. The wife, just a girl, has lost her mind. How and why, Harriet didn't know. She said it was pitiful, though."

Licking molasses from his lips, the minister thought. "Sours. Sours. I know them. They're in one of my congregations." He sighed. "Four. What a shame. We'll have to have a homesman."

"What's that?"

He put down his cutlery. "That's what I call him." Last year, Dowd said, there were three demented women, wives, on his circuit, and by spring something had to be done with them. Two were actually dangerous, homicidal, and the other one kept running away. "Well, I got the three husbands together—they're responsible, after all—and had them draw lots. The one who lost was the homesman. The other two chipped in and supplied the rig and team and supplies—the entire matter kept as secret as possible. The homesman gathered the three women and took them back across the river to Hebron, Iowa. Last year the man who lost turned out to be a fine fellow name McAllister, a good Christian. He had them in Hebron in five weeks, and without much difficulty as I recall." In Hebron, the minister continued, the Ladies Aid Society of the Methodist Church was run by a sterling woman named Altha Carter, wife of the Reverend Carter there. She had raised funds by appeals to congregations back east, and when the unfortunate women arrived with McAllister, they were passed into the care of three volunteer members of the Society, who in turn escorted them by railroad eastward, home, which was wherever they had family or close relatives. He paused, and pulled his dried-apple pie closer. "I presume they do something like this other places out here. It's not much of a system, I admit, but show me an alternative."

Mary Bee had listened. "Three, last year. I never heard a word of it."

"Things like that aren't talked about. They're just done."

She brought the pot from the stove and refilled their cups. "Bless you," she said.

"Bosh. Necessity the mother of invention, you know. Oh, I suppose someday we'll have all the trappings of civilization, insane asylums and so on. But we've been a Territory less than a year, and building an asylum is one of the last things a legislature gets around to. For now, this is the best we can do. I must say, though, it asks a lot of one man."

"Eat your pie."

He was glad to, and soon applauded the banquet by sitting back in his chair and groaning. "Best dinner I've had in a month of Sundays. Bless you."

"I dine like this every day."

Neither smiled. They sat through another silence looking at each other. Each surprised the other. His hair was a bright, startling red, and salted. She had a woman's eyes, but her big, square face was based on a man's square jaw.

"Where will you head now?" she asked.

"I'd better go see Sours, the poor boy."

"I'll go over to the Belknaps in the morning. I'll take a hindquarter of the antelope."

Dowd thought. "Tell Vester to be at Kettle Church a week from today. In the afternoon. We'll hold the drawing then. I'll tell young Sours today, and I'll see that Petzke and Svendsen know. A week from today."

"Vester won't do it."

"He must."

"If he loses the drawing, he won't," said Mary Bee. "He's lazy. He's ignorant. He's a whiner. Theoline's the one. She's been his backbone."

The minister frowned, pushed back his chair, rose, and began to wrestle into his coat. "He must. He's responsible for her, just like the others. I could say several things about him myself, but I will not be uncharitable. The Lord wouldn't like it." He tied his coat closed with twine. "Do what you can with him tomorrow," he appealed. "I'll appreciate it." Winding his muffler, this day around his neck, he stepped to the door. "I'll go get my gallant steed."

After a minute or two, Mary Bee put on her coat and went out into the warm wind. Dowd was just leading his nag from the stable. "I'm full as a tick," he said. "I doubt Rosinante will carry me."

They smiled, and once again clasped hands. "I'm so glad to find you hale and hearty," he said.

"And I you," she said. "My love to Mrs. Dowd, if you please."

"Surely. I'm sorry to bring such sad news. If you please, don't dwell on it."

"How can I not?"

"Because it happens out here. It just happens. Every winter. Last year three, this year four. I'm surprised there aren't more, conditions being what they are. I don't know how any of the women bear it." He took up the reins and hopped aboard and looked down at her soberly. "I don't know how you do it, my dear. Honestly. Living alone, I mean."

"I can do anything," she said.

"I believe you," he said. "Well, let us lift up our hearts. A melodeon. Spring," he reminded.

"Yes, spring."

Alfred Dowd rode away in the direction opposite his coming. After half a mile he stopped and turned in his saddle to see if Mary Bee Cuddy was watching him go. She was. She waved, and he did. His wave was a salute.

She saddled Dorothy, her trusty mare, the next morning and rode the two miles to the Belknaps, the antelope haunch, wrapped in sacking, tied on behind her cantle. Vester came out to meet her. She gave him the meat and advised him to hang it high in his stable or the wolves would have it. Then she said she'd just heard yesterday, from Reverend Dowd, about Theoline, and wanted him to know how shocked she was, and how terribly sorry. Vester said so was he. She inquired as to Theoline's condition, and he said the same, crazy. He still had to hand-feed her and carry her to the outhouse and mind the girls and do the cooking and whatnot until he was tuckered most of the time. Mary Bee dismounted. What in the world had caused it? Vester shifted the haunch to a shoulder and said he had no idee, but he'd been troubled about Line as far back as last fall. She complained about the weather and losing their crops. She talked little and ate less. And she got the notion God was angry with them, so the baby coming would be crippled or have a harelip or something bad. Oh, and she had headaches and was cranky. Mary Bee shook her head and started for the door of the house. Vester said no, she wasn't to go in, he didn't want anyone gawping at his wife in such a state. Mary Bee swung round, vexed, and said she was the dearest friend Theoline had, and she would see her no matter what. Vester cursed. She told him to hush up and take care of that meat, and opened the door and went in.

The three girls, Junia, Aggie, and Vernelle, were waiting. They leaped at her like little animals full of fear, hugging her waist so hard they almost threw her into the stove; and they were crying, and it was all she could do to keep from crying with them. She wouldn't allow herself to look yet at the bed. After a time, taking their shoulders, she told them to go into the back room, she wanted to talk with their mother, now, please, girls, go, and snuffling, they obeyed. They were good girls.

Mary Bee looked round. The place was a shambles. Then she went to the bed.

Theoline Belknap lay on her back. Her eyes were fixed on a corner of the roof. Her hair was a rat's nest. Her wampus was food-stained. Her feet were bare and filthy. Each of her wrists was tied by a picket rope to an upper bedpost. Mary Bee untied the near rope, then leaned over her and untied the far. She sat down on the side of the bed and rubbed both wrists, raw and swollen.

"Theoline," she said, "this is Mary Bee."

"Undo," responded Theoline.

"Undo your arms? I have, dear."

"Undo, undo."

"Do you know me, Theoline?"

"Undo, undo, undo, undo."

Mary Bee bent and turned the woman's face toward her. Theoline's eyes remained fixed on the roof.

"Line, dear, I'm Mary Bee, your friend."

"Tha."

"Don't you know me?"

"Tha," Theoline said. "Tha, tha, tha, tha, tha, tha, tha, tha, tha."

Mary Bee looked away and sat a spell. Inside, she went void. At length something flared in the void like the strike of a match in pitch dark. It was anger.

She rose, pulled the hung quilt aside, and went behind it to the girls. She knelt. She opened wide her arms and swept the sisters into them, close. There were still some sniffles. "Now listen, girls," she said. "Your mother's very sick, but she loves you just the same, as she always has. You must love her, too, and help her as much as you can. Here are some things you can do for her. I've untied her arms. I want you to undress her, heat some water, and give her a nice bath, with soap, face to feet."

"Right on the bed?" Junia asked.

"Right on the bed. Wash and dry her hair, too, then brush and comb it. Then find clean clothes for her, and underwear—they're probably in her trunk—and dress her again. And while you're doing this, smile at her and say kind things. Do you know a little song you can sing?"

"We know 'Away in the Manger,'" offered Vernelle.

"That would be fine," said Mary Bee. "And when you've finished all that, do some chores for your father, too. You are now the ladies of the house. Sweep it out. Wash the dirty dishes. Take the bedding outdoors and air it. Show him how grown-up you are. Will you do that? For him? For me?"

They nodded, gravely, awed perhaps by the number of their assignments.

"Good," she said. "And remember—love your dear mother." She let go of them and stood. "Now, you get busy as bees. Give me your foreheads."

They raised their faces. She kissed each one on the forehead, then left them. Passing through the front room, she couldn't bear to look again at Theoline. Outside, Vester had hung the meat and stabled her horse and was returning. Mary Bee noticed she had clenched her fists. It was anger again, flaring higher in the void. It must have found kindling. She must damp it down before it reached her heart.

"I've untied her."

Vester scowled. It had irked him to stable her horse. He had not thanked her for the antelope. "Who said to? No tellin' what she'll do."

"I assure you she's harmless. Besides, you may not have her much longer."

"How's that?"

"That's one reason why I'm here. I have a message for you from Reverend Dowd." She opened her fists into hands and began to explain the necessity for a homesman, but Vester soon interrupted her. He knew all that, Dowd had told him. Very well, she said, the drawing would be held at the church next Tuesday, in the afternoon, and he should be there, the other three husbands would be. Vester asked what drawing. Why, to decide which one of the four would take the four wives back east, across the Missouri, to Hebron, Iowa, whence they'd be escorted home. Whoever lost the drawing would take them back, the other three husbands would supply wagon, team, and supplies. That was the way it was done last year, when three women had lost their minds over the winter, and Reverend Dowd proposed to try it again this. Vester stared at her, then stated flatly he wouldn't do no such a thing. Christamighty, he knew Petzke and Svendsen—the one was a damn Dutchman and the other a Norskie— Sours he'd never heard of—and he wasn't hauling their women anywhere. She could tell Dowd to find another fool. Mary Bee said he must be there for the drawing. He was as responsible for his wife's welfare as the others were for theirs. Vester said he wouldn't, and nobody could make him, this was a free country. "Then what will you do with Theoline?" asked Mary Bee.

That stumped him.

She started for the stable. It was a tiny triumph, but the anger burned in her unabated. In the stable she glanced at a swelling on the flank of the ox next to her mare, which had to be warbles, which needed

41

coal oil. When she led the mare out Vester had followed, whining. He swore he wanted to do what was best for Line, but what if he went to the drawing and lost? Heading east with a load of women, being gone for weeks, who'd see to his stock and his girls? Mary Bee said she would. Well, what if he wasn't picked? He was so hard up he couldn't chip in a sack of meal or a red cent for the trip. Why, he'd just been into Loup last thaw and taken out a chattel mortgage, and he had to get a crop in this spring or lose everything. If he had any more bad luck, he whined, come summer he'd quit and pack up his girls and goods and head back for Kentucky, where a feller had a chance. Couldn't she get it through her head how he was whipsawed? If he was picked in the drawing he wouldn't go, and if he wasn't, to his shame he couldn't ante up a thing—either way he come out behind. Just what in holy hell was he s'pose t'do?

She heard young voices singing in the house, singing "Away in the Manger." What she'd have liked to say was oh, Vester, all we have brought out here to this wilderness is our lives and a little seed of civilization. We have planted that seed. Unless we tend it, it will die, and if it dies, we are no better than brutes. Taking these poor women home is civilized.

Instead, she said, "Go."

"I won't."

"Tuesday," she said.

Now he was angry. He hadn't budged her.

"I won't."

"Then I'll go in your place," she said. "I'll draw for you. If I win, I'll provide what you can't afford. If I lose, you'll start east with your wife and the other three. You have to."

"Damn if I will!"

"They'll make you."

"I've got a long rifle!"

Mary Bee mounted up, reins in one fist. "In the meantime, love her."

"Love 'er! After what she's done t'me? I give 'er no cause t'go crazy!"

"You gave her another baby."

"The Lord's will!"

Now her anger blazed, and Mary Bee Cuddy felt the heat of it in her heart. "It wasn't the Lord bedded her!" she cried. Her look after that was like a cut of the reins. "Vester," she said, "you are a damned poor specimen of a man." And she nudged Dorothy with a knee and rode off.

Vester Belknap cupped both hands around his mouth and hollered. "I am, hey? Leastwise I don't dress up like a woman!"

This day it turned cold again and spit small, sparse flakes as though it disremembered how to snow.

This time Charley Linens and John Cox and Martin Polhemus picked up Henry Caudill on the way. Henry was a good man with a gun. When he joined them he had a package wrapped tight in white paper. They asked what that was. He said sulphur.

They asked what it was for. Henry said for just in case. The four rode south and west toward the Kettle River until they came to Andy Giffen's stove-pipe and a curl of smoke rising from it, then down into the ravine, keeping well upside of the stove-pipe. Here they tied horses to a runt tree, and slipping rifles, sneaked down the ravine into a thick tangle of gooseberry bushes that faced Andy's dug-out from maybe sixty yards off. When they figured they had enough cover of the bushes, they readied rifles and let Charley Linens take the lead. He shouted.

"Moore!"

The door and window of the dugout were closed.

"Briggs!"

He was talking to himself.

"Hey, you, jumper!"

That did it. As they watched, the door opened a crack and the window a crack.

"This here's the same bunch was here the other day!" Charley shouted. "Andy Giffen's friends! Andy's due any day now, and we want you off this claim! We got four guns to your one, so you be smart about it. Come on out with your hands up and we'll see you on your way, much obliged, no harm done! Come on now!"

They waited a minute, two.

"Shit," said Martin Polhemus.

He raised up on his knees, poked rifle barrel through the bushes, set stock to shoulder, and fired at the dugout door. Then the rest did the same, some firing at the door, some at the window. It sounded like a battle. The ugly horse in the stable took fright or fury at the gunfire and started snorting and screaming like a woman in labor. But they had bitten off more than they could chew. Briggs or whatsisname was as rapid with a rifle as he was with a handgun. He jumped from door to window and back again and that barrel would snake out an inch or two and he'd fire and snake back and they never thought a man could be so accurate aiming and firing so fast. His bullets clipped branches close to their faces. They went by like a hot breath. John Cox got a twig in the eye and said "Ow!" and stopped firing. So did the others.

They sat back on their buttocks in the snow. They were scared. They knew what they had to do, but how the hell to do it was the question.

"Goddam him," said Martin Polhemus. He was breathing hard and sweating.

"Boys, listen," said Henry Caudill, who was a soft-spoken man. "We've got us a mossback here. We can't shoot him out. He's got sod and wood between us. So why not smoke him out? That's why I brung that pound of sulphur."

He told them to let loose again. While they did, he'd run up the ravine, get his sulphur, climb on out, and drop it down Andy's stovepipe. They looked doubtful. Henry said give it a try. He said back where he came from, mountains down in Missouri, that's how they got a bear out of a hole, smoked him out. Then when he came out bellering and half-blind, they'd kill him easy as falling off a log.

"Why not?" said John Cox, rubbing his twig eye. "I'm cold and hungry and it's a long ways to supper."

"I don't want any of us shot," said Charley Linens.

"Him neither," said a grim Martin Polhemus. "I want that sonvabitch strung from a tree."

So they gave it a try. Three of them blasted away at the dugout again while Henry Caudill peeled off up the ravine. Then they hunkered down in the gooseberry bushes and waited and watched the dugout and could see nary sign of movement. The afternoon began to die on them. It grew dark sooner in the ravine than up on the flatland. Then, suddenly, the dugout door swung wide open and the window, too, and thick yellow smoke billowed out from both and they expected to see Briggs come out coughing and half-blind. But he did not. The dugout disappeared completely in a yellow cloud. Martin Polhemus hitched up and fired off a couple rounds into the cloud, and to their disbelief, a couple more banged right back out of the cloud and sliced the bushes close by.

That made Martin Polhemus so mad he rose up and took a chance. "You et enough smoke yet, Briggs?" he hollered. "You had enough?"

The jumper hollered right back. "You damn dumb sodbusters! Go on home!"

Martin sank down and swore a blue streak.

Henry Caudill slipped back from on top and they bunched up and looked at him, squatting.

"You still want him out of here?" he asked.

They did.

"All right," said Henry. "We can't shoot him out or smoke him out. You come by my place next week and pick me up. I'll have Thor Svendsen with me. Strong as an ox. But he's maybe got some gunpowder."

"Gunpowder?" they all said.

"Why not? That's the sure way. We'll blow him out like a stump."

"I'll bring the rope," added Martin Polhemus.

"Rope?"

"He ain't blown dead, I want him down by the river. At the end of a rope. Dancin' a jig."

If the reference was to religion, it was called "Kettle Church"; if to education, "Kettle School." It served both purposes. A building bee enlisting every man and boy in the neighborhood had erected it in a single day on a rise not far from the river. Logs for walls were hauled from the river bottom, chinked with blocks, and pointed up with clay. The roof was made of sod and branches. Mary Bee Cuddy's hundred dollars bought the niceties: a door, two window frames and glass, a stove, a carpentered pulpit for the preacher, a dozen slates and sheepskin erasers, and a grab bag of books. Every second Sabbath, winter permitting, and this one had not, Reverend Dowd held services of a sort he called, with a twinkle in the eye, "non-denominational Methodist." But the wider function of the building was instructional. School was divided into three terms of eight weeks, fall, winter, and spring, although this year the winter term had been canceled for reasons of weather and love. The children could not come for cold and snow. Teacher could not come because she had married at Christmas. She was Miss Clara Marsh, late of Vermont and early to the plains. Rather than the result of love, however, marriage for her was probably the lesser of two evils. This was a subscription school. Her fee was a dollar a child per term, plus her keep, and with seventeen scholars signed up, she should have had, by the end of the fall term, seventeen dollars. She did not. She had ten dollars in hand and seven in hope. Worse, she had spent the term boarding and rooming with the parents of her pupils, moving from sod house to dugout, sleeping three to a bed with wiggly youngsters, subsisting on a diet composed in the main of cornmeal mush, corn samp, corn cake, corn dodgers, and corn bread, which had undermined her constitution. Marriage, therefore, even to a balding widower who needed a workhorse wife, might have seemed to Clara Marsh a sensible alternative to poverty and broken health. She was asked. She said yes. There was no winter term at Kettle School.

Mary Bee was the first to arrive.

She stood for a spell, deciding not to start a fire in the stove even though there was ample wood in the box. What had to be done would take only a little while. A long, broad board was slotted on pegs inserted in the logs on two sides of the room. On this crude desk, books and slates and erasers were neatly stacked. The benches, for classes and congregations, were hewn logs with pegs driven in for legs. Near the stove was a wooden water bucket and a rusty dipper. She seated herself on a bench in front of the movable pulpit.

Garn Sours entered.

He stared at her in surprise, managed to nod, then sat on a bench near the door, his back to her, bent over, studying the dirt floor, a picture of misery. He was twenty-one or -two at most. Her heart sank. That he could lead four women unsound of mind, his own wife included, several hundred miles over trackless prairie, feed them and care for them and bring them safely to haven, was inconceivable.

Again she surveyed the room. It occurred to her to envy Miss Clara Marsh. Both of them had come west full of faith, beans, and foreboding, but Marsh had been the luckier. Her school had every amenity compared to the one south of Wamego over which she, Cuddy, had presided for a year. No desk, no slates, few books, a stubborn stove, and a pinch-penny board that failed, every term end, to pay her the full dollar a day it had promised. That school had come equipped, in addition, with two oafish louts of sixteen who tyrannized the younger children and would have made pedagogy impossible had she not one day, at one stroke, shown them what stuff she was made of. A band of Pawnees camped in the vicinity. She carried a rifle to school every day. While the autumn was still warm, a rattler four feet long found its way into the room. Calmly, scared half to death, she took charge. Herding the hysterical children away from the snake, she seized her weapon, tossed a book near the reptile to make it coil and rear to strike, aimed, and with a single bullet shot off its head. At once she earned the louts' respect and saved the term. Yet playing heroine did not endear the profession to her. She, too, like Marsh, ate more corn than was fit for cattle. She, too, like Marsh, lay sleepless in ticky beds with grubby, bad-dream bedfellows. But unlike Marsh, no balding knight-at-arms appeared to save the maiden in distress. Instead, in the spring, money had come in the mail—two whole whopping thousand dollars of it—and she was free. The last day of school she wrote a note to the school board and told it, politely, to go suck an egg.

Otto Petzke and Thor Svendsen came in together.

They gaped at her, then nodded recognition, said "Miss Cuddy," retired to a bench far from her and from young Sours, whom they ignored, and began to wonder together what in tarnation a woman was doing there.

To pass the time she rose and examined the books stacked along the desk. There were Clark's grammars, Webster's spellers, Ray's *Mental Arithmetic*, McNally's geographies, and McGuffey's and Hilliard's readers, but not really enough of any one title. There were also a few hymnbooks.

In walked Alfred Dowd.

He, too, stared at her, spoke to the three men, then strode directly to her. He kept his voice low. "What are you doing here?"

"Vester couldn't come."

"Wouldn't, you mean."

"I'll draw for him."

He frowned. He took off his hat and laid it on the pulpit. "I don't like this," he said to her. "It isn't right."

"It can't be helped."

He addressed the others. "Otto, Thor, Garn, come here to me, please." They came forward, clumsy in heavy coats and boots, and seated themselves on the bench behind Mary Bee's. The minister was still frowning. "Miss Cuddy is here today in Vester Belknap's place. He was unable to be with us, I don't know why, but I don't see that it will make any difference."

He opened his mouth to speak again, then stopped. This he repeated. Then he began to unwind his muffler, being very slow about it. Mary Bee understood that her friend simply did not know what to say. The gravity of the moment undid him. She looked at the two older men and the one young. How they did not want to be here. How they did not want to do what one of them must. She perceived in their faces a queer mix of resignation and apprehension. The latter—dread on the part of each that he might be the one chosen by chance—she could almost smell, along with a congregation of other odors cooped up in the small room: of chalk and animals, urine and smoke, paper and manhood. Suddenly a wind came up outside, a minor wind. It made a sound like that of a woman crying, or a man whining.

By the time Alfred Dowd had removed his muffler and hung it on the pulpit, he had found his words. "Well," he said. "Well. This is a painful occasion. I am your pastor, and I grieve for you. Four fine women. Wives and mothers. Asked to give beyond their power to give. I hope you understand that dementia is not uncommon out here, and certainly nothing to be ashamed of. I assure you the Lord God is with you in your sorrow. And will be henceforth, when you must be both father and mother to your children. All four families have been stricken—I include Vester's." He stopped. He was going round and round the barn and knew it. He cleared his throat. "I've spoken to all of you about the system. We draw lots. One of you will escort the women east, to Iowa. The other three must provide the conveyance, the team, and the supplies. It's a method that succeeded last year, and I have no doubt will this. Now." He dug in a pocket, picked up his hat, and dropped something in it. "I've put four kernels of corn in here. Three are yellow, one is black. Whoever draws the black goes east. Now I'll shake them up." He held the hat by its brim, revolved it, then held it out high. "Shall we defer to the lady? Miss Cuddy, will you draw first?"

"No, thank you," she said. "Vester isn't here. I think he should draw last. I'll defer to Mr. Sours."

"Oh," said Dowd. "All right. Garn, will you draw?"

The youth rose, stepped over the first bench, almost tripping himself, reached high into the hat, and sat down with a groan, holding up a yellow kernel for all to see.

"Otto?" Dowd invited, moving toward him.

Otto Petzke hesitated. He had an Old Country habit of resting his right hand against his neck under his brown beard. He took it out now, stood, reached, and fumbled in the hat then opened his hand. *"Lieber Gott,"* he murmured, thrust a yellow kernel at the others, and sat down again, heavily.

"Thor?" said the minister.

Thor Svendsen looked at Mary Bee, then loomed to his feet, shoved a big hand into the hat, and withdrew it, closed. He brought the hand to his chest before opening it, then rumbled with relief, extending the hand like a platter, palm up, to show the yellow kernel.

All looked at Mary Bee.

"He won't go," she said.

"He will," said Dowd.

"He told me he won't."

"If he loves God he will."

"He's got to!" cried Garn Sours.

Mary Bee stood. "I told him you'd make him. He said if you try, he has a long rifle."

"He must," repeated Dowd. "Or the whole system breaks down."

Otto Petzke jumped up and raised a fist. "He will so do it! I will thrash him!"

"We also have rifles," threatened Thor Svendsen. "Three of them! We make him all right!"

"Oh, my, my," Dowd despaired. "We can't have bloodshed. I never expected—"

"I'll go," said Mary Bee.

Had it not been for the wind outside, the silence would have been absolute.

"You can't," said the minister.

"Yes, I can," she said. "It makes sense. Vester can see to my stock."

"A woman," muttered Thor Svendsen.

"I can ride as well as you. And handle a team. And shoot," she said to them. "And I can cook. And I can care for the women better than you."

They looked at each other. Alfred Dowd stepped behind the pulpit and leaned forearms on it. He seemed more shocked and bewildered than they. "We simply cannot allow this," he said.

"Would you trust him with them?" she asked.

"Vester is just as responsible for—"

"Would you really?"

This was inarguable. He looked away.

"She's right!" cried Garn Sours. "Miss Cuddy, this is just mighty white of you!"

Her legs were sapped of their strength then, and she sat down on her bench.

"When would you go?" asked the minister.

"As soon as I can. We'll have better weather now. A week, ten days. So I can be back in time to get in a crop."

"Miss Cuddy, you are a fine lady," said Otto Petzke, almost bowing to her.

"That is right," agreed Thor Svendsen. "You tell us what you need, we will get it." Still nodding agreement he stooped to her, suddenly, cupped a hand to her ear, and whispered, "But you watch out for my Gro! Do not put your back to her! She will kill you!"

Trying to absorb that, she heard herself insisting on a well-built rig of some kind, covered, and a good team, maybe a pair of geldings, which wouldn't give out on her, plenty of provisions, and a grub box with utensils. She heard their assurances. Dowd read aloud to her a name and address on a piece of paper, which he gave to her: "Altha Carter, wife of Reverend Jonas Carter, Ladies Aid Society, Methodist Church, Hebron, Iowa." She put it in a pocket. He said he would send off a letter to Altha Carter right away, saying she was coming with four passengers. She listened while he instructed the three husbands to prepare papers for their wives, the names and addresses of close relatives to whom the women might be entrusted back east. Mary Bee, he said, would carry them with her for Altha Carter. He advised them to dress their wives warmly and simply for the trip, nothing fancy, and she heard herself adding that they should send blankets and pack in a sack a few toilet articles such as comb and brush and soap, also a handtowel or two and a change of underclothing. Dowd snapped fingers. What was to be done about Vester Belknap? Mary Bee said she'd let him know what had been decided. Very well, then, he said to the men. He hoped they had heeded because he might not see them again before Miss Cuddy came by to pick up their wives. He asked her again how long, and she replied she'd prefer to start in a week. One last thing, the minister said. The less said about the journey and this whole tragic episode the better—for their own sakes and that of the other women in the neighborhood.

Otto Petzke and Thor Svendsen and Garn Sours thanked Miss Cuddy, and told her everything would be ready for her in a week, she could count on it, and they and their families would be grateful to her always, and clumped to the door with Dowd. She heard the door close, and looked to see Alfred Dowd returning. He sat down on the bench beside her. The day was darkening fast, and hence the room. He took her big hands in his.

"My dear lady," he said. "This is incredible, and splendid. Why, why did you do it?"

"I thought I had to."

"Why?"

"Vester won't. Sours is a boy. I saw how the others didn't want to. I'm free."

He reflected. "Remember what I said about the four wives? Asked to give beyond their power to give? Have you asked too much of yourself? Are you truly up to something as difficult as this? As dangerous?"

"Yes."

"I believe you. But if you have second thoughts, let me know. We can draw again. Or I will go in your place if I have to."

She was silent.

"Very well." He released her hands. "What's done is done. It's so like you."

He leaned forward and rested elbows on knees, thinking. His boots were muddy, the first spring mud she had seen. She noticed how hollow was his stubbled cheek, and how apparent was the bald spot at the back of his head. He was getting on, yet never slacked his pace. There must be men, too, she thought, on the ragged edge. She had heard of a middling young bachelor named Winbegger, up near Loup, who hung himself.

He spoke. "If you leave in a week, I may not see you before. So while I can, I'd better tell you about the women. What drove each of them over the brink. Mrs. Belknap's case you know. But the other three."

"Must you?"

"I think so. If you're to tend them, to understand them, shouldn't you know as much as you can?"

"You're right."

He told her about Arabella Sours.

He told her about Hedda Petzke.

He told her about Gro Svendsen.

"And there they are. Your charges," he concluded. "Now you know the worst." He waited for her reaction. There was none.

He went to the pulpit, put on his hat, and rewound his muffler. "Aren't you going now?" he asked. "If you are, I'll ride partway with you."

"No," she said. "I'll stay. To think."

"Of course." He moved to her and put a hand on her shoulder. "Goodbye, my dear. Thank you for all of us. If anything should go amiss, get word to me. Or if you should reconsider."

"Goodbye, Alfred."

He stepped lively to the door, and then, before opening it, turned back to her a second time. "Let us pray," he said. She bowed her head. He placed a gentle hand upon it. "Heavenly Father," he prayed, "look down upon Thy daughter. Bless her in this undertaking. Grant her Thy strength. Guide her with Thy grace. Let her bring them home. I beg Thee in the name of Thy Son, who gave his all for others. Amen."

At last she was alone.

As day faded from the windows she sat still on the bench, hands folded in her lap, a wide-shouldered woman wearing a rabbit hat and a black melton coat and a man's hickory shirt and ducking trousers and good four-dollar boots. The hat, close-fitted, with earflaps she could hook on top when it was mild, was her pride. She had shot the rabbits, scraped and dried the skins, cut them to her own pattern, and sewn them with #8 waxed linen thread. The wind outside warned her not to think about what she had offered to do. Instead, she forced herself to consider summer and fall. She would have sixty acres into wheat, which she calculated would bring forty to fifty cents a bushel. Hogs, she guessed, would go for three dollars a hundredweight come fall, so she intended to buy shoats this spring and fatten them on corn she had saved from last year's crop. She planned also to put in some pumpkins. Two or three loads would fetch a fair sum in town, and what she couldn't sell she would feed to her cattle. Cattle took to pumpkins the way horses took to apples.

There was an early line in Genesis: "And the earth was without form and void; and darkness was upon the face of the deep." She took the word "deep" to mean the void, which was dark. What had happened to her lately she thought of as going void. She was suddenly empty inside, absolutely void. In her was a great, dark deep. Then one of two things occurred in the void. A match was struck, a light flared, and soon she was full of flame. That was fury, as she had been furious at Vester Belknap. Or, like a seed, a crystal of ice formed and grew, and soon her deep was solid ice. That was fear, as she had feared the snake. Going void was fear more often than fury, she had found, especially on long winter nights in her house when wolves howled and she was alone as now, sitting on the bench, emptying inside, and feeling the first crystal form. She shivered. She stood up and went to the door. Once outside, in near dark, she decided to relieve herself before starting, so walked around Kettle School to the outhouse at the rear. She entered, closed the door, opened her coat, pulled down her britches and the drawers made of Queen Bee Flour sacking, and seated herself over the hole. The second she did so, she thought of Theoline Belknap. She cried out in horror. She sprang up, pulled herself together, buttoned coat, and burst from the outhouse, running. Now she was solid ice inside, solid fear. She untied Dorothy from the hitch rail, mounted, wheeled the mare and gave her a bootheel in the flank, then another out of the trot into a slow gallop.

It was not only what Theoline had done.

It was what Mary Bee Cuddy had done.

For she knew she could not. Alone, by herself, she couldn't possibly handle a team and wagon and feed and nurse and protect and comfort four such cases all the way to the Missouri River, not alone, not by herself. She knew in her soul she couldn't possibly. What woman in Christendom could?

She must have help.

Andy Giffen would have gone with her, gladly, but Andy Giffen was back east after a wife.

What was she to do? Choke on her pride and ask Alfred to draw again? Beg the others, even young Sours? Get down on her knees and shed tears before Vester? Let poor Alfred attempt it and fail? Pretend to take sick and be unable?

No, she must have help.

In the name of God, who?

She had routed herself across the snow to tell Vester what had been decided, and get it over with, but now, after a mile, she reined Dorothy north and east, toward home, and eased her back to a trot. It was night now, and she shuddered with cold and unhooked the flaps of her rabbit hat and rode on, full of fear.

By the time she reached home, three miles later, she was in panic, short of breath, gulping cold air. As fast as she could she watered her mare, stabled and unsaddled her and forked her rack high with hay, then rushed into the house. She lit two candles and set them on opposite sides of the table. She threw off her hat and coat, restarted a fire in the stove, took off boots and shirt and trousers. From the chest of drawers she took out the very best dress Theoline had made for her, one of lustrous maroon taffeta that complemented perfectly, she thought, her dark hair. This she kept up with combs most of the time, but at a party she let it down for this dress and tied it with a maroon ribbon. The dress was floor-length, there were ruffles of maroon lace at the sleeves and around the high neckline, and it buttoned at the bodice. She pulled it on over her head now without buttoning, and seated herself at the table, unrolling and spreading out a five-octave melodeon keyboard she had made from a length of muslin. It was an excellent replica, actual size. The white keys were outlined with, the dark keys stained with, a dye derived from walnut shells crushed and boiled. She smoothed the cloth keyboard, placed her hands, and began to play and sing, when her breath returned, in a deep, contralto voice. She loved music. As she played and sang she felt the ice melt in her, the fear recede, and the void fill slowly with her own warm, strong, real self.

She had come to do this often in the endless evenings of this winter. Mary Bee Cuddy believed sometimes that it had preserved her sanity. She sang hymns and ballads, sad songs and sacred, and finished the recital with her favorite ballad, "Take Thee This Token."

There were five of them this night: Charley Linens, John Cox, Martin Polhemus, who brought rope, Henry Caudill, and the new man, Thor Svendsen, whose wife was in a bad way and who did have a pound of gunpowder.

They had clouds overhead, but scudding clouds, and in the separations they had moonlight. They talked little. Charley Linens set a steady pace. Each one had a sense of finality. They had plenty of light and gunpowder and men enough to be rid, once for all, of the jumper. Martin Polhemus put it well: "Boys, we're a-going to blow his ass to Kingdom Come."

They located Andy Giffen's stovepipe up on the flat, and Caudill dismounted with the paper sack of explosive. He would be the exploder. He said he'd give them ten minutes, give or take a minute, then drop the charge down the pipe and hurry on down to see the fun.

They left him and rode down into the ravine and tied horses to the runt tree, slipped rifles, and sneaked along like Indians past the stable. But they couldn't fool the jumper's hard-mouth horse. When they went by he let out some mean snorts. Once into the cover of the gooseberry bushes across from the dugout they laid down flat, side by side in the snow, and fixed on the wink of light at one edge of the window. They were counting along with Henry Caudill.

That gunpowder, when it hit the fire in the stove, made about the most splendiferous boom they had heard in their born days. Clods of sod catapulted across the whole ravine into the bushes and chunked down around them. After that was over they hoisted themselves to their feet and honed their eyes to see what had happened.

The job was done all right. Half the front wall of the dugout was blown away. There was no door anymore, no window. There was no trace of stove or stovepipe. They figured the iron of the stove, blown to bits, must have cut the man to pieces. They had saved Andy Giffen his claim, but he would have, on return, a sight of work to do on his house.

Henry Caudill joined them puffing and said well, let's get up close, make sure he's dead. So rifles at the ready they started in a bunch toward the half-hole that had been the front of the dugout. They got within a few rods and stopped in their tracks as though they had been hit over the head.

Because just then the moon came out and so did Briggs. He sort of staggered out of the hole and staggered around in a circle like a man blind, deef, and dumb. He didn't know where he was or the day of the week. And he was a spectacle. His face was smoke black. His hair was concussed every whichway.

All he had on above was longjohn, and it was black, too, and below were his pants, which were black in the first place, and even his two bare feet were smoky. Suddenly he lurched toward Henry Caudill, arms out as though to get hold of something and hang on, whereupon Henry jammed him hard in the ribs with the business end of his rifle.

"Hold on there, Mister," said Henry. "I would take pleasure shooting you."

Briggs backed off and Charley Linens said, sharply, "Everybody get around him. Pen him up!"

This they did, and every time he lunged again he ran into a rifle. And there they stood, five God-fearing farmers, surrounding him, breathing hard. They were edgy. The fact was, they were afraid of him, and had been since that first afternoon when he snaked his gun. And even though they had him helpless now, dead to rights, they had no particular notion what to do with him. One did, though.

"Oh, I am glad of this," said Martin Polhemus. "I am glad the sonvabitch ain't dead. I told you fellers before, I aim to see him dance. That's why I brung rope. Let's get him mounted up and down to the river under one of them big trees. Then let's see him swing and get on home."

"Well, I don't know," said Charley Linens.

"I do," said John Cox, normally a peaceable man. "I vote with Martin. I got a warm bed waiting."

"Count me in," said Henry Caudill. "How d'you stand, Thor?"

Svendsen, the tall, spare Norskie who had provided the gunpowder, was decisive. "Hang him. If we let him go, he will jump more claims. If we hang him, he is over."

That was logical. "All right," said Charley Linens. "I'm not easy with it, but I'll go along."

Agreement set them stirring. John Cox kept the prisoner covered. Henry Caudill struck up the ravine to bring the horses. Linens and Polhemus and Svendsen went to the stable to bring out the jumper's horse and for the life of them couldn't. He was wild as a catamount cornered. He ripped and reared and kicked and tried to bite and made a terrible racket. What they had to do, finally, was go get Briggs and nudge him into the stable and alongside, and that quieted the bastard beast down. They haltered him and led him out and helped Briggs up on him and tied his hands behind his back and his ankles under the horse. Caudill brought their mounts. They climbed on and, leading the roan, rode on down the ravine a quarter-mile to where it opened out into the north bottom of the Kettle River, which was frozen over. Here was a fine stand of trees, cottonwood and sycamore mostly. Here was where they'd cut the timber for the church-school. And here they selected a big sycamore with a long limb that suited their purpose to a T. They dismounted and moved horse and rider under it. If the rider knew where he was or what was going on he gave no indication. Being handy with rope, Henry Caudill looped and knotted the noose. He slipped it over Briggs's head and way up under his jaw and slung the coil up over the limb, then yanked it into a fork, then looped the free end around the tree trunk and began to take up slack ever so carefully until he had the line not too taut to choke but taut enough to raise Briggs's head so he was sitting up straight and staring straight ahead like a soldier at attention. Then he wound the line around the trunk thrice and secured it with a slipknot and cinched it up just so. Then they all stood back to take their satisfaction.

"I'm the one hits that horse out from under him," announced Martin Polhemus.

"How'll it work?" asked John Cox.

"He won't have much of a drop," explained Henry Caudill, the man from Missouri. "It won't break his neck. It'll just shet off his wind. I reckon he won't die for two, three minutes. Not entirely."

"So long, you sonvabitch," said Martin Polhemus to Briggs, moving up close. "I'll hit this goddam horse so hard he'll run from here to Ioway."

"Hold on." This was Charley Linens. He walked over to the trunk of the sycamore and laid his forehead up against it a spell, then turned and walked back to the others. "Boys, listen to me," he said. "This here's lynching, plain and simple. I never killed a man before, and I don't care to now. I was praying the Lord, and what I got was, don't do it. Don't lynch him. Let him hang himself."

"How is that?" asked Thor Svendsen.

"Why, leave him be," Charley responded. "Let him set just as he is. That rope's tighter'n a bowstring. Sooner or later that horse'll walk out from under him and he'll hang himself and we won't have blood on our hands."

"Shit," said Martin Pohemus.

"Martin, you mind what I say." Charley Linens rubbed his hands together. "Do we want something we have to be forgiven for later on? What if we're not? Forgiven, I mean." He appealed to the rest. "Think about it, boys. We're all believers. He's a goner anyhow. 'Vengeance is mine,' the Lord said. Well, let's go on home and let the Lord have it."

No one said a word after that. They kicked at the snow or stared out at the ice on the river. Martin Polhemus was the first, unexpectedly, to throw in his hand. He plodded to his horse and grabbed the reins and hauled himself disgustedly into the saddle.

"Shit," he said.

The others went slowly to their animals and mounted. But instead of leaving, they sat for a time in the dark under the tree and had a last, interested look at their handiwork. There he sat, bareback, bound and silent, upright and stiff as a poker, a rider going nowhere to see nobody about nothing. If he so much as looked down or sideways the rope, which had no give to it, would eat into his throat. Charley Linens was right. In an hour, or two, or three, that infernal, four-legged thing he was up on would spook or go off to graze and the confounded claim-jumper would do what the law of gravity decreed. He would damn well drop.

Martin Polhemus shook a fist at him. "So long,

you thieving sonvabitch. All I wish is we'd hung you up by the nuts."

"Hey, Jumper," said Henry Caudill. "Sorry, but there won't be no claims you can steal in Hell. That country's all settled."

John Cox piped up. "Might as well tell us now, Mister. What in Jehu's your name?"

Of course he had no answer. They wheeled out from under the sycamore and away up the ravine through intermittent moonlight. Each man probably asked himself whether they had made a mistake or not, whether they should have hung him and cut him down and buried him then and there or whether they had done the right thing after all, leaving him be, and just as probably had no answer to that either.

She set out for Loup early in the morning. A man named Hessler had stopped by her place the preceding afternoon with a message from Alfred Dowd: the wagon and team and supplies were ready and waiting at the blacksmith's.

Morning of the day before she had gone over to tell Vester Belknap even though she dreaded to. She did not go in the house to see Theoline or the girls. She told him about the drawing, that Petzke and Sours and Svendsen were there and she had drawn the black for him and since he had declared he wouldn't, she had volunteered to go east in his place. It was well she had not expected gratitude from the Kentuckian. To cover his conscience, he covered her with scorn. She was as crazy as the wives. She'd never get there. She'd bog down in the middle of nowhere and they'd all starve to death or be taken captive by goddam murdering Indians. No, he loved his wife too much to trust her to any damn female in the Territory. She heard him out, then said that was the situation, she was going, take it or leave it. Her rig would be ready any day now, and she'd start gathering the women immediately. She would stop at his place last of the four, to see if he had changed his mind. That would be his last chance. If he did change it, he should have a paper for Theoline with the name and address of her kin back home, and blankets, brush, comb, soap, hand-towels, and clean underclothing. If he didn't, if he held her, so be it, her care and keep were his. Vester sent her on her way with a string of language too lewd to ignore. She turned in the saddle and thumbed her nose at him.

Mary Bee Cuddy had not made a trip into town since November. She had a long list of needs and treats compiled through the winter, but that buying could wait until her return from Iowa. She had a sunny day for the ten miles. Snowdrifts were caving in like cakes. Running water gurgled in the gullies. She lost count of skinny rabbits. Her mare Dorothy knew spring when she saw it. She pranced.

Seen by a bird, Loup would have resembled buffalo droppings. Seen from terra firma, it was a scatter of shacks and small buildings, some of sod, some of logs, some of both, dropped here and there about a hollow, and through it twisted a main trail of mud and manure. It had a general store and drygoods in which the mail, when it came, was distributed; a bank, with a counter, a desk, and a safe; a saloon with a whiskey barrel and a bar made of planks over sawhorses; a feed yard in which horses and mules were bought and sold and cattle and hogs were slaughtered on local demand; and Buster Shaver's establishment, consisting of a log smithy, a plank shed, and a stable roofed with brush. In good weather there might have been a hundred people and dogs in Loup any day but Sunday; in bad half that number, counting dogs.

Mary Bee's mail disappointed. She had but one letter from Dorothy, her married sister in Geneva, New York, who wrote every month without fail, and a flyer from a nursery in Fort Wayne, Indiana, urging her to put in an orchard of apples, plums, cherries, etc. The gall of them. She'd ordered several of each tree from the very same flyer from the very same nursery last year, and the saplings, when shipped, were in such poor condition she couldn't persuade them to grow. Writing for her money back had been like writing to a stone wall. The gall of them. The clerk in the general store told her he'd heard there was a ton of mail backed up in Wamego, but the big back-up was in St. Joe. Apt to be another month, he said, before the pipe opened. She bought a dime's worth of cheese and crackers for her lunch.

Buster Shaver set up shop in Loup before there

was a Loup. The town attached itself to him the way a litter attaches itself to a sow. He had two trades, transportation and information, and both were basic, transportation to the economy and information to the curiosity. He could shoe a horse and inform you who was ill and reinforce an axle and inform you who was close to foreclosure and make a singletree and inform you who was pregnant and hub a wheel and inform you who was to blame.

"Hullo, Mar' Bee. Hey, you heard about the jumper?" He had the hind leg of a spavined old sorrel tucked up and was trimming a hoof.

"Hello, Buster. Which one?"

They might not have seen each other since November, but there was no need to get gushy. Mary Bee and Buster were members of their own mutual-admiration society.

"One over to Andy's. Name of Briggs."

"Oh. No, I haven't."

"They lynched 'im last night."

"They what!"

"Blew 'im outa the dugout with gunpowder, hung 'im, buried 'im. That's all she wrote."

"Mercy! Who?"

Buster grinned. "They didn't leave no callin' card." He let down the hind leg. "Say, wanta see yer mules?"

"Mules!"

"That's right."

If there'd been something to sit down on, she

would have. "Damn them! Mules? Oh, no. I asked for a good team. They promised—"

"Petzke and Svendsen."

"Yes." ●

"But they got you a span of mules—bought 'em cheap, I hear. Well, c'mon, time the three of you got acquainted."

Buster walked her out of the smithy. A man in his fifties, he was short in the legs and long in the arms and thick in the shoulders, causing some to liken his appearance to that of an ape, though never in his presence. He walked her into his stable and there were the mules. Mary Bee looked at them hopelessly. "I don't know a thing about mules!"

"Who does?"

"Are they sound?"

"Sound enough."

"Are they kickers?"

A straight face. "I asked 'em. They said no."

"Why does that one twitch his ears?"

Buster was up a tree. To gain time, he reached down and flicked dried mud from his leather apron. "I expect," he theorized, "because he's thinking. It must hurt a mule to think, and as his mind is between his ears, he twitches 'em to relieve the hurt." He sighed. "Anything else?"

"Damn them."

"The mules?"

"Otto Petzke and Thor Svendsen. How do you harness mules?"

"Same as horses. How else?"

"Show me."

Buster started, she helping him with bridles and collars until she said, "Wait a minute. This is shaft harness, not tongue. I asked them for a good strong wagon, not a buckboard. What have they—"

"Hold on. Let's finish up and hitch 'em up, then you can have a fit."

They finished, Buster backed the span out of the stable, and using the traces as reins walked them around behind the plank shed, Mary Bee following.

"My Lord, what's that!"

She was as bowled over as she had been by the mules. The vehicle resembled a big box on wheels. Away from everything, on flat land, it would stick out like a sore thumb. From a distance, it might have been a hearse. Closer up, there was something ominous about it, even fateful. It was the kind of rig in which criminals would be carried, or soldiers being slow-marched and drum-rolled to a firing squad. Just to look at it lowered your spirits.

"Called a 'frame wagon,' " said Buster. "I swapped a Moline for it last year, then didn't know what to do with it. Just set here in the snow. So them two clodhoppers come along, Petzke and Svendsen, lookin' for a wagon, an' I thought, just the ticket for them wimmen. Sold it to 'em cheap. Set some new spokes, coupla new felloes, put on one new tire, cut the windies bigger so's the passagers can take notice, greased 'er up, an' she's ready t'go, round the world."

Mary Bee wasn't having a fit, she was moving

slowly round the wagon in search of a reason to refuse it. The box was perhaps twelve feet long and five wide and eight high off the ground, its top, bottom, and sides framed entirely of three-quarter-inch hardwood plank which had weathered dark gray and smooth. Up front was a footboard and a seat with a storage compartment beneath. The top was set up for storage of bedrolls, provisions, and such, with a folded canvas tarp and a coil of rope and tie rings. Into each side of the box two windows a foot square had been cut. At the rear were double doors and a step, on one side of which was lashed a six-gallon water keg. There were tie rings at the rear, too, in case other animals had to be trailed. And this whole rig rolled on sixteen-spoke, iron-tired wheels as high as carriage wheels. When Mary Bee had circumnavigated it once, she opened the doors at the rear and stepped up into the box.

Buster backed the mules into place, hooked up the shafts, ran the traces from the collar hames through the fills back to the doubletree, pulled the reins from the bits through the rings and tossed them over the footboard, then went to the rear of the wagon and climbed in to join Mary Bee. A plank bench with hinged top and storage space underneath was built into each side of the wagon. He slid along beside her while she inspected the grub box, essential to travel. She found most of what she would need: tin cups and plates, forks and spoons, matches, salt and pepper, saleratus, butter and grease in closed cans. She missed a spider, pots and pans, a coffee pot. Buster said she was sitting on them, under the bench. Oven? Up top, he said. Toward the front, between the benches, was an assortment of sacks and one large closed can. In them, he said, were cornmeal, beans, potatoes, salt pork, and in the can, molasses. He pointed at the open doors. "I put a slide-bolt on them doors."

"Why?"

"To lock the ladies in."

"Why would I have to?"

"Stop an' think."

She thought a moment. "Oh," she said. Then she thought of something else. "Picket pins."

"Four of 'em. Under the seat up front."

She leaned back against plank and looked around the interior of the wagon. The gray wood walls seemed to imprison her. "Oh, my," she said.

"Oh, my what?"

"It's time. So suddenly. To start. I'm not sure I'm ready."

Buster leaned forward and looked out the window opposite at the sunny morning. "You scairt?"

"A little."

"Mar' Bee, listen," he said. "You've got a passable rig an' mules an' you yourself. You're as good a man as any man hereabouts. An' you're doin' a hell of a fine thing. So do it."

"I will." She looked out the window opposite her at the sweet sunny morning. "Does everybody know?"

"Yup."

"What do they say?"

"They don't. People'll talk about death an' taxes, but when it comes to crazy, they hesh up."

Both reflected. Buster stuck a finger in his mouth and moved it around as though tallying how many teeth he had left and calculating how long they were good for. Then he slapped hands on leather knees, got up, and backed out of the box and down the step. She did likewise. He closed and locked the doors. He went up front and took the nigh mule by the bridle and led the span and wagon out from behind the shed, tied her mare to a ring at the rear, came round front, gave Mary Bee a boost up to the seat, and handed her the reins.

"Goodbye, Mar' Bee," said Buster Shaver. "Folks ask me why I never did marry. Well, I never did marry due to I never met one like you."

He turned abruptly and headed into the smithy as though he didn't trust himself to say more or stay longer.

Mary Bee tightened the reins and clucked and waited and clucked again and this time the mules put shoulders to collars and moved.

On the way out of Loup she met and passed two town women walking in, hoisting their skirts above the mud. She might have nodded, or spoken, but they took one long look at the frame wagon and, knowing where it was going and what it would carry, their own kind, turned their faces from it.

*   *   *

She stopped at the Linens place. Charley and Harriet knew what she was up to, everyone did. She told Charley she would start the gather in the morning, she expected to be gone four or five weeks, and would he please tend her stock? He said he'd be glad to, he'd look after her place like it was his own, and by the way, he wanted her to know how much he admired her sand. He'd never set eyes on a frame wagon. He looked inside and asked if he couldn't stow the provision sacks on top for her, and she said she'd be grateful. While he was busy Harriet came out to say goodbye, and when Charley finished loading and covering with canvas and tying down, Harriet suddenly put her arms around Mary Bee and hugged her hard and retreated into their sod house in tears.

Mary Bee drove on, and within a mile of home it struck her that this was her last day to be free for a long time. She changed direction. She thought she'd have a look at the gunpowder damage done to Andy Giffen's dugout. It was only three miles out of her way, and the spring day still sparkled.

She took an immediate liking to the mules. The off mule, the thinker, who twitched his ears often, was the more interesting, but the nigh mule was the worker. His nose was always an inch ahead of the other's. He'd be the one she could depend on.

She stood up once and looked behind the wagon at poor Dorothy being hauled along willy-nilly by the bit in her mouth, a new experience for her and surely a mortifying one. Then it struck her she was in the same fix, being hauled along by a wagon and women gone mad and a husband who wouldn't do his duty and her own foolish heart rushing in where angels feared to tread. A new experience, yes, but scarcely mortifying. Terrifying was the apter word.

She reached Andy's stovepipe and held the mules under tight rein down into the ravine, along it past the stable, and pulled the span up before the wreckage of the dugout. She was appalled. To save Andy's claim from the jumper they had had to destroy his dwelling. Lynching was too good for the man—she thought Buster had called him Briggs. From a coat pocket she took out the dime's worth of cheese and crackers bought in town and ate her lunch. Somehow, sitting on the high wagon seat, eating, reminded her of the night last September she had given Andy dinner at her place, inviting him especially, gussying up in her maroon taffeta, putting together a sumptuous repast, and afterward, daring to get out her muslin keyboard and play and sing for him. Rocking in the Boston rocker, drawing now and again from the jug of whiskey he had brought, her guest seemed to enjoy himself. She could have loved Andy Giffen. He had beautiful black eyes. He was tall and strapping. He was twenty-nine, he'd said so, and the difference between that and thirty-one was nil. Then she ceased to sing and made him a proposition. Why not marry her? Why not throw in together—land, animals, implements, lives—the whole ball of wax? Why not use her capital and know-how to improve his claim as she had hers? As partners, they must prosper. If there were children, so much the better. Looked at from any angle, it made sense, so why not marry? She waited, breath held. Andy had a long pull from his jug. He said he intended to go back east for a wife. She would not take no for an answer. She pressed on, pleading a case, biting her lips, humbling herself. Andy stood up, unsteadily, and put jug down on table hard. He was a little drunk. "Miss Cuddy," he said, "I 'preciate the offer. And supper. And concert. And all. But I can't marry you. Will not. Won't. I ain't perfect. But you are too bossy. And too plumb damn plain."

The sound of ripping startled her. It came from down by the Kettle. It was like the sound of a length of fabric, silk or taffeta, being torn end to end. Or the sound of river ice splitting bank to bank. On impulse, mouth full of cheese and crackers, she took up the reins and wheeled the mules and started down the widening ravine for the river. For one thing, she wanted to put Andy's house and bride behind her, and the shame of that evening. She had been heartsore for weeks. For another, she wanted to see the ice split, a sure sign of spring. For still another, she longed to see trees, many trees, miraculous trees.

The wagon reached the river bottom and the stand of sycamores and cottonwoods. Suddenly, nearing a great sycamore, the mules dug forefeet in and stopped, ears forward. They wouldn't budge. They alarmed her. She jumped down from the seat, slipped back to Dorothy, got her rifle, and walked, rifle ready, step by cautious step around the tree. Then she stopped, rooted to the snow. A puppet on a string on a horse.

It seemed to take her forever to comprehend—the man, the horse, the rope.

The man sat shoulders slumped but head unnaturally erect, held so by the noose, with bare blackamoor face and hands and feet, hands bound behind him, feet tied under the animal's belly. Face, hands, and feet had been blackened by smoke.

The horse was plug-ugly, a roan with a rat tail, its face and four stockings speckled white. It looked Indian. Head down, fore- and hindquarters sagging, it seemed about to founder, as though all that held it up was the loop of its rider's tied legs.

Finally the rope, taut up to a limb and through the fork down to the trunk and around the trunk thrice to a slipknot. Now she understood. This must be the jumper, and the men last night, whoever they were, had not in the end lynched him. They had determined he would hang himself, or the horse would. When the horse moved out from under him, he would hang. Or the horse would die and fall, and the man would fall and die. Last night! It must be noon now, or later. Hours! He should be dead now. He might be.

"You," she said.

His eyes opened, then his lips.

"Help me."

"You're not dead."

"Help me," he rasped.

"Why should I? You tried to jump Andy Giffen's claim. You deserve to hang."

He closed his eyes.

She moved a step closer, into the shade of the tree, considering what to do, and then, as though suspended herself, was dropped down, down, by an idea.

"Suppose I do," she said. "Suppose I save your life. What will you do for me?"

His eyes opened. "Any. Thing."

The more she thought, the more possible it seemed, and the more it seemed she had no choice.

"If I set you free, you'll do anything I ask. Is that right?"

"Yes."

"So you say. Swear it."

"Swear."

"Swear to Almighty God."

"Swear to God."

She stood a minute more, shaken by the risk, angry that she had no alternative. "All right," she said. "I'll save you. I have a job of work for you. But if you make one move to harm me, I'll shoot you."

It was said. She circled him to the sycamore trunk, stood rifle against it, slipped the knot, and unwound the rope. At the release, the jumper's chin dropped. She moved out from the tree and eased the rope down from the fork until it was free and on the ground. She approached horse and rider, and squatting, rifle propped against her, untied his ankles, then rose and untied his wrists, then backed off quickly, rifle up.

"Take off the noose," she said.

He raised one arm, and the other, awkwardly, as though it pained his joints, and fumbled at the noose until he could lift it over his head and let it slide. His horse had not moved. Next he tried to dismount, but raising his right leg unbalanced him and he toppled off the horse and crashed into the snow and lay as though unconscious. She waited. After a bit, still on his back, he moved arms and legs up, down, and sideways to restore circulation, and when he had, dragged himself onto his knees and with a hand on the horse's flank helped himself to his feet and stood turning his head to get the kinks out of his neck.

Mary Bee watched him like a hawk.

He did a strange thing. He coiled the rope. Either he was not a man to waste good rope or he wanted this as a memento.

"Need to go house," he said hoarsely, hanging the coil over a forearm. "Find some things."

"Go," she said.

"Get your wagon," he said.

She frowned but started out and around the tree and after only a few steps heard him. He was passing water on the sycamore trunk. Either he had to or he wanted to show contempt.

By the time she got up on the wagon, rifle on the

seat beside her, and had the mules moving again, he was leading his horse by the halter up the narrowing ravine, plodding barefoot through the snow. Twice he stopped to have a coughing fit and blow his nose with his fingers, a man's habit she hated, that and spitting. When they reached Andy's place he led his horse on into the stable, presumably to give it a feed, then returned to the ruined dugout. She sat on the wagon waiting, rifle across her lap, and watched him hunt around beyond the half-wall of sod for whatever useful he could find. She couldn't believe herself. What in sin and salvation had Mary Bee Cuddy gone and done? What did an oath sworn on a stack of Bibles mean to a claim-jumper? Only the Lord knew how many other kinds of criminal he was. Would he rape her or kill her or both? Or simply leave her with a laugh? What might he do when she had to tell him, eventually, where they were going and why? Should she whip the mules away, now, and pay alone, on the trail, the price of her idiocy? The sun passed beyond the western rim of the ravine and she sat in shadow, shivering.

He came out of the dugout dressed, his face as smudged as ever. He had found a slouch hat, boots, a ragged red scarf to sling around his neck, a coat of cowhide worn in places down to the leather, and something in each hand. He came toward the wagon, dropping what appeared to be a tin of sardines into a pocket, and then, opening his coat, shoved under his belt a big repeating pistol with a blackened wooden grip.

"You can put away the rifle," he said. "I can blow you off that seat anytime I'm a mind to. What kind of rig is this?"

"A frame wagon. For passengers."

He turned and walked away to the stable and returned leading his horse, saddled, and slung the coil of rope on top of the wagon, then mounted up and looked straight at Mary Bee. He had eyes as brown and bottomless as ponds in a marsh.

"Well?" he said.

"We'll go to my place. Is your name Briggs?"

"Might be."

"We'll stay the night there and set out first thing in the morning."

"You said a job of work."

"I'll tell you when I'm a mind to."

If she did once, she looked back over her shoulder twenty times to see if he was still there, following, riding that rat-tailed roan, and every time, he was.

When they topped the rise to her place she told Briggs to unhitch the mules and stable and feed them, and also her mare and his horse, and also see to her other stock.

He sat his horse and stared at her. She might as well have been talking Hottentot. She knew a loner when she met one. Of course a loner wouldn't understand an order, or even a suggestion, but what was exasperating, he had never heard of cooperation either. Such a man lived by himself on the globe and believed it turned for his comfort and convenience. She jumped down.

"Or if you don't care to, I will," she said. "And then your supper'll be an hour late."

She took her rifle and went on into the house, and from a window watched him unhitching the mules. When he led them to the stable, she went to the outhouse. By the time he came back for the other animals, she was busy at the stove. When, later, his chores done, he started toward the house, she met him at the door, barring his way with soap, basin, and a towel. He washed, but triumphed—he went to the outhouse after washing rather than before. Entering the kitchen, he handed her basin and towel ceremoniously, and took off scarf and cowcoat to reveal a black, rusty suitcoat ripped at one sleeve and two sizes too big for him. This he left on, as though he were dining formally, and pulling the pistol from his belt and placing it on the table, he sat down, ready to be served.

She gave him a decent supper: fried salt pork, green beans she had grown and dried, corn bread and sorghum, and coffee, which he sipped repeatedly to convince himself it was real, then gulped down and pushed his cup at her for more. He wolfed his food. He had abominable manners, using only his knife and fingers, spilling beans on the floor and eating them anyway, and when his plate was empty, and he had sopped it with bread and eaten that, he tilted onto the back legs of her good chair and belched.

It was darkening. She lit a candle and finished her own meal while the jumper appraised the furnishings of her house.

"This job of work," he said as she put down her cutlery. "Time I knew what I'm in for."

"I'd be grateful," she said, "if you'd not use my good chair that way."

He let the front legs down with a thud and planted elbows on the table. "Well?"

"My name is Cuddy. Mary Bee Cuddy."

"Where's Cuddy?"

"I am single."

He discovered something between his teeth, dislodged it with a fingernail, decided it was edible, and added it to his supper. "The job."

"Very well. Over this winter, four women, wives, in the neighborhood have lost their minds. Their husbands can't care for them properly. They must be taken to Iowa, where some church people will take them on to their families. It—it's a very sad situation. They were fine women, they still are. It's just that, well." She reproved herself with a frown. "Well, anyway, I offered to take them across the river. The husbands went in together and provided me with the mules, the frame wagon, and supplies for the trip. I plan to start in the morning."

"You saying the Missouri?"

"Yes, I am."

"Hell, that's five weeks from here."

"Mr. Briggs, I am as particular of my ears as I am of my chairs. This is my house, and I will not sit still for profanity in it."

"Hell."

"When I sit at your table, you may turn the air blue if you wish. But not at mine."

"I can see why you're single."

Had she been a man, Mary Bee would have thrown him bodily out the door. And his clothing after him. And his gun.

"To continue," she said, "I know I can't do this service by myself. Not and care for the women, too. I must have someone who can guide, and hunt, and spell me at the reins, and help me with the animals. That's why I set you free. That's your job. And you have sworn to do it."

She waited. She fixed her gaze on his big repeater, and on the walnut grip, which had been so badly singed by the explosion that it must blacken his hand every time he touched it.

"Five weeks," he said. "Four crazy women. A lot more'n I bargained for."

"But worth your life, surely."

"Depends."

"On what?"

"On what comes along."

"I see. That's another thing. I will have to depend on you, and so will the women. If you have any intention of abandoning us somewhere on the trail, I want to hear it now. You are a man of low character, Mr. Briggs. If you've lied to me, tell me now, before it's too late."

Briggs regarded her. For a moment she feared she had gone too far. But if she had insulted him, he would deny her any satisfaction from it. She recalled his passing water on the sycamore tree as a sign of contempt. He regarded her now with a look which had in it elements both of that contempt and of indifference. He was a man in control. He feared nothing, even words. And the source of his strength was his ignorance. Finally he got to his feet, slowly, took his weapon from the table, and belted it. "Thanks for the kind words, Sister," he said. "You are no prize yourself, though. You are plain as an old tin pail and you have got a viper in your mouth." He slung his scarf and cowcoat over a shoulder. "This is the most tomfool traipse I ever heard of—and a lot more'n you can swing alone." He placed his slouch hat on his head at a slight, almost comic, angle. "But you sleep easy. I'll set out with you because I said I would. Might as well—I'd be on the run around here anyhow. And I'll look out for your cuckoo clocks the best I'm able. However, I will up and leave when, where, and if I please. Now, if you don't mind my asking, where's my goddam bed?"

Mary Bee sprang up, face burning, marched into her bedroom, tore a blanket from the bed, marched back, and pushed it at him.

"Your bed's in the stable," she snapped. "Goodnight and good riddance!"

He accepted the blanket, turned, eased himself out the door, then kicked it shut with a thud.

She heated water and did the dishes. Then, hoping he had been to the outhouse, she went to it herself, worrying every step there and back.

At last she had an opportunity to read the letter from her sister she had picked up in Loup that morning. Dorothy was well, as were Harold, her doctor-husband, and Adam, their six-year-old, and guess what, she was expecting again!

A hard tap at a window and Mary Bee fairly jumped out of her skin. She took the candle over and it was Briggs, of course, wanting in. The night was cold, he shouted, and he had the catarrh bad. She said no, absolutely not.

He replied he was coming in anyway. She must have a bed in the loft.

She took up the rifle and threatened to shoot him if he entered.

He entered, blanket about him, and climbed the ladder to the loft while she stood, finger on trigger, like a complete ninny.

Her situation, as she saw it now, was desperate. Not only was he a fearless man, he was a brazen. He had called her bluff, and safely could again. If she shot and killed him, he couldn't help her; if she didn't, he could help himself—to whatever he desired. Big and strong she might be, as tall as he, but she would be no match for him in the end. She fled into her bed fully clothed, candle near, rifle at her side and pointed at the doorway. She dared not close her eyes. And sure enough, in the wee hours, she heard the ladder creak. The wolf on the fold. She sat up and aimed the gun.

"What're you doing?" she cried out.

He came to the doorway.

"Going out to pee!" he hissed.

After he had done so, outside her front door no doubt, and climbed back into the loft, she was so humiliated that she fell asleep, and when she woke it was light and he was descending the ladder and closing the outside door.

She made flapjacks for breakfast, or as some called them, "suckeyes." Occasionally she watched the jumper through the window. After chores he filled from her well the wagon water keg, then moved back and forth bringing various items from the stable and stowing them in the box under the front seat. She called him in, and when he was seated at the table she set a stack before him. He drenched it with molasses. She brought her own stack.

"The sleeve of your coat's torn," she said, declaring a truce. "Would you like it mended?"

He shook his head.

"What were you putting in the wagon?"

"Hammer. Nails. Shovel. Ax. Stakes. So forth." His mouth was full. She had to reach for the molasses. "This morning?"

"Yes. We'll stop in Loup first."

That stopped his fork.

"Why?"

"I have an idea. You said last night you'd leave us whenever you please. I can't have that. So I've thought of a way to keep you with us to the Missouri. To make the job worth your while."

"What?"

"I'll tell you in Loup."

"Then where?"

She went to the stove and poured the last of her batter. "I have it mapped in my mind. You should know their names. Mrs. Petzke, Mrs. Sours, Mrs. Svendsen, and Mrs. Belknap. We'll pick them up in that order, two today, two tomorrow—they live far apart. Can you eat another flapjack?"

He nodded.

She brought his plate, served him, filled his cup and her own, and sat down again.

"I think you should know something about our four passengers," she said. "I'll start with Theoline Belknap, my nearest neighbor to the west and a dear friend. Let me tell you what happened." She sipped coffee. "A couple of weeks ago, during a blizzard, Theoline had a baby girl. She is forty-three. It was her sixth child. Her husband was in town and she gave birth without help. She then took the baby to the outhouse and put it down the hole. Her husband found it later, dead. Now she is completely out of her mind. She can't speak or feed herself."

Mary Bee waited for reaction. Her star boarder finished his flapjack.

"Then there's Mrs. Petzke," she began.

"You taking your horse?"

"Of course. You're not interested in Mrs. Petzke."

"No, I'm not." He drained his cup, rose, and collected his clothing. "Who'll look after your stock?"

"Charley Linens. My neighbor to the east."

"All right, I'll harness and hitch. You clean up in here and pack for yourself and make us bedrolls. If we're going, let's get to it."

He was out the door before she had time to be provoked. She did up the dishes quickly, then thought to pack. She would have liked to use her portmanteau and take a proper outfit in which to meet, eventually and triumphantly, Altha Carter in Iowa, but there simply wouldn't be room. He might even pitch it away. Instead, she settled for a velvet sewing bag and the few things she had prescribed for the wives, plus her sister's last letter, ten dollars in greenbacks, and folding in finally, on whim, her precious cloth keyboard. Precious little opportunity she'd have to play! Once or twice she looked out the window at the cloudy, inauspicious day. Briggs had already tied mare and roan to the frame wagon and stowed their saddles on top, and was now backing the harnessed mules between the shafts. He stopped, coughed, and bent over with coughing, which was followed by much hawking and spitting. He was indeed plagued by catarrh. She made their bedrolls, stripping two blankets from her bed and two from his in the loft, rolling hers around the sewing bag and tying both with cord. She opened the stove and smothered the coals with ashes. She emptied the water bucket out the door. She pocketed several boxes of ammunition for her rifle. Then, too suddenly, she was ready. She looked around her, at her lovely house, and to her dismay her eyes filled with tears. If she didn't take care, she'd sit down at the table and have a good boo-hoo and join him with her face a swollen fright. As though that mattered when she was plain as an old tin pail. She drew a deep breath. Tears were out of the question. A smatter of self-pity, however, she could allow. This was the day Mary Bee Cuddy set forth to do the greatest kindness of her life. Did she have trumpets? She did not. A cannonade? She did not. All she had to honor her heroism was a cloudy day and four dumb animals waiting and a fifth hawking and spitting. She put on her coat and rabbit hat, picked up bedrolls and rifle, latched the door behind her, strode to the wagon, dumped the bedrolls inside and her gun in the box under the seat. Briggs was examining the mules' teeth.

"D'you know much about mules?" she asked.

"Some."

She climbed to the seat. He was still studying teeth. "Will they get us there?"

"They're old. Old mules, their teeth wear down from chomping their bits."

She nodded at the off animal. "This one twitches his ears a lot. He's the thinker." She nodded at the nigh. "This one does more than his share. He's the worker."

"She," corrected Briggs. "She's a mare mule, other's a horse mule, male."

"Oh," was all Mary Bee could say.

He came back and would have climbed aboard but something turned him. "Hold on," he said, and walked off to the stable. She heard thumping, like the sound of a hammer. When he returned he had four strips of leather cut from the traces of another harness, strips thirty inches long or thereabouts with two nail holes at each end. So that he could put them under the seat, she had to rise.

"What're those for?"

"To strap 'em in."

He dropped the seat onto the box.

"Strap them in? Why?"

"They're crazy, that's why. They might need to be tied down."

"I'm sure they won't."

"They might get to clawing and biting. Or run off altogether."

"They'll do no such thing."

Briggs hauled up beside her on the seat. "Just how in hell do you know?"

He was right, of course. How would they behave? Might they quarrel? Might they try to flee? She recalled Mr. Svendsen warning her not to turn her back to his Gro— "She will kill you!" Or might they be as dear and easy to manage as retarded children? She hadn't an inkling. Her knowledge of madwomen was as extensive as her knowledge of mules. She penalized him for being right by not saying a single word to him almost the whole ten miles into town. A mile from it he reached, took away the reins, pulled up the span, and jumped down from the seat.

"You're going into Loup."

"I have business."

"Then get down and lock me in the wagon."

"Why?"

"I just cheated one rope. I don't care to bet on another."

"I don't understand."

"Think about it."

He made her feel an ignoramus again.

"Oh. You might be recognized."

He walked to the rear of the wagon. She came down, saw him inside, and easing between the trailing horses, hers and his, locked the doors with the slide-bolt. As she headed for the front, he spoke through one of the windows on that side. "You've got money."

"Some."

"I don't have. Here's what you buy me. Three boxes of paper catridges for a Navy Colt's .36, and caps. Star tobacco. And a jug of whiskey."

"Whiskey?"

"Snakebite."

Mary Bee put hands on hips. "Oh, no. Bullets and tobacco, maybe, but no whiskey, not a drop."

"Why not?"

"Think about it."

He was actually annoyed. He stuck his head through the window and knocked off his hat. "Why not?"

"I can't have you getting drunk around four defenseless women."

"If I don't get drunk around those women, I'll lose my own mind."

She picked up his hat. He withdrew his head and she handed the hat through the window. "No," she said. "I won't."

Inside, he sighed. "Then be dry and be damned. I won't go east with you," said he. "Goodbye, Cuddy."

She was much more than annoyed. "You have to, Briggs. I saved your life."

"Thank you."

She stomped a boot. "You swore to God!"

"I'm a man of low character."

The last mile into Loup she plotted a perfect revenge. He was locked in the wagon, he hadn't realized he was her prisoner. What she'd do was drive to the center of town, stand on the seat, and announce, at the top of her voice, that inside her wagon she had the varmint who tried to jump Andy Giffen's claim—a crime at least as low as rustling cattle or thieving horses. That would attract a crowd. The jumper, his name was Briggs, had slipped the noose once, she would go on to the crowd, larger and more murderous by now, but she had him this time, and she was sure there were men enough and trees and rope in Loup to make certain of him. Then she would descend, slide the bolt, sashay off, and let the local vigilantes hang him while she idled away an hour in the general store imagining death by strangulation and admiring millinery.

She tied the mules to a tree across the way from the general store, waded through mud, went inside, emerged after a few minutes, waded through mud back to the wagon, and via a window delivered to her prisoner three boxes of cartridges and three plugs of Star.

"And now," she said, "a jug of whiskey." And she added, "The saloon's best—Old Tabby."

She smiled as he took the jug through the window. Half a revenge was better than none. He must have heard the story, which was told about practically every saloon in the Territory and its proprietor. In Loup, as elsewhere, whiskey dispensed by the general store was judged to be of higher quality than the saloon's, which had come to be called "Old Tabby." The proprietor got whiskey by the barrel from Wamego, and according to the story doubled its volume with water but maintained its potency by adding dead rats caught by his cat. Then the cat disappeared, having run out of rats perhaps, and the saloon-keeper, desperate to keep some teeth in his elixir, was suspected of using the unfortunate feline instead.

She spoke to the window. "What's your first name?"

He stayed out of sight. "That's my business."

"I have to know."

"Why?"

"I told you—I have an idea how to keep you with us, all the way to the Missouri. I'm going to the bank, and I have to have your name."

The bank sank in. "Let's say George."

"George. George Briggs. All right, I'll be back soon."

The Bank of Loup boasted a counter, a desk, a safe, and Mr. Clemmons, President and Cashier. The story told about it and him, as apocryphal probably as the one about the saloon proprietor and his cat, had also been told at one time or another about every wildcat bank and banker in the Territory. Footloose, and looking for a professional living, Clemmons had wandered into town, rented a clapboard front, installed a safe, painted BANK on the window, and opened for business. The first day a man came in and deposited a hundred dollars. The second day a second individual deposited two hundred. By the third day, Clemmons had acquired enough confidence in his bank to deposit a hundred himself. It was a good story, but Clemmons had the last laugh. He turned out to be a crackerjack banker and a man of total probity. He had survived for two years now. He held mortgages on much of the best farmland in the area, at interest rates averaging five percent a month. Like all wildcatters he issued his own paper money, notes on the Bank of Loup elaborately printed with a promise of redemption in greenbacks or in gold or silver specie, and his currency was acceptable everywhere. Finally, his customer service was high-grade. Miss Cuddy asked to withdraw three hundred dollars from her account, was immediately obliged with six fifty-dollar banknotes and informed that this reduced her balance to two hundred four dollars. Saying she wished to mail the money, she was offered the desk, a pen, ink, and an envelope. This she addressed as follows: "Mr. George

Briggs, c/o Mrs. Altha Carter, Ladies Aid Society, Methodist Church, Hebron, Iowa." Miss Cuddy rose then, was shown to the door by the President of the Bank of Loup, and wished a good day.

Her step on return to the wagon was slow. The envelope seemed heavy in her hand. With two of the three hundred dollars she had planned to buy a beautiful cherrywood melodeon and bench. She held the envelope up to the wagon window.

"Read this."

His face appeared. He frowned at the rectangle almost fiercely. It was an expression she had seen many times. He couldn't read, so surely couldn't write. Names or words written or printed he could recognize only by repetition or association.

She turned the envelope front to her and read aloud from it: " 'Mr. George Briggs, care of Mrs. Altha Carter, Ladies Aid Society, Methodist Church, Hebron, Iowa.' " She looked at him. "I've put three hundred dollars in this envelope. I'll mail it at the store now. When we reach Hebron safe and sound, Mrs. Carter will have it for you. Don't you think it a fair sum?"

"I reckon."

"I reckon, too. Have you ever in your life earned three hundred dollars for a few weeks' work?"

He answered her question with his own. "Why not let me have it now?"

"Oh, no."

"Why not carry it along?"

"Oh, no."

He turned away.

She crossed the street again, then stopped, as deep in thought as she had been in mud. It would in fact be safer to carry the money with her. You couldn't trust the mail. Besides, he could leave them anytime on the trail, ride on ahead, identify himself, and collect the envelope from Altha Carter, who'd have no way of knowing its purpose or what it contained. She opened her coat and buttoned the envelope inside her shirt. When they reached Iowa, she would make a little ceremony of presenting it to him herself. Decided, she recrossed the street, mounted the seat, and drove out of Loup.

After a mile or so she stopped, unlocked the rear doors, and let Briggs out. He stretched his limbs and took the reins to spell her.

"You sent the money to George Briggs."

"I did."

"That's who I better be, then."

"You mean you're not?"

"One name's as good as another out here."

He drove for two hours, northwesterly, while she made a list in her mind. Twice they inquired the way at sod houses. Then they topped a long rise, and Mary Bee had him pull up, and pointed.

"That must be the Petzke place." She turned to him. "From now on we'll have women with us. There are some things I want to say. First, you said you're not interested, but I don't care. I want you to know what happened to Mrs. Petzke—Hedda, I think her name is."

She told him. The man beside her listened, or pretended to, bringing from a pocket of his cowcoat a plug of Star and gnawing off a good chew.

"There, now you know," she said. "I'll tell you about Mrs. Svendsen and Mrs. Sours as we pick them up." She frowned. "Oh, yes, the second thing. I am aware that you can't read. I knew it when you looked at the envelope. If you'd like me to, I'll teach you how. Somewhere, at some house or school, I'll get a book or two, and I'm quite capable, I'm trained as a teacher. So whenever you're ready, I'll be."

She waited. There was a sound high above them. They looked up, and over the white earth the sky was spread like a great, gray tarpaulin and under it, northward, aimed a black arrowhead of geese.

"Three," said Mary Bee, counting with her fingers. "By this time tomorrow we'll have our load. From then on, I will be in charge. I will make the decisions. I am responsible. You are simply to help me however you can. Is that clear?"

It was like lecturing a mule, the only difference being that the man chewed his cud in response while the mule twitched his ears.

"Four," said she sternly. "You may not now, but one day, when we've got them safely home, you'll see what a grand and glorious thing you've accomplished. Money aside, it may be the only unselfish thing you ever do." She fervored up her voice. "And one day, one day, Mr. Briggs, you'll thank the Lord He gave you the opportunity."

He spat loudly over the side. "School's out," he declared, and started the wagon.

N.W. 6, Section 25, Township 10, Range 22W.

She hugged him tight and would not let him go. He asked her what was the matter.

"Those wolves," whimpered Hedda Petzke.

Otto Petzke tried to joke her out of it. "All you must do, open the door and holler *'Raus! Raus!'* and they will run away."

"No, no," she whimpered.

He understood now that she was truly frightened. *"Schatzlein, schatzlein,"* he murmured in her ear. Otto Petzke was forty, his wife, Hedda, thirty-six, they had been married sixteen years, and still he called her "sweetheart." He had an idea.

Entering the house, he came out with his shotgun and a shell. He had his rifle in the wagon in case he could shoot a buffalo. Hedda had never fired a weapon, she shrank from it, but he showed her how to break the gun and load it and, after much coaxing, to put it to her shoulder and aim. Then, standing behind her, placing her finger on the trigger, so that she would know the sound and kick, he tricked her and pulled it. At the explosion and recoil she cried out and collapsed at his feet, and he thought she'd fainted. But she had not, and when he lifted her she threw her arms around him. They stood together several minutes, their boys, Rolf and Jergen, fifteen and fourteen, watching them impatiently from the wagon, the ox team breathing steam. It was early-morning light. Father and sons were going to the Couteau, eight miles south, to cut wood in the river bottom, for they were out of wood and almost out of hay for the stove and this was only February and only their second thaw. Otto Petzke looked aside at their sod house. The snow had drifted on the north side as high as the roof. What had become of the small, sturdy, spark-eyed woman who had come west with him three years ago? It was this long *verdammt* winter, or maybe Gerda's dying. She was thin now, she spoke only when spoken to, lifting a finger tired her, she was a stranger in their midst. And he recalled: when the wolves, hunting in packs, howled outside nights, she turned to him in bed and hugged him as she did now, desperately.

He forced her from him, holding her arms.

"We go," he said. "Here is what you do. In the house I have put out two boxes of shells. If they come near, open the door and shoot the gun, anywhere. They will run away *schnell,* quick, I promise it. We be back tomorrow, I promise it." He put the shotgun into her hand.

"Nein," she said, and let it fall.

He strode from her to the wagon.

But she did not see them go. She ran, leaving the weapon in the snow, into the house.

To keep busy that day she sewed, patching the seats and knees of Otto's and the boys' spare overalls with flour sacking. It was also to keep her mind off the coming night.

She was very lonely. She missed the virile voices

of her husband and her boys. She wished they had a
ticking clock.

They had come west from a farm south of Springfield, in Illinois. Otto longed for free land and a
fresh start. His farm was mortgaged. He hungered
for adventure, too, but this he could not put into
words except to talk now and then about buffalo.
So he sold out and bought a wagon and oxen.
Hedda made him wait until the baby was born, a
girl, Eva, and then they set out across Iowa, husband, wife, two boys, a girl, Gerda, and the baby,
Eva, nursing. Crossing the Missouri by ferry at
Kanesville, they joined several other wagons to follow the Platte River, the most traveled trail. Here
they lost Eva, the baby, to fever and fits, and buried her beneath a tree beside the river. They left
the train then, and turned northwest, and after a
month more Otto found his land. He filed two
claims, each of a hundred sixty acres, half a section,
one a homestead and the other under the "timber-
ing" provision, and paid the fee of fifty cents an
acre. The soil was sandy there, and he concluded to
try potatoes along with corn and wheat. By the end
of the second summer he favored potatoes over
corn and wheat by forty acres. The Petzkes prospered. And to top it off, Otto found adventure. He
shot and killed the only buffalo seen in those parts
in years, a stray bull. He skinned it out, butchered
it, kept the hump and a hindquarter, took three
quarters to the three nearest neighbors, and came
home drunk for the first and only time in his married life.

In the afternoon it started snowing.

She was very lonely. It was not so bad in winter, with her family about, but the rest of the year, when she was alone, she talked to herself. Now she had not seen another woman for four months, even her nearest neighbor, Mrs. Iverson, four miles away. She had not gone into Loup with Otto since August. Mrs. Iverson told her about a farmwife up north in the Territory who went into the fields summers and lay down among the sheep, to have company.

She forgot to go to the stable to feed the stock until it was near dark. Then she ran both ways, and to the outhouse, and running back stumbled over the shotgun. She snatched it up, hurried it into the house, dried it off, and stood it against a chair by the boxes of shells Otto had put out.

It was snowing hard and getting cold. The thaw was over. They might not be home tomorrow.

At dark she lit the old hussy. This was a bowl of sand with a stick upright in the center and a wick wound around it and filled with skunk oil. Otto had shot a fat polecat that gave two quarts of oil. By this light she cooked herself a supper of *schnitz und knep,* dried apples and dumplings, and drank a cup of rye coffee with bran essence to make it taste like real coffee.

There were precious few hay cats left. She stoked the stove with some, saving most for morning, and got into bed fully dressed except for her boots.

They were gray wolves. Some weighed as much

as fifty pounds. As the winter wore on they began to hunt in starving packs of five or six to be sure of their prey. They attacked anything alive. Mr. Iverson had told Otto what they did to cattle during blizzards. Covered with ice and snow, the cattle were jumped on and knocked down and couldn't rise, and the wolves would rip into their bellies and eat until they had eaten a hole big enough for one or two to crawl into and shelter themselves from the storm. Hedda Petzke knew in her soul they were more than wolves. They were messengers of God.

She dozed, then went rigid at the howls outside, not close but not far.

She slid out of bed and by the light of the old hussy took up the shotgun, loaded it, and creeping to the door, opened it a crack, put the gun to her shoulder, poked the barrel through the crack, and fired. The explosion deafened her, and the recoil bumped her backward. She closed the door. When her ears could hear, the howling had stopped.

After that she couldn't sleep but lay still, the shotgun beside her on the bed and loaded.

Later, she heard scratching at the wooden door. How could she open it to fire outside without letting them leap through the crack onto her? It was hung on leather hinges. If they jumped at it, two or three of them, the way they did at cattle, might they not tear it off the hinges?

She had insisted that they bring their bed with headboard and footboard of solid oak, hers and Otto's, from Illinois. It was their wedding bed. The scratching continued. Partitioned off by a hung blanket, the boys slept behind their parents on a bed of strung rope and poles braced by the sod walls.

She sprang out of bed, gun in hands, and moving around the bed, putting the headboard between herself and the door like a wall, laid the weapon over the headboard and, stooping, aimed it at the door.

Wolves were born hunters. They knew someone, something alive was inside the house.

Suddenly there was a great crash of glass, of the window glass beside the door, and she turned the gun barrel toward the shower of glass and pulled the trigger.

Inside the house the roar of the weapon was even louder. When her hearing returned, she listened. She couldn't see the animal. Had she killed it? Wounded it? Or missed it altogether? But the silence was more fearful to her than sound, and after a minute she sank to the floor behind the bed, tore the hung blanket down about her, and began to sob. Later, as light entered by the shattered window, she still sat there, bundled, shaking cold.

In full morning she roused herself. The wolf that had leaped through the window lay dead at the foot of the bed. It was thin, its ribs could be counted, and its head was bloody. She opened the door and, taking it by its tail, dragged it outside. She went to the stable to feed the stock, and to the outhouse, through heavy snow drifting down under a sky the color of dishwater. They couldn't be home today, not hauling a wagonload of wood. She would be alone another night.

Somehow she passed the day. There was no use lighting the stove, not with the open window. She ate nothing. Her right shoulder was sore from the kick of the shotgun. From the trunk she took a packet of letters from her two sisters-in-law in Illinois, received and treasured over the past two years, and read them aloud one by one to hear the sound of a voice. The Petzkes had not had mail since November. There was an old German saying, *"Reden ist Silber, schweigen ist Gold,"* "Speech is silver, silence is gold." It was not true.

In the afternoon she made ready. Using some sticks behind the stove, she pegged up a blanket over the window, then stacked two chairs, one atop the other, in front of it. She fed the stock again. It had stopped snowing. As the day darkened, she moved a third chair behind the headboard of the bed, lit the old hussy, placed the boxes of shells on the boys' bed behind her, easy to reach, then wrapped herself in another blanket and seated herself on the chair, loaded gun across her lap.

Hedda Petzke waited.

She had not done enough to save Eva, her baby, sleeping now in a lonely grave beside the Platte. She had not done enough to save Gerda, her four-year-old, laid low last summer by a rattlesnake bite. She had gone on the run at Gerda's scream by the stable, killed the snake, which was a yard long, with a hoe, carried the child into the house, and run into the fields screaming for Otto. They gave her whiskey, then Otto saddled up and galloped to the Iversons, caught a chicken, galloped back, and together they tore the hen apart and bound the heart over the bite, by the ankle, to pull out the venom. The nearest doctor lived eighteen miles away. All night they gave her whiskey and kept the heart over the bite, but in the morning Gerda died. They buried her near the house. Hedda had lost both her girls. She had failed them. He knew that, too. It was why He had sent the wolves as messengers. "Vengeance is mine; I will repay, saith the Lord." Romans 12:19.

The howling started, close by this night.

She unwrapped the blanket, crept to the door, opened it a crack, and fired. The howling stopped. She sat down again behind the headboard.

But they stayed near, circling the house probably. Could they scent her through the blanket?

Suddenly the blanket over the window billowed. She jumped to her feet and aimed.

The blanket dropped, the stacked chairs were smashed over, and a gray shape, leaping, was tangled in the chairs. She fired. The shape writhed and then lay still over the chairs, near the foot of the bed.

Reloading the weapon she began to cry softly. After a time she could truly hear them, whining about in front of the house. She remained standing, crying. What would they do now? They were too wary to try the window again. Gun pointed at the window she stood, stiff with cold, until her eyes blurred with tears. She could not have that. She willed herself to stop crying, which she did, but to vent her fright began to whine like the wolves.

Suddenly she heard something above. They were on the roof. Searching for a way to get past the gun, to reach her, they had climbed the drifted snow on the north side of the house to claw a hole in the roof and jump down upon her.

The clawing continued. Bits of wood and dirt dropped on the bed. Whining, she raised the gun and aimed it at the roof.

Her arms ached. A clump of wood and earth and legs fell suddenly, awkwardly, out of the roof.

"Grüss Gott!" she screamed, and fired.

The charge of shot flung the animal sideways onto the table, tipping over the table and dowsing the light.

In the darkness she whined with fright and fumbled for a shell and broke the gun and reloaded and couldn't see where to aim but sensed another messenger of God descending and fired where instinct told her and the messenger, wounded, yelped and thrashed upon the bed. It snarled and snapped in agony, crawling up the bed to tear her limb from limb and to avenge her dearest dead. She could see its awful eyes, closer, closer. She could breathe its foul breath, closer.

Her men came home in the morning. They saw the broken window, the dead wolf outside the door, and inside they found the carcasses of three more, one caught in chairs, one on the table, one on the bed. They found the shotgun and shell casings behind the headboard. But there was no sign of wife and mother. A frantic Otto ran shouting to the stable, Rolf and Jergen to the outhouse. Then they returned on the run and for some reason Otto threw himself down and peered under the bed. *"Lieber Gott!"* he gasped. It took two of them to pull Hedda Petzke from under the bed. Her arms, legs, body, were rigid. It was like a paralysis. They had to help her rise and sit upon a chair. She couldn't speak, but made strange whimpering sounds. The pupils of her eyes were dilated. She did not know her husband or her sons. *"Schatzlein,* sweetheart," mourned Otto Petzke over and over, her hands in his, tears in his eyes.

They must have been on the lookout, for they emerged from the sod house long before the wagon reached it and stood like soldiers in rank, three of them, father and two stout boys in their teens. They were ready, too. Otto Petzke held some envelopes, one boy a bundle, the other a bedroll. Neither boy, probably, had ever before seen a frame wagon, but they didn't stare, standing erect and Germanic as their father, and Mary Bee's heart went out to the three. She knew what the wagon would mean to the four families, visited in turn. Its coming would be dreaded and welcomed alike. Its going would have the finality of death.

She stepped down from the seat and greeted Otto,

then indicated Briggs, who, she said, would assist her on the way. Petzke introduced his sons, Rolf and Jergen, and said the three of them had been waiting since Reverend Dowd came by yesterday and said Miss Cuddy would soon be there. He gave her a packet of envelopes tied with a string. On the front of the first was the name "Karl Koenig," Hedda's older brother, who lived not far from Springfield, Illinois. Inside, he said, was a letter from himself to Karl which explained everything. The others were letters from Hedda's sisters-in-law. Karl, he was certain, would take his sister in and do what he could for her, otherwise her younger brother, Albert, would. He lived and farmed near Karl. Hedda had been close to her sisters-in-law, writing back and forth. But if neither family was able, there must be an asylum near Springfield, that being the state capital. Petzke gave her also a folded sheet inside of which was eight dollars in greenbacks, all the cash he had. It should go to Karl or Albert, he said, whichever brother accepted his Hedda.

They were grouped between the house and the wagon, near enough to the latter, Mary Bee thought, for Briggs to hear what was being said. She wanted him to. She asked Otto Petzke what his wife's condition was, could she travel. The homesteader said the same, the same, almost as she was when they found her under the bed after the night of the wolves. He prayed to *Gott* every day that she would be herself again, but she couldn't be. Fear had changed her, maybe for life. She couldn't talk, she

made sounds only. If he held her up, she could
move her legs to walk, as to the outhouse, but
couldn't move her arms. She would sit still on a
chair by the hour. She must be fed by hand, like a
child. And nights were worse. He would let her
down into bed and there she would lie, seeming not
to sleep, eyes big with fear. He didn't see how they
could take her so far, how they could care for her.
And it was all his blame, that was what tore him to
pieces inside. He had known how she hated guns,
he should never have left her alone to cut wood
when it might snow and the *verdammt* wolves would
come. And now, as he condemned himself, Otto
Petzke's round, stoic face cracked, and Mary Bee
sensed that if she let him continue, he would break
down.

"We must be going, Mr. Petzke," she said. "Why
don't you bring her out?"

"I get her, I get her," he said, almost with relief,
and strode into the house.

Mary Bee spoke to the boys. "Will you please
put her things in the wagon? There's a slide-bolt at
the back, and leave the doors open."

While they tromped through the mud and snow
to the wagon she opened her coat and buttoned into
her shirt, along with the envelope from the bank,
the packet of letters to and from Illinois and the
sheet with money. When they camped this night,
and it was dark, she would hide them all in her own
bundle.

Suddenly he rushed outdoors, a wild man, arms

raised high, tears rolling down his cheeks, and turning aside, fell to his knees and began to attack the house, pounding at the sod wall with his fists.

"Nein! Nein!" bellowed Otto Petzke. *"Nein, nein, nein, nein!"*

Returning from the wagon, Rolf and Jergen stopped in their tracks, staring at their father, wondering if he, too, had lost his mind.

"Go in, go in, boys," ordered Mary Bee. "You bring her out. Quickly!"

Otto Petzke remained on his knees. Having exhausted himself, he spread both hands against the wall of the house he had built with those hands, then laid his head against it as he might have his wife's bosom, sobbing.

The boys brought out their mother, arms about her waist, lifting her a little to spare her legs the weight, legs that dangled and skipped as her boots bumped the ground. She made no sound. Her coat was much patched with sacking. They had pulled down over her head a kind of woollen cap with bill and earflaps. Mary Bee glimpsed a worn white face and holes for eyes and that was all. Rolf and Jergen swept her around between the trailed horses and up to the open doors of the wagon. Then they had trouble getting their burden over the step. Mary Bee hurried to help, conscious that Briggs stayed seated, as unconcerned as though they were loading cordwood. Jergen jumped up inside the wagon, Rolf and Mary Bee hoisted the woman, and Jergen, inside, somehow seated her on a bench, then sprang down and out. Mary Bee closed the doors, slid the bolt, ducked under Dorothy's trail rope, went to the front of the wagon and climbed up beside the driver. Hedda Petzke's sons tramped after her like tongue-tied schoolboys, faces upturned. Only now did they understand what was happening to them, and its meaning.

"Take care of your father," she said.

Mary Bee bit her lip. This had been a leathery, loving family that had suffered together on this far frontier and survived until today. Taking away its center, its soul, was she saving or destroying it? She didn't, couldn't, know. As though to sear the scene in memory, she let herself have a last, fleeting look—at the boys' miserable faces, at the bereaved husband kneeling by the wall of his home, empty now—then pinched her eyes shut against her own tears. Unable to give voice, she dug an elbow in Briggs's ribs. The wagon started. When it had rolled perhaps a hundred feet, she heard the pitiful cries behind them.

"Ma! Ma! Oh, Ma!"

W. 10, Section 22, Township 6, Range 18W.

Through the gray afternoon, through crusted snow and drab water the wagon rolled, Briggs keeping the mules to the task. Inside the box, Mrs. Petzke was silent. It was but four miles or so to the Sours place, which, they were told, when they asked directions at a claim, was a dugout. On the way Mary Bee told Briggs about Arabella Sours. He appeared to listen but might not have attended a word. She said she'd never heard of such a terrible thing happening to a couple so young. She'd met Garn Sours, she said, and he couldn't be much more than twenty. His wife could be no older. They must watch him closely, she warned. She had no idea what he'd do when Arabella was actually taken from him. Briggs spat over the side.

At first they couldn't locate the stovepipe and had to drive concentric circles till they spotted the pencil line of smoke rising, it seemed, out of the snow. Then, when they reached the rim of the ravine opposite the Sours dugout below, Briggs refused to take the wagon down. If he did, he said, he wouldn't guarantee to get it out, not with only two animals and this load. And just how, Mary Bee demanded, did he propose to get the wife out? Briggs looped reins around the footboard and leaned back against the box. If she was young, he said, she could walk. If she couldn't, and the husband could, he could damn well carry her.

The slope was steep but Mary Bee could walk it, though she sat down once, hard, on her backside and could imagine Briggs's amusement. No one came from the dugout to meet her. She was greeted instead by two slat-sided pigs, a boar and a sow, which were confined, in lieu of a pen, to a hole in the ground dug with steep sides. They grunted at her and sloshed around in water a foot deep, on the surface of which floated some slops. She knocked at the door. Garn Sours opened it and, recognizing her, shook her hand awkwardly and let her in. The dugout interior was small and dim, the dirt floor uneven from sweeping, a pan was piled with tin plates and cups with leavings in them, and the odors in the place sickened her. She took care to push the door wide open.

"Well, there she is, ma'am," said Garn. "My wife. Belle."

Arabella Sours sat in a straight-backed chair, the only chair. In her lap she held a frayed rag doll with a dangling arm. She was small, and thin as a rail. Her heart-shaped face was that of a woman half again her age. Her flaxen hair was tangled.

"How do you do." Mary Bee smiled. "I'm pleased to meet you, Mrs. Sours."

Mrs. Sours stared at the window.

"She won't say nothing, Miss Cuddy," said her husband. "She just sets and looks out the windy. It's like her body's all stiffened up—I have to tote her to the outhouse, undress her nights, dress her mornings."

"I see. How long has she been like this?"

"Ever since. Doc Jessup said she'd get old all of a sudden, and I guess she did." Garn had seated himself on the bedside. His jaw had a hang-dog set. He made Mary Bee think of an overgrown eighth-grader who believed he'd been punished for something he hadn't done. "I don't even know her no more," he declared.

"How old is your wife?"

"Nineteen."

"And you?"

"Twenty-one."

"I see."

"My, but she was beautiful a bit ago, Miss Cuddy."

"She may be again, Garn, once she's home." Mary Bee gave him her full attention, determined not to look again at the girl. She had come too close to tears over Hedda Petzke. "What will you do when she's gone? I mean, from now on."

He shook his head. "I dunno. I sure can't go it alone."

"Why not? Other men have out here. I've had to myself. It isn't easy, but it's possible."

He was not in a frame of mind to believe her or anyone.

"Well, I've come to take her," said Mary Bee. "What about papers for her?"

From a pocket he took a sheet of lined paper, unfolded it and handed it to her. "That's got her name and address in Ohio, where we all come from, and the other names. She's got her folks and a big family—three brothers, three sisters, some married. She'll be cared for."

Mary Bee opened her coat and buttoned the sheet into her shirt. As to the other things, he was unprepared, and she had to help him make a bedroll of the two blankets he could spare and sack up comb and soap—she made sure of a comb—a towel and a change of underclothing.

"There's this, too," said Garn. "Her grandma's wedding gift. It must be worth a lot. I reckon it should go with her."

Mary Bee opened her palm for it and studied it closely. It was a pink cameo pin. The head and face of a girl was carved in relief, her features delicate, and on her head was a crown, so that the resemblance was to a young queen. The pin had been cherished, Mary Bee surmised, and the girl much envied. She lived in a palace. She would have one child or two. She would never be workworn, never grow old before her time. Forever would she reign, and be forever fair.

"It's beautiful," she said. "I'll keep it for her and see she takes it home."

Arabella's coat was adequate, but the bonnet was not, and so Mary Bee covered the girl's head with two knitted scarves, tied under her chin.

"There," she said. "I think we're ready." She faced the young farmer. "Garn, let me say something. There's a chore you can do for her after she's gone. If you love her, clean up her house. Air it out. Air out your bedding. Sweep. Wash up your dishes. Until you decide what to do, keep your home as clean and tidy as she would have. It's the least you can do. Don't you agree?"

He was sullen. "Yes, ma'am."

"All right, then. The wagon's up on the rim. Can you carry her?"

"Yes, ma'am."

They started, his wife in his arms, her rag doll in hers. But halfway up the side of the ravine he slipped to his knees, rose, and slipped a second time in the wet snow. He couldn't go on. Mary Bee panted to the rim and mad as a hornet screeched at the man on the wagon seat, who'd been observing the effort.

"Mr. Briggs! Will you interrupt your leisure long enough to lend a hand? Now!"

Briggs spat his gob over the side, climbed down in his own good time, and sidestepped the slope to Garn Sours. The two men made a chair of their arms and together hoisted the girl up to the wagon. Mary Bee had the rear doors open, and it was a simple matter to place her inside on the bench with Mrs. Petzke. Mary Bee closed the doors, slid the bolt, and did not trouble herself to introduce Briggs, who took the driver's seat and reins.

"I wish you God's comfort, Garn," she said. "I know and you know this is the best thing we can do for her." She reached for his hand and shook it. "We'll be back in a few weeks, and you'll hear from me through Reverend Dowd that she is safe and sound."

"All right, ma'am," he said, his face still full of injustice.

Mary Bee had taken her seat and the wagon had started when a strange thing occurred. Someone called. Briggs and Mary Bee turned, and through one of the windows in the side of the wagon opposite her husband, Arabella Sours had thrust an arm, raised it, and was waving a farewell.

"Goodbye!" she called to no one. "Goodbye!"

Garn Sours ran around the moving wagon to her side and slowed to a walk.

"Goodbye!" called Arabella.

"I know who you're waving to!" Garn yelled in anger at his wife. "It ain't me!"

"Goodbye!"

"Or you wouldn't leave me like this!" the young husband yelled, walking alongside the wagon, fists clenched, tears spilling down his cheeks. "You had no cause to lose your mind! We could of had more kids! You don't love me—you don't give a tinker's damn!"

"Goodbye!"

With his reins Briggs switched the mules to a trot, and the wagon rumbled. Mary Bee turned forward, wishing she could stop her ears.

"Go on home and play with that damn doll!" sobbed Garn Sours. "Leave me up against it! Belle, for all I care you can just go to hell!"

Again the wave of the arm through the window as he fell behind the wagon, again the plaintive farewell to persons only Arabella Sours could see.

W.4, Section 14, Township 3, Range 5W.

Morning brought a day as dreary as the day before and the day before that. An endless sky of iron cloud seemed to weigh upon the wagon as it creaked across the endless land.

From more than a mile away they saw the man standing before his house. He saw them, too, and rather than waiting, went into the house.

She had time then, covering the mile, to tell Briggs what had happened to Gro Svendsen. There might be trouble getting her, she added. She had met the husband, Thor, and he had warned her not to turn her back on his wife, in her condition she was dangerous. She hoped and expected, Mary Bee said, that if there was trouble, he, Briggs, would come to her aid without being asked.

They drew up to the sod house, which was bigger and better built than most, and waited, as was customary. Svendsen did not come out. Mary Bee said he was probably getting his wife ready. After several minutes she stepped down and knocked at the door. After another minute Thor Svendsen opened it.

"Good morning, Mr. Svendsen."

"Good morning, Miss Cuddy. It is good to see you. Come in, come in. She is ready."

Gro Svendsen was tied to a chair with a rope that went round her arms and upper body twice and was knotted at the back.

So shocked by the sight was Mary Bee that she turned, reflexively, to Thor Svendsen. "Thank you very much. I mean, for the wagon, and the mules. They are just—fine."

"Good, good. Otto Petzke and me, we put in the money. The others, nothing."

Mary Bee was still at an utter loss. "May I ask, why is she tied?"

"Oh, she would kill me. Sixteen years we are married, and she would kill me."

"You can't mean that."

The tall Norwegian, a lean man with long arms,

spread them wide, helplessly. "God will strike you down, she says to me, her husband, and she is God. So she thinks." He spoke in a singsong, swinging his long arms and huge hands. "Oh, she would kill me. I tie her all day and feed her, and all night in bed, her legs also. I told you, do not turn your back."

"She speaks, then." Mary Bee forced herself to face the woman, who was fully dressed in heavy coat and boots and a braided cap of felt. "I'm glad to meet you, Mrs. Svendsen. I am Mary Bee Cuddy."

Gro Svendsen had ears and eyes only for her husband. Her eyes were bright with hatred.

"We have no children," said the man unexpectedly.

"I'm sorry, I didn't know," said Mary Bee.

"I have bad dreams."

"Oh?"

"Of trolls."

She got gooseflesh. Until now he had seemed normal. For an instant she thought of calling Briggs. "Well," she said briskly, "if she's ready, we should be starting. I have Mrs. Petzke and Mrs. Sours in the wagon now, and we'll stop for Mrs. Belknap this afternoon. Do you have her papers?"

He bent over the bed, which was made. On it, in a neat row, were a bedroll, a bundle, and an envelope. He gave her the envelope.

"Here are the names, and where they live. Her two cousins, in Minnesota. May be they will take her, may be not. They have an asylum in Minnesota."

Mary Bee said that was fine, she would pass the

names on to the people in Hebron. "Now, how can we take her to the wagon?"

"I do it, Miss Cuddy," said Thor. "You bring those things, open the door."

Mary Bee picked up bedroll and bundle and opened the door. Svendsen moved cautiously to his wife, leaned, and slipped the rope over the back of the chair. She sprang to her feet as though to attack him, but her arms were still bound to her upper body and he was able to swing her about and bind her to him with his long arms as well. Twice-tied, she struggled, making fierce noises like those of a trapped animal, but he walked her, propelled her, with him in long strides through the door. Mary Bee followed, then had to run to unbolt the rear doors of the wagon and open them. Gro Svendsen was a tall woman, as lean as her husband, and strong, and once she almost tripped them up, but he staggered her to the wagon and wrestled himself and her up the step and inside and seated her with a thud. Taking bedroll and bundle from Mary Bee, he dumped them in, then bolted the doors, walked a few steps away, and stood breathing hard.

"There," he said. "It is done."

"Can't we untie her?" asked Mary Bee.

"No, no. What would she do to the others? No." And just then Thor Svendsen noticed the man on the wagon seat. "Who is that?"

"A man who's going with us. Surely you understand, Mr. Svendsen, I can't—"

"Wait." The farmer walked to the front of the

wagon. Briggs had averted his face. "You," said Svendsen. "You!"

Briggs turned to him.

Svendsen took one look, then strode for the house in a straight line. He was inside and out in seconds, and he had a rifle in his hands.

"That man, I know him! He is the dirty claim-jumper from Andy Giffen's place!" Svendsen advanced on the wagon. "He will not go! With my wife or any woman!" He put the rifle to his shoulder and aimed it at Briggs. "You! Come down or I shoot you!" he roared.

He was quite capable of it, Mary Bee knew that, and knew that Briggs's gun was under his belt, under his cowcoat, and knew further that if he tried to reach it, he'd be killed. Her mind whirled like a vane.

"Wait! Wait, Mr. Svendsen!"

She ran forward and vaulted to the seat so that she stood between Briggs and the rifle and ordered him under her breath. "Stand up! Behind me!" He stood. Swiftly she raised the seat lid, lifted her own rifle out of the compartment, raised the weapon to her shoulder, and aimed it at the man below.

"If you shoot him, I'll shoot you, Mr. Svendsen!" she cried, her voice shrill. "I don't want to, but I will!"

"Get away from him!" roared the farmer.

Her arms were weak, and it was hard to hold the rifle steady. Svendsen's aim was at her now, and the little black hole at the end of his gun barrel seemed to enlarge. "No, I mean it!" she cried. "I can't do this alone! I need him!" And under her breath she urged Briggs. "Get us moving! Now!"

Briggs sat down. The wagon started. She cried out again to Svendsen. "I'll watch over your wife, Mr. Svendsen! I promise!"

He did not fire. Still standing, Mary Bee propped a boot on the seat so that she would not be thrown down as the mules were urged into a trot. At length, when they were a hundred yards away, then two, the man by the house lowered his rifle. She collapsed onto the seat by Briggs, disbelieving that she, Mary Bee Cuddy, had threatened another human being with a weapon, and had been herself threatened. She looked back. Thor Svendsen stood before his home as bewildered, as helpless, and as alone as he had ever been.

A rider dotted a ridge on a course parallel with theirs, and when he changed course to meet them, and his nag and his gait were familiar, and she waved and he waved, Mary Bee guessed it was Alfred Dowd and it was. He came in on Briggs's side. She introduced them. By a twist of the mouth, a narrowing of the eyes, the circuit rider recognized Briggs's name, she guessed that, too. He surveyed the frame wagon and span of mules and said they looked as serviceable to him out here as they had in town, at Buster Shaver's. Were they? Mary Bee said they were, she was content, and they already had Mrs. Petzke, Mrs. Sours, and Mrs. Svendsen inside and were on their way to the Belknaps'—of course, she still didn't know if Vester would let Theoline go with her. He had sworn a blue streak he wouldn't. Well, he would now, said Dowd. He'd be only too glad to have his wife gone. He, Dowd, had heard talk of it day before yesterday, so yesterday stopped by the Belknaps' and confirmed it, and guess what? This time Mary Bee couldn't. Had she heard of a family named Tull south of here maybe thirty miles? She had. Well, Otis Tull had a homely harelip daughter, Jenny, seventeen years of age, and Vester had paid Otis fifty dollars of his mortgage money for her and brought Jenny home with him.

"No," said Mary Bee.

"Yes," said Alfred Dowd.

"The poor thing," she sympathized.

"Indeed," he concurred. "Living in sin at seventeen. Vester old enough to be her father. Disgusting."

Briggs let the gossip go in one ear and out the other. To pass the time, he contemplated earth, sky, and the hind ends of the mules.

"I'd like to speak with you a moment privately, Miss Cuddy," said the minister. "Will you step down?"

She descended and walked back beyond the trailing horses. Dowd rode back and dismounted, holding reins. He was concerned, he said. Briggs was the name of the claim-jumper supposed to have been hanged.

"This is the man. I saved his life. In return, he's given his oath to help me."

"Bosh. His oath wouldn't amount to a hill of beans. He'd murder all of you in a minute."

"I don't think so, Alfred. He's a conniving man, not a murdering. Petty crimes, not big ones."

"You're sure."

She hesitated. "Enough."

"Why?"

"I have to be."

"And?"

"To make sure, I've sent money ahead for him, in care of Mrs. Carter. He knows he'll have it in Hebron, when we arrive."

"Money."

"Makes the mare go. And the mules."

"I can't believe it yet. You. Our homesman." He sighed. "None of us will know a moment's peace until you're back. And by the way, I've also written Altha Carter, informing her you're about to start." He looked at her solemnly. "Well," he said. He opened his mouth, then closed it. She recalled the afternoon at the school, when she and the men had assembled for the drawing. The gravity of the occasion, the muddle of his emotions, had undone the minister momentarily. "Well," he said, "we part." Today he had no muffler to wind or unwind. "God bless you and keep you." Abruptly he turned and led his nag forward, pausing to peer into each of the two windows on that side of the wagon. When he came abreast of the driver, he halted. "Mr. Briggs," he began, then began again. "Mr. Briggs, you bear an awesome responsibility. To the unfortunate women in this wagon and to the lady at your side. Ahem. I hope and expect you will discharge it faithfully."

Briggs stared down at him as he might have someone selling snake oil.

Dowd stepped lively around the mules and alongside the wagon, then peered into the other two windows. Mary Bee had followed him forward and was taking her seat beside Briggs. The minister hopped onto his nag and laid a hand on top of the wagon. "Let us pray," he said, essentially to those on the seat. Mary Bee bowed her head, Briggs did not. "Lord God, to Thy care and love I commend these women. They are three now, and will soon be four. Today they begin a journey through the wilderness. They will want. Feed them. They will weary. Lift them up. They will be sore afraid. Give them Thy shield. At journey's end, O God, let them come to Hebron in peace of mind, in serenity of spirit. Let these, O God, Thy dear and troubled children, come to Thee. Amen."

Mary Bee raised her head and turned around. Alfred Dowd was riding away at a good hickory. She watched him, but for once he did not wave.

Briggs dozed. It had not been the dullest day of his life, loading and hauling lunatics and looking down the barrel of a rifle.

"There's the Belknap place," said Mary Bee, one-handing the reins and pointing. "Mine's over that rise and up the next, you remember, so we're almost back where we started. The last stop, thank heavens. I'll be so relieved to have all four and be on our way. I told you about Theoline, didn't I? And her baby?"

Briggs nodded.

"And you heard Reverend Dowd. Vester's always been shiftless, but I never dreamed he could be so carnal. A harelip girl, and poor Theoline still in the house! Can you imagine?"

Briggs nodded.

"So he's changed his mind about letting her go with a woman. I'm sure he has. He'll be delighted to have her gone, and nice as pie to us, mark my word. Don't you agree?"

Briggs's head did not move.

"Don't you?" she prodded.

Briggs nodded.

She frowned at him. "And the moon is made of green cheese, isn't it?"

Briggs nodded.

"Wake up," she snapped. "Look there."

Someone with a scarf over her head was running from the door of the sod house across to the outhouse.

"Hmmm," said Mary Bee. "That is not one of his girls. I know, that's Jenny Tull! She's ashamed to meet me, poor girl, and Vester doesn't know I know he's taken her in and doesn't want me to find out. Ha, ha. Won't I teach him a lesson, though."

Vester Belknap came out of the house immediately the wagon stopped, and reached it in time to assist Mary Bee grandly to the ground. If he'd worn a hat, he'd have removed it.

"Miz Cuddy, nice t'see you. Been waitin' on you since the parson stopped by an' said you'd be along."

He almost bowed.

She almost smiled.

"Well, now, Line's all ready," he said, having a quick study of the man on the wagon seat.

"How is she, Vester?"

He put on his sorrowful face. "Near the same. She'll feed herself, but she still don't talk sense." He recalled something. "One thing she done—you won't believe it."

Couple of mornings ago, he said, he woke up to find blood all over Line and the tick, her tick. He'd put a straw tick on the floor for her nights. Well, what she'd done was bite through her wrist, the big vein along the big outside bone of the forearm.

Mary Bee stared, speechless.

Yup, tried to kill herself, Line had. Blaming herself, he figured, for killing her babe.

"Dear Lord."

Anyways, he and the girls got busy and bound up both her wrists with sheeting torn in strips, the one to stop the bleeding, the other so's she couldn't bite through that wrist. And when she, Mary Bee, found the bindings on Line's wrists, under her shirt, that was what they were for. And they'd better be left on, he advised, because she might try t'kill herself anytime.

Mary Bee shook her head. "You were right to tell me. Where are the girls?"

"Oh, inside." He gestured at the house. "No use havin' 'em out here under foot, cryin' an' carryin' on when their ma goes."

Vester had interposed his bulk between her and the door. Mary Bee sidled around him and could see Junia, Aggie, and Vernelle at the wavery window, noses flattened. She nodded to them. To their father's annoyance, they tapped a greeting on the pane. At the same moment she could see, in full outline, what Vester was up to. The coming of the wagon and the carting off of his wife were to him a game of Hide and Seek—the whole point of it being to prevent her from discovering that he had bought a new wife to replace the old one, who, though legally married to him and still resident in his house, was shatterpated. To that end, he had ordered his girls to hide indoors lest they blab and give him away, while Jenny Tull had been instructed to run to the outhouse and hide there, out of sight, until Mary Bee, the Seeker, was gone. Getting her to go, as soon as possible, he would handle himself right now.

"Now here's her things, Miz Cuddy," he said, lumbering to the house, picking up a bedroll and a bundle and bringing them to her. "An' here's a paper for Slade's Dell, Kintucky, where she's s'pose t'go. Got a sister'n brother there. Now you put them things away an' I'll fetch 'er right out—how's that?"

Before she could say yea or nay he had gone into the house. She buttoned the paper away, took bedroll and bundle to the wagon, opened the doors, smiled at each of the three women, and turned as Vester, one arm about her waist, bustled Theoline out his door and across the muddy stretch toward the wagon. The woman's eyes darted here and there, but her step was firm and directed. Mary Bee was determined to speak to her, to see how she reacted.

"Hello, Theoline. I'm glad to see you looking so well. Do you remember me, Mary Bee?"

"Ti," said Theoline. "Ti, ti, ti, ti."

"Oh, you want t'talk, she'll talk yer arm off," said Vester, helping her into the wagon and seating her beside Mrs. Sours. He backed out and down, huffing, and heaved a long, sad sigh as Mary Bee closed and bolted the doors. "Don't see as how me and the girls kin live without our Line," he said. "But I know this is the best thing for 'er. An' I have you t'thank, Miz Cuddy, takin' 'er home—what a goodly, Christian thing t'do. An' speakin' of that, cain't I see t'yer stock while you're gone?"

"Thanks very much, but no thank you," said Mary Bee. "Charley Linens will."

Suddenly she slipped past him. It was time to seek. She marched in a straight line toward the outhouse, stopping ten feet away. "Jenny!" she called.

She was not answered.

"Jenny Tull!"

She could almost see, through the wooden door,

the frightened, disfigured girl hiding inside. Did she know what Theoline Belknap had done there?

"Jenny, this is Mary Bee Cuddy," she announced loudly enough to be heard at the wagon and even in the house if anyone was curious enough to crack the door and listen. "Welcome to our neighborhood. I live just two miles east of here. I'm going away now, for a few weeks, but when I return, I want you to know you'll have a friend. Goodbye."

When she swept back to the wagon in triumph, Vester had moved forward to stand by the seat, found out and red-faced. She climbed up on the driver's side.

"That was mighty smart, Miz Cuddy," he sneered at her past Briggs. "But pot cain't call the kettle black. I see you got yerself some comp'ny, too, fer the cold nights. Who's this plug-ugly?"

In Briggs's right hand appeared his big Navy Colt's. He, too, had played the game. Mary Bee didn't know where he'd hidden the gun, behind him or under him or in a fold of his cowcoat, but here it was. Vester stood stock-still, his eyes widened by the weapon. A rifle might not have daunted him, but he was a stranger to handguns and the kind of men who carried them. Briggs leaned out and down and with the barrel of the repeater gave the homesteader a sharp tunk on the forehead, just above the hairline, insufficient to fell him but hard enough to split the scalp. Briggs laid the gun on the seat and wiped the black from his right hand on his coat. Dark blood trickled down Vester's forehead, over the bridge of his nose, and fell in drops from the tip. Briggs handed the reins to Mary Bee, she clucked to the mules, and the wagon moved away. Vester Belknap stood like a dumb animal, bleeding. Briggs spat over the side.

Thus the wooden box on wheels commenced its passage over the plains. The wheels made two sounds. Where there was posthumous snow, they crunched. Where there was not, and the miles were mats of damp brown grass and the iron tires cut through to soil, they rumbled. And counterpoint to these sounds, before and behind, were the trampling of the mules and the thuds of trailing animals, mare and rat-tailed roan. Mary Bee Cuddy had the reins, Briggs beside her. Four women rode within the box, passengers and prisoners, locked in with their belongings. On top, tied down under a tarpaulin, were bedrolls and sacks of provisions and saddles for the trailing horses. Underneath, suspended from a cross-brace, hung a bucket of axle grease. Staring from its windows, its square and sightless eyes, the wagon tended eastward toward a place where gray sky and mottled earth met and made a long, long line. After an hour or two of travel, a new sound reduced the rest. One of the women began to wail, grievously, and went on wailing until Mary Bee said she couldn't bear it, asked Briggs to stop, climbed down, and stepped back to a window. It was Mrs. Svendsen, least likely of the four, whose arms she had untied. "Please stop, Mrs. Svendsen," she asked. The woman continued. "Mrs. Svendsen, I asked you to stop. Please do." The woman did not. "Stop!" cried Mary Bee through the window at her. "This instant! You stop!" Mrs. Svendsen stopped.

Mary Bee went up to the seat, wheezing as though she couldn't catch her breath. When she did, she spoke to Briggs. "That was dreadful. I couldn't endure it." He looked at her, amused. "What'd you think this was, Cuddy? A church picnic?" Soon, however, Mrs. Svendsen began to wail again, and was echoed by another woman, then another, and presently the voices of all four, Gro Svendsen and Hedda Petzke and Arabella Sours and Theoline Belknap, joined in discord. It was a lament such as these silent lands had seldom heard. It was a plaint of such despair that it rent the heart and sank teeth into the soul. Mary Bee pressed hands to her ears. Tears streamed down her cheeks, the tears she had damned up yesterday and today. It was as though the tragic creatures in the wagon could now, finally, discern what was happening to them: that they were being torn from everyone they loved, their men, their children born and unborn; and from everything they loved, their flower seeds and best bonnets and wedding rings—never to return. The wagon rumbled. Mary Bee wept. Briggs pushed the mules. The women went on wailing. Wailing.

THE
TRAIL

IN the neighborhood they were called "Norskies." Among their own kind they were known as "Vossings" because they had originally come to the New World from the Voss district of Norway. They were hard-headed people. They let their sweat speak for them. They feared only God and prairie fire.

Thor and Gro Svendsen came to the Territory from Minnesota, selling the farm there to Syvert and Netti Nordstog, Gro's parents, staking out one claim in the Territory and buying the adjacent from a homesteader who had frozen his feet crossing a swollen stream. A doctor amputated his legs with a skinning knife and a hacksaw.

The Svendsens built a sod house and stable, turned eighty acres with a breaking plow and planted sorghum, put down a well and found water at twenty feet, and prospered from the beginning. They toiled from light to bed and had rain enough and money in the Bank of Loup and loved each other and lived with tragedy.

Gro was barren.

It was the central fact of their life.

She was thirty-six now, Thor thirty-eight. The calendar pages curled. The bed turned its back on them. Sexual intercourse, which had once been an act of love, and later a chore as customary as bringing a cow to a bull, had become after sixteen years of marriage a deed done in silent desperation. Their childlessness was not from lack of trying. Every night, except for those of her periods, husband threw a leg over wife, drew up her nightgown, mounted her, worked upon her as though he were hammering a crowbar or swinging an ax, spilled his seed, rolled away from her, and slept. Neither uttered an endearment. Neither kissed the other. Thor could not conceive why Gro could not conceive. How could a field, a virgin field, plowed and planted now uncounted times, fail to yield a crop? What poison was there in the soil? She must be at fault. Had he not done his duty? Why would she not do hers?

Now and then, after supper dishes, while she bent by candlelight to her task, mending sheets, weaving a rag rug, Thor would stare long at her through the spectacles he had bought from a salesman who peddled the neighborhood every year. After trying on many pairs, you settled on one and bargained for it. Two dollars was not too dear a price to pay to save your eyesight. "I have given you my seed," Thor would say. "You do not accept it."

"I am sorry."

"I should have big, strong boys to help me. You should have girls. Soon it is too late. Soon we will be old. What then?"

She would bite her tongue.

"All have children. All but you."

After a time she would say, "I am as God made me." And add, "As you married me."

He would look away, but they took his bitterness and her sorrow to bed with them.

And so to atone, to prove to him she was not a good-for-nothing, Gro Svendsen did the work of three, a mother and two of the daughters she could not have. She worked in the fields with Thor when he could use a hand. Often she fed the stock and forked out the stable. She planted and tended a vegetable garden. She mended bedding, kept them in candles, baked, made her own clothing from yardgoods, washed outdoors and ironed in, fried, made soap from wood ash and grease drippings, dried corn and beef, salted pork and cucumbers, patched overalls and jeans, stewed, churned butter, stuffed fresh ticks for the bed, kept the house clean, swatted flies, gathered herbs for medicines, battled bedbugs in the walls, and opened her door and larder to hopeful wagoners headed west as well as the sad folk headed east, homeward, in defeat. In between she did her utmost to keep herself presentable. She prized a small mirror and stared into it when Thor was gone, trying to recall the bride to whom it had been given, and was every time inclined to cry.

She did cry, frequently, when alone, but tears could not relieve her. Thor spoke the truth. She must be to blame. He gave her the gift of his manhood, and her body would not accept it. Over the years guilt grew in her like a gross, unwanted child. Guilt made her heavy. Guilt waddled with her. Her stomach went sour. She vomited often in the morning. She had headaches. She was without hope. Time would not deliver her of the abomination in her womb, she was certain, no matter how unsightly she became, no matter how long she lived. And as guilt must be her only child, so must it be her secret. She would bite her tongue through before she breathed it to her husband. She thought of killing herself.

Then, in Minnesota, in the early autumn, her father, Syvert Nordstog, died, and Netti, her mother, wrote saying she couldn't manage the farm by herself, she was too old and lonely. She proposed selling it and coming to the Territory to live out her life with her daughter and son-in-law. She would turn her savings over to them and help Gro all she could. The Svendsens had to decide.

Gro was in favor. "She has no one else, poor soul. And she will have three, four thousand easy."

Thor pushed up his spectacles and rubbed the bridge of his nose. "Where will she sleep?"

Gro knew at once what he meant. "In the loft. She sleeps sound."

Over the rear half of the sod house there was a loft floored with poles where they stored things, and a ladder. Gro could stuff another tick.

Netti Nordstog came to them with the first snow. How changed she seemed from the mother Gro had known, how frail she was, how old. She couldn't climb the ladder to the bed made for her in the loft, and had to sleep with Gro while Thor roosted overhead. She was a comfort, though, to Gro, and another pair of hands. She could cook and clean and sew and add a new voice and presence in the evenings when sycamore logs snapped in the stove and wind raged about the corners of the house. She was like a second candle burning. Mother and daughter had never been as close.

It was the most savage winter any of them had known, even in Minnesota. As the days dragged and blizzard followed blizzard and snowdrifts piled as high as his head, Thor piled resentment within himself. Gro understood. An old woman had got the best of him in a bargain. She had jumped his claim to his own bed and cheated him out of his manhood. Granted, she had given them good money, but more greenbacks in the bank were not worth a single hair of a child's head. Sometimes, at night, as her mother slept at her side, Gro could hear him toss and grumble in the loft. It was more than dreams of trolls. If he had grudged Netti Nordstog in the beginning, he hated her now. Gro dreaded an explosion.

And then in February, as though Thor willed it, Netti was taken desperately ill. It wasn't the ague, she did not turn yellow, there were no agonies of fever and chills, it was something inside, the failure of an organ, the liver or a kidney perhaps. She was in fierce pain down deep. The doctor was thirty miles away, and Thor could not be expected to risk the ride. Gro nursed her mother day and night, using the only specific she had, a patent medicine called "J. L. Curtis's Compound Syrup of Sassafras," which, according to the label, was a surefire cure for "Consumption, Hives, Bronchitis, Spitting of Blood, Whooping Cough, Lumbago, Cholera Morbus and Other Maladies Too Numerous to Mention," and dosed her patient also with teas made from wahoo and snake roots. She tried mustard poultices, too, about the neck, wrists, and ankles. But at dawn of the third day, while yet another blizzard overwhelmed the house and Thor snored in the loft, Netti Nordstog passed away, holding on to her daughter's hand for dear life.

"Thor! Thor!" Gro sobbed him downstairs, and the two conferred. There could be no funeral now, for the neighbors, even the Caudills, their nearest, could not be notified in this weather, nor could they summon the circuit rider, Reverend Dowd. All that would have to be put off, but she must be buried now.

Thor shook his head. "Ground's too hard. Solid three foot down."

"Then how?"

"I see to it. You lay her out."

"How?"

"Freeze her."

"Freeze her!"

Thor poked up the embers in the stove and added kindling and a log. "She can't stay in here. Soon she will stink."

Gro gasped. "You wished her dead!"

"I did no such."

"You hated her!"

"Lay her out, woman!" Thor roared.

Gro washed her mother, combed her hair, dressed her in her best silk faille dress, laid a cloth wet with vinegar over her face to deter mortification, and crossed her arms over her bosom. Thor dressed, and carried the body out into the blizzard, then returned, stomping and shaking snow.

"Where?" Gro demanded.

"Never mind."

"Where!"

"In a drift. Near the house."

"Oh, God!" Gro sat down in a chair, covered her face with her hands, and rocked herself. "My mother! In the snow! Like an animal!"

That night Thor got into his rightful bed and expected sex. Gro sprang from the covers and screamed at him from behind the stove. "No, you do not! When she is buried proper, yes! Now, not!"

Thor sat up in bed. "It is my right! Do you not want a son?"

Her response was to rush past him, climb the ladder, and sleep in the loft.

And there she slept from then on. Husband and wife did not exchange a word after that.

Then they had a thaw, and the first day of it Thor tried digging a proper grave, to no avail. Strive though he might after clearing the snow, his spade bounced off the frozen earth as though it were rock. After a few minutes of this, he saddled up and rode over to the Caudills to discuss the problem with Henry. While he was gone, Gro left the house and, shedding tears, swept at the drifts with a broom in search of her mother but could not find her.

The next morning, after chores, Thor saddled up again and rode fourteen miles to Loup. Henry Caudill had suggested gunpowder. Ten pounds of it, in his opinion, would blow a hole wide and deep enough. To be on the safe side, Thor bought eleven pounds at the general store, and fuse, and did not reach home until two hours after dark. Gro still slept in the loft.

In the morning, with a crowbar, Thor drove two holes three feet deep and four feet apart in the place where he had cleared the snow, and filled them almost to the top with gunpowder. Since he was a thrifty man, he saved a pound of powder and set it away in the stable. He then cut the fuse in half, ran the two lengths into the holes, tamped them shut with clods, struck a match, lit the fuse ends, and ran for the house, making it just in time.

There was a muffled explosion.

Gro started. "Gunpowder," said her husband. "I have made a grave with gunpowder. It is the best I can do. Now I bury her. You want to come?"

Thor went outside and looked at the hole. It was ample for a small woman. He got a horseblanket from the stable, with a shovel located the right drift, and disinterred the body. It was frozen stiff. He rolled it up in the blanket, placed it in the hole, and went to work with the shovel.

That night, when both were ready for bed, Gro started up the ladder to the loft, but Thor took her by an arm and held her fast.

"No," he said. "Now she is in the ground. Now you will lie with me."

She came down the ladder and got into bed. He followed, drew up her nightgown, threw a leg over her, mounted her, worked upon her, spilled his seed, and rolled away.

To his surprise, she left the bed by crawling over the foot and came round to stand beside him.

"God will strike you down," she said, then climbed the ladder to the loft.

Thor Svendsen's dream saved his life that night. In some small hour a troll rode a bear through the forest toward him, and he woke with a start. He heard a creak. His eyes adjusted to the dark. His wife was descending the ladder. He lay still and watched. Once down, she moved behind the stove and came out with something in her hand. As she approached the bed, even without his spectacles he could see the long blade of his skinning knife. She raised the knife high. He readied himself.

As she plunged the knife downward, toward him, he hurled himself out of the bed against her, bulling her backward into a chair by the table, tipping it over and Gro with it, knocking the knife from her hand. He snatched it up and sat with it on the bed. His wife got up without a word and climbed into the loft. He had no sleep the rest of that night.

In the morning they dressed, and while she got breakfast Thor went out to do the chores. When he returned and reached the door, something, an instinct, caused him to open the door slowly and to hunch as he entered. It was well he did. She had hidden behind the door, and as he passed the door's edge, she swung at him with the hatchet kept by the stove to split kindling. The blade buried itself in the door.

Thor Svendsen saw red. He wrestled her into a chair, held her struggling with one arm, while with the other hand he opened her trunk and found a pillowcase, then bound her to the chair by the neck.

He stood, breathing hard and glaring at her. She glared back, her eyes glazed with hatred. It was then he realized his wife was insane.

They were to traverse almost the entire Territory, and Briggs set a course due east. Mary Bee preferred to follow the river valleys, which ran southeasterly, in hopes of encountering people who would aid them on their way, the more people the better. He contradicted her. The fewer the better.

"Why?"

"Because we're hauling an odd lot of freight."

"Freight!"

"You call it what you want. It's freight to me," he said. "Stop to think. We can meet three kinds of people out here. Who?"

"Well, wagon trains, I suppose."

"And you suppose those men'll want their wives to see what becomes of women in these parts?"

Mary Bee sat silent.

"What other kinds?"

"I don't know."

"Freighters. Men. Haven't had a woman lately. Who else?"

Mary Bee scowled.

"I'll tell you. Indians. After they lay me low they'll have a high old time with the five of you."

He let her reflect and then, having won the argument, had the right to the last word. "So I'm shooting straight for that river, and I'll shy away from anybody. The fewer the better."

But she was a woman. "They are not freight. They are human beings."

"They're crazy."

"They are precious to the Lord."

"Well, they are to me, too, Cuddy. Three hundred dollars' worth."

They saw, now and then, a sod dwelling or a school or the smoking stovepipe of a dugout, and Briggs avoided them as carefully as he did the bloated carcasses of cattle frozen to death in the winter.

After three days they had established a routine.

Like the horses, the mules were picketed at night, or lariated as some called it, and woke the party mornings by braying like bugles. Briggs unpicketed them, along with the mare and his roan, and let them roll and run and play bronc and try to bite and kick each other. He couldn't feed them grain, but even damp and dead the bluestem grass had some nutriment in it. One at a time Mary Bee took three of the women away from the camp, behind bushes if there were bushes, to relieve themselves, during which Briggs got her fire going again. Having lost the use of her legs, Arabella Sours had to be carried, and he did this. Mary Bee heated water and washed the women's hands and faces and combed their hair, then cooked breakfast. Mrs. Sours and Mrs. Petzke had to be hand-fed. After the meal Mary Bee washed dishes, packed the grub box, rolled blankets, and loaded bedrolls while Briggs harnessed and hitched the span and tied the trailers. Together they placed their passengers in the wagon and moved on. Mrs. Svendsen's arms were still unbound. Rough riding seemed to have knocked the rage out of her.

They took turns at the reins. Briggs spoke seldom. Among other pastimes, Mary Bee counted lone trees. Stands of timber were usually found along creeks or in river bottoms, cottonwoods and sycamores, ash and elm, but occasionally a lone tree seemed to have planted itself on the plain and grown to full majesty. How it was there was a riddle without an answer, unless by bird dropping. She loved these solitary trees. They were dauntless. They comforted and inspired her. The second day she counted four of them, the third day two. They made two or three stops daily. During one the animals were watered and the keg filled at a creek or spring. During another, when opportunity presented, Briggs would take the ax and cut a supply of firewood and toss it up on the tarp. A midday stop was scheduled to permit the women, Mary Bee in charge, to relieve themselves, Briggs again carrying young Mrs. Sours and her doll. They took turns at hunting, too, she one afternoon, he the next. She saddled Dorothy, took her rifle, and rode out as free as the breeze, hoping for big game, antelope or a buffalo stray, but settling, as he did, for prairie chickens or jackrabbits, which weighed up to seven pounds.

They camped in late afternoon, Briggs choosing the site. Mary Bee got a fire going, unloaded the grub box and Dutch oven, dressed and prepared the game. He untied, unhitched, unharnessed, and picketed the four animals. She had never seen anyone as fussy about picketing. First he looked for good grass, then walked round and round on it and stomped the earth until he was satisfied it was solid enough and would hold. Then he drove the four pins in so deep with an ax that nothing less than a hippopotamus could have dislodged them, and it was all he could manage to pull them in the morning. Once supper was eaten and the dishes done and the women taken to bushes or out behind the stock, beds were unrolled for them under the wagon box in case of rain. Every several days, when there was a stream nearby, Mary Bee put the women into clean underthings, washed their dirty, and spread them out to dry. If they weren't dry by sun-up, she spread them on the tarp atop the wagon and weighted them with stones. From the start Briggs insisted each woman be tied to a wheel spoke by a wrist for the night. That got her dander up. These were people, she declared, not animals, no need whatever to picket them. And what, he inquired, if one or more of them set out in darkness for hearth and home? Fiddlesticks, they wouldn't. How did she know they wouldn't? Was she ready, in the morning, to ride to hell and gone to find them? If she could? And if she couldn't, what then? So they were tied. Mary Bee bedded down near them. Briggs slept by the fire, and slept cold, he complained. She had dealt him two damn skinny blankets. Sometimes in the night the whicker of a mule or horse waked her, and when she looked over at him he lay on his side, her rifle near, staring into the embers of the fire, thinking. Thinking? Was he capable of cerebration?

Each hour of the hours each day on the wagon was long enough to go round the world at the equator.

If only she had a fife to toot.

If only she had Mr. Emerson to read.

If only she had a hatpin to jab into the stick-in-the-mud beside her on the seat.

"Why are you a claim-jumper?" she jabbed one morning.

"It's a living."

"How much of a living? How much would you have got for jumping Andy Giffen's claim?"

"Two hundred."

"That isn't much."

"For laying up three, four months it is."

"What would have happened when Andy came home?"

"He couldn't drive me off. He'd have to go to the lawyer in Wamego, man I work for. Buy his own place back, maybe a thousand dollars, or get tied up so long in court he'd starve."

"Despicable."

"Dumb."

"Dumb?"

"He forgot to file."

Another morning she tried the mules. "Will these mules make it to the Missouri?"

"I don't expect."

"Why not?"

She'd hit his nail on the head. "They'll lose too much flesh," he said. "Those sodbusters who put this outfit together for you should've had some sacks of corn on top. There's not enough good in this dead grass. Out here stock should have a quart or two of shelled corn every day. Some say oats, but oats'll get musty. Not shelled corn. Best feed there is, man or beast."

Anything to keep him talking, to hear another

voice. Anything to occupy the mind. "The one twitching his ears, he knows he's the subject of discussion. He's the Thinker, the other's the Worker. But they should have names. What shall we call them?"

"I don't use names."

"Oh. What d'you call your horse?"

" 'Horse.' "

" 'Horse,' " she said.

" 'Horse,' " he repeated.

"That's all," she said.

"That's all," he repeated. "I don't care to get too choice of anyone or anything."

"I see." She considered that. "Well, my mare's name is 'Dorothy,' after my sister."

She waited. That gave him a lead, and if he had a smithereen of social instinct he'd take it, he'd inquire politely about her sister, or her family, or her origins. She waited in vain. He was an utter dolt. And so, eventually, she took her own lead, plodding through her past as though she were following a plow up and down a field while his eyelids drooped and his head sank. Dorothy was her older sister, two years older. They had no brothers. Dorothy was happily married to a doctor, had a little boy, six, and was expecting another child, she'd just written as much. She lived in Bath, on Lake Keuka, in upper York State, where both girls had been born and raised. Their father was a tanner, and she could still remember the smell of the acid when he came home evenings from the tannery. Her mother died when she, Mary Bee, was twelve. She attended the Troy Female Seminary, taught primary school in Massachusetts and New Hampshire for eight years, and then applied to Catharine Beecher's National Popular Education Board in Boston to be tested and inspired and transported out west, her way paid. To serve God and her church, to light a candle of learning in the darkness of the far frontier— these were her intentions. That she hoped also to have some adventures and to catch a strong, handsome, educated, industrious, virile paragon of a husband went without saying to anyone, certainly to Briggs. She was accepted and soon, with her friend Miss Clara Marsh, transported to the Territory by rail, steamer, and stage. In the winter of that dreadful year at the school south of Wamego, word came that her father had passed away, and in the spring came her inheritance. Within weeks she had bought a claim from a new widow and started putting in a crop. The driver's chin reached his chest.

"Am I keeping you awake, Mr. Briggs?" she asked.

His head jerked erect.

"Why, no, Cuddy," said he, touching the brim of his hat. "You are putting me to sleep."

One day he turned the wagon down into a stand of timber to water the animals and fill the keg. As soon as they stopped by the considerable stream, Mary Bee jumped down, walked stiff-legged to the nearest tree, a black walnut, and flung her arms around it, holding it in her embrace for several minutes. Perhaps what she missed most, she told

Briggs defiantly, cheek to trunk, was trees, the trees she had known and loved in York State—maple and beech, poplar and birch, spruce and cedar, in all their multitudes. She let the women out and put them back. Then, as they moved away through the timber, Briggs held up the mules. Ahead of them, atop four poles cut from young trees, was a scaffold of saplings lashed together and to the poles by rawhide thongs. There were three such platforms. On each lay a shape the size of a human wrapped in a buffalo hide. Corpses, said Briggs. Winnebago. This was how they did it. They sat for a moment in stillness. A crow cawed, distantly. Briggs eased the wagon alongside the nearest scaffold and climbed back on top, over the gear on hands and knees. He leaned, got a grip on the buffalo hide encasing the corpse, and yanked on it until it pulled free and dumped the body off the scaffold. Before it thudded on the ground Mary Bee had exclaimed in horror and averted her eyes. Briggs shook the hide, whacked it on the platform to get the dust out of it, spread it on the wagon top to air, and resumed his seat and driving. That day, whenever Mary Bee chanced to see the hide, she felt sick at her stomach. That night, at bedtime, Briggs laid his two blankets over the hide and rolled up in all three. In the morning he announced he had slept warm for the first time.

She had all her valuables in the velvet sewing bag now: a sheet with the name and address of Theoline Belknap's sister in Kentucky; the packet of letters and the name and address of Karl Koenig, Hedda

Petzke's brother near Springfield, Illinois; the paper
with the names of Arabella Sours's numerous family in Ohio, and her pink cameo pinned to a piece
of cardboard; the envelope with the names and
addresses of Gro Svendsen's two cousins in Minnesota; the cloth melodeon keyboard; the last letter
from Dorothy; and the envelope the banker had
given her containing six fifty-dollar notes on the
Bank of Loup and addressed to Mr. George Briggs,
c/o Mrs. Altha Carter, Ladies Aid Society, Methodist Church, Hebron, Iowa; plus her own ten dollars
in greenbacks. By day the bag was rolled up in her
blankets. By night she slept with it. In her bones
she knew she had been right to bring the three
hundred dollars rather than mailing it, but the same
bones told her indubitably that if Briggs laid hands
on it, he would abandon them forthwith. If he was
the other things she believed him to be, he could
certainly be a thief. A man of low character. An
ignoramus. A stick-in-the-mud. A dolt. A brute—
only a brute could have split Vester Belknap's scalp.
She had ransacked her vocabulary for the one noun
that would perfectly peg him. Most of the men who
came to the plains were good men, hardy and brave,
God-fearing and ambitious, family men. Oh, there
were exceptions, lowest on the scale, the outlaws
and ne'er-do-wells. The in-between batch consisted
of culls, inferior in every aspect, taking what they
could, contributing nil. Eureka. She had her noun.
The claim-jumper was a cull.

The next morning the mules, harnessed and

hitched, would not go. Mary Bee had the reins. She clucked till her tongue tired. Briggs sat impassive beside her. She stood up, grasped the reins, and gave each beast a smart switch on the croup. Neither budged. The Thinker twitched his ears. The Worker was adamant. She gave them a second switch. They would not go. She consigned them to Perdition. She switched again. They stood stubborn as—as mules.

"Damn!" she cried, and sat down.

Briggs got down and unhitched them, and taking the span by both bridles, trailing the reins, led them out of the shafts and around the wagon in a wide circle, backed them into the shafts, hitched them up again as though for the first time that morning, handed Mary Bee the reins, and took his seat.

She clucked.

Away they went.

She looked at Briggs, who was looking at her, and he did something so startling she could have fallen from the seat.

He gave her a wink.

As the long miles hissed and grumbled under the wheels of the frame wagon, she studied her four charges with great interest, making daily entries in a kind of mental notebook.

There was no change in the condition of Mrs. Petzke, who had been terrorized into insanity. Her paralysis persisted. She could walk only with an arm about her waist, moving and supporting her, and could take nourishment only if fed by hand. She seemed never to sleep. Mary Bee would peer in at her as she lay under the wagon at night, tethered by a wrist to a wheel spoke, and her eyes were always open, the pupils always dilated. Sometimes she whimpered. It was as though the poor woman was still besieged by wolves, and would be as long as she lived.

Mrs. Sours seemed to have lost permanently the use of her legs. Briggs carried her to meals and to relieve herself. Awake or asleep, she clutched the rag doll. She was scrawny, her cheeks pale, her flaxen hair had no luster, and incredibly, for a girl of nineteen, she showed no animation. Mary Bee fed her, too, by morsel, with her fingers. She opened her mouth for food like an infant, but ate without appetite. Her paralysis seemed to be as much of the will as of the body, and to Mary Bee she was the most pitiful of the four.

The dangerous one, Mrs. Svendsen, turned out to be anything but homicidal. Now that she had been removed from the presence of her husband, the hate that had glittered in her eyes was gone and she seemed entirely harmless. When spoken to, as Mary Bee did, she made no response except to say, from time to time, and in a placid manner, "God will strike you down." She was frequently sleepless at night, turning and tossing under the wagon with sighs and groans, due perhaps to an inner agitation which did not manifest itself by day.

Among the women Mrs. Belknap, dear Theoline,

was the most obviously demented. Her rest at night was fitful, and while awake she often babbled softly in a language intelligible only to herself. She threw her eyes about at random. She ate like a bird. She understood nothing said to her, and Mary Bee gradually developed a theory: Theoline must remain demented, because if her mind cleared, and guilt entered, she would kill herself. There must have been at least one rational moment, then, a moment when her murder of her baby had been revealed to her in all its horror, or she would not have bitten through the radial artery in her forearm. Mary Bee took care to change the bandaging on that wrist every several days, and to keep the other bound in case Theoline's mind cleared again.

These were observations she could make when they were out of the wagon. When they were inside, after she had closed and bolted the rear doors, they were hidden to her, and she had no idea how they reacted to the confinement and to each other. There was one curious thing: when she opened the doors at each stop, none of the women had moved en route. Each sat in exactly the same place on the bench and on the same side that she had taken all along. And each was separated from the woman beside her and across from her by several inches, so that there would be no physical contact no matter how rough the ride. It was as though each of the four was determined to stake out her own space, her own inches, to isolate herself in her own individual Hell.

It was late March, but there had been no shift of season. Winter would not go. Spring would not come. Instead, ten like days shuffled from one end of the plains to the other. They were divided only by darkness. Every day of the ten the sky was gray, the air still and swollen. Every day a gray wagon crawled under a gray sky from one part of the plains to another. Every day the land lengthened before it.

Then late one afternoon there was a breeze, from the north, and welcome to it. But soon it became a wind, and Briggs sniffed it. They were going to have a blow, he said, he didn't know what kind, but a hell of a big blow. He stopped and stood on the seat but could find no river bottom or sheltering timber or even a deep draw. He continued until he could drive the wagon down into a buffalo wallow, which would give them close to three feet of advantage. He ordered Mary Bee to hurry, to get the women out of the wagon and under it, together with their bedrolls and his and hers. While she hurried, he unlashed the tarpaulin and cleared the top of the wagon, and when the women were out, he hauled out the grub box, shoved it under the wagon, and loaded the interior with everything from the top, blocking one north window with a sack of cornmeal stood on a saddle, the other with a sack of beans. By now the day was blackening to night, suddenly, and the wind was growing to a gale. He got hammer and nails and, with Mary Bee holding it, nailed the tarp to the north side of the wagon to cut off whatever was coming, rain or hail. Finally, he unhitched and unharnessed the span and the roan and mare, and rather than picketing them, tied the four animals to wheel spokes on the south side of the wagon. Here they'd be close, and in the lee, and though they might suffer they wouldn't scare off and go gallivanting. He and Mary Bee went under the box then, and got themselves and the women into blankets just as the storm smote the wagon with a blast that hoisted both north wheels entirely off the ground.

It was an ice storm, a phenomenon of the plains. Clouds of ice particles almost as fine as flour were hurled across the level land by a roaring gale. Neither man nor beast could confront them. In the open a person's face was covered with ice instantly, his eyes frozen shut, his breath taken away, his clothing so penetrated by ice that his whole body was encased. Only the protection afforded by the wagon and the tarpaulin saved these travelers. As it was, the tarp began to flap and whipped them violently until they got hold of it and pulled it inward and weighted it with their bodies. Even with lee shelter the animals suffered terribly. In an hour their bodies were sheeted in ice; in two hours their heads were the size of bushel baskets, made into masses of ice by their congealed breathing. Soon after, neither mules nor horses could support the heavy cumbers and lowered their heads to the ground. For hours the storm assailed the wagon and those beneath it. The six humans clung together in a kind of clump, blankets and a buffalo hide around and over them. Mary Bee could have no knowledge of what went on in the women's heads, whether or not they were frightened. She was. There were moments when it seemed the wind would muscle the entire wagon into the air, the animals tied to it, and hurl it Heaven knew where. She tried to imagine her fright away by imagining herself away, not under a wagon on the prairie with four madwomen and a cull of a man but with a trusty captain on a stout bark on some romantic sea, tempest-tossed. Only once did she ask herself what would have happened in this emergency had she started out alone with the women, had Briggs not been there—and dared not answer the question. Toward morning the wind ceased to blow as abruptly as it had begun, and the only sound on earth was the breathing of animals through holes at their noses. It was black night yet, but presently the black washed to gray and then a great golden sun was lifted over the horizon, the first sun they had seen in eleven days, and in minutes its rays turned the world of ice into one made of diamonds. It blazed with a brilliance almost divine. The ground, for instance, was three inches deep in white fire. The six squinted. A cranky Briggs was first out from under the wagon, and after a bout of catarrh, hawking and spitting and cursing, then turning his back and passing water in plain sight, he said he wanted them moving, no food, nothing, so get to it. Using the flat of the ax like a club, he knocked the ice off the mules and horses, off the harness and the tarp. Mary Bee unloaded the wagon and got the women into it. She climbed up on top, and he heaved saddles and supplies up to her. She lashed down the tarp while he tied the mare and roan and hitched the span, and in fairly short order they were out of the wallow and crunching east again through light so bright it hurt the eyes. But within three miles they were past the ice and the ground was its old patch snow and brown grass again, as though the storm had never been. The sky was blue, not gray. The air had a remembered warmth. Mary Bee thought she saw a robin and a mockingbird. It had been the deadliest winter the Territory had known, taking an awful toll of its people, as witness the women behind her; but this storm, His storm, though limited in area, had at last blown down winter's walls and let spring in, real spring. She was grateful to her God.

Near noon she made Briggs stop, opened the grub box, and gave everyone a cold corn dodger. She had just regained her seat and bitten hungrily into hers when screaming inside the wagon brought her down again. She ran to the doors, unbolted, and flung them open.

At first she couldn't see clearly. Mrs. Sours and Line Belknap, nearest the doors, were cowering in fear, heads covered by their arms. She pulled them outside, then realized that Mrs. Svendsen was attacking Mrs. Petzke, had thrown her down on the bench and was beating her with her fists.

"Help!" she cried to Briggs, and jumped inside to

stop Gro Svendsen. She struggled with her, but Gro was a wild woman and strong, and before Briggs could reach them Mary Bee was shoved out of the wagon and borne to the ground and being beaten viciously.

Suddenly the woman was hauled upward. Gro Svendsen's felt cap had fallen off, and Briggs had her by the hair of her head.

He swung her about and with his free hand gave her a sharp slap on the cheek.

The fight went out of her. The hatred in her blue eyes faded. She sagged.

Briggs bound her with his arms and lifted her over the step and into the wagon and dumped her on a bench like a sack of beans.

He went to the front of the wagon, under the seat, and brought back hammer, nails, and the four leather strips he had cut from harness traces at Mary Bee's place just before leaving. In the box again, he hammered eight nails through the hardwood planking, four on each side, and fitting a strip across Mrs. Svendsen's body and arms just above the elbows, pushed the hole in each end of the strip over a nailhead. She was strapped to the wall tightly. She could move neither of her arms and had to sit upright.

"No, no," choked Mary Bee. Tears rolled down her cheeks, which were bruised. Her ribs ached from blows.

Briggs stepped down and, taking Mrs. Sours inside, strapped her against the opposite wall.

"You will not!" sobbed Mary Bee.

He proceeded to do likewise with Mrs. Petzke and with Line Belknap, then exiting the wagon, hammer in one hand, an extra nail protruding from his mouth, closed and bolted the doors.

"I won't have it!" cried Mary Bee. "They're not prisoners, they're precious human beings! The Lord's creatures! Let them go!"

"They're crazy as bedbugs," said Briggs around the nail. "And I intend to get 'em to Ioway before they kill each other."

"You must never touch them again!"

"I'll do what needs doing," he replied, and heading for the front end of the wagon, put away hammer and nail and took the seat and reins.

"You'll do as I tell you!" Mary Bee cried at him. "I am in charge! I saved your life!"

"Suit yourself," said Briggs, starting the mules and moving the wagon away.

She stood her ground. He wouldn't dare.

"Stop!" she shrieked.

It was inconceivable that he would leave her here alone, without food, water, mount, or friend, but minutes passed and he did exactly that. She must run after the wagon, she had no choice, but pride rooted her, and fury. Then the vehicle disappeared, driven down into a draw evidently, and she was in fact abandoned.

All at once the dark familiar deep was in her. She was going void. But when she shivered, and felt the first crystal of fear form in the void, she commenced to run, headlong, in panic. Her heavy boots and coat burdened her, and she could not run far. Soon she was exhausted and slowed to a walk, and in a while came to the edge of the draw. There, below, was the wagon. He had stopped it out of sight to wait for her, cocksure she would, she must, follow. She descended to it in long strides, reached the front end, and climbed to the seat beside the driver. Without a look or word he clucked to the mules.

Mary Bee was utterly winded. She sat upright, as though she were strapped to the seat, gasping for air. She heard, high above, the plaintive cry of a killdeer.

That night, camped, the women fed, dishes done, the stock watered and picketed, Mary Bee sat for a time by the fire, a blanket round her shoulders. Briggs, too, sat by it, easing himself. Immediately after supper he had got out the whiskey he had forced her to buy for him in Loup, and now he sat crosslegged on blankets and buffalo hide taking pulls from the jug. He was in fine fettle. It had been a jimdandy day for him. He had saved the party from an ice storm, slapped Mrs. Svendsen into submission, had his way about strapping the four into the wagon, and made a grown woman run after him like a child being punished. He had even been helpful at supper, washing faces and hands and spoon-feeding Mrs. Petzke and Mrs. Sours, humming to himself as he unlashed the tarp and threw down bedrolls.

"I was in the Dragoons," he said.

She couldn't believe her ears. It could only be the whiskey.

"Comp'ny C, First U.S. Dragoons."

"Oh?" She was cautious. She wanted to know more but did not want him drunk.

"Fort Kearney."

"I see." She glanced at the women behind her under the wagon. They were asleep, each one tied to a wheel.

"Yep. Had us a real fracas one time down in Kansas. Kiowas."

She knew little about the United States Dragoons, although she gathered they were trained and equipped to fight both mounted and on foot.

"Hell of a time," he said.

"Tell me."

The warmer night had let him take off his cowcoat and hat. She recalled the black, rusty suitcoat with its ripped sleeve. He slipped the big revolver from his belt, laid it close by, tilted the jug again, and wiped his mouth with the back of his hand.

"Went out to Fort Leavenworth, C Troop, from Kearney. They put t'gether a supply train six-mule wagons, fifty of 'em, an' a herd three hunderd horses. T'take 'em down t'Fort Union, New Mexico. C Troop escort. Y'know how they trail a horse herd?"

"No."

"Strings of forty horses led by herders."

"I see."

"Well, we had Kiowas like fleas. Trailin' us. War

paint. Sassy. Big as life an' twice as natural. Wanted those horses."

"I see."

He rubbed his chin. "So one night camped on the Arkansas River, the Cimarron Crossing. Teamsters picketed three hunderd mules an' herders picketed three hunderd horses. In sand. Sand. An' did a damn poor job. Drove the pins halfway in, two or three lariats t'one pin. Hell, they wouldn't hold a prairie dog! An' sure enough, that night Kiowas stampeded the whole bunch. Away they go. Whooeee! Trampled the wagons t'pieces an' got the stock tangled in lariats an' crippled up with flyin' pins an' the Kiowas chasin' 'em whoopin' an' hollerin'." He paused, staring grimly into the fire. "Oh, my, but weren't we riled. Blew the bugle Boots'n Saddles an' away we went after 'em. Sun's comin' up now, gettin' light. We caught Kiowas here an' Kiowas there, in bunches, tryin' t'drive our horses, an' killed 'em. They had bows'n arrows'n we had muskets'n pistols. Rounded up our animals an' drove 'em right through the goddam Kiowas' camp. Come night we had most of our horses an' mules an' killed more'n thirty Kiowas an' busted their camp t'hell." He grinned at her in triumph. "Pretty fair job of work, huh? Comp'ny C, First U.S. Dragoons!"

He waited, grinning, as though for applause, like a youngster after a recitation.

"How interesting," said Mary Bee, and went off to her bedroll by the wagon. She made her bed and slept, how long she had no idea, but a shout waked her.

"Whooeee!"

Her back was to the fire, and she whirled over to see an astonishing sight. Strong drink, she supposed, affected different men differently. Briggs had built up the fire and was on his feet by it—dancing. Of all things, of all people, George Briggs was dancing. And unlike the recital of the dragoon story, this seemed to be a performance for his own pleasure. It was a kind of jig, or hoe-down, and he pounded his energy into it without stint. He banged his boots, he clapped hands, he flapped his arms like wings around himself, and as he danced began to sing some words of "Weevily Wheat" in a loud, besotted voice:

I don't want none o' your weevily wheat,
An' I don't want none o' your barley,
Take some flour'n half an hour
An' bake a cake for Charley.

The higher up the cherry tree,
The riper grows the cherry,
The sooner that you court a gal
The sooner she will marry.

O Charley, he's a nice young man,
An' Charley he's a dandy,
Every time he goes to town
He brings the girls some candy.

Mary Bee turned over. The women were awake. They lay on their sides under the wagon watching the dancer. In the firelight their eyes glittered.

Spring sent winds to bluster the face or sail a slouch hat from a head.

Spring scudded the clouds or let them graze like sheep a new blue sky.

Spring dropped dark veils of rain in the distance or flattened the mules' ears with a flood.

Spring damned the plains with thunder and lightning or blessed them with sunny hours so sweet the heart gave thanks.

The snow melted. The gray wagon splashed eastward through puddles. Briggs pushed the party harder.

Late one afternoon they saw, a mile or two to the south, an emigrant train headed west, a short train of six ox-drawn wagons and a small herd of perhaps fifty head of cattle. As they watched, the train commenced to circle for the night, and Mary Bee had an idea. She'd saddle up, ride to the train, and ask if they couldn't camp with the emigrants. It might do the women good, she thought, to spend a few hours with women who were normal, who'd treat them with compassion, it might have a wholesome, healing effect. Briggs said no. In the first place, he didn't care to rub shoulders with any damn pilgrims, and in the second, their four women wouldn't be welcome. Mary Bee wanted to know why in the world not. Because, he said. Because the husbands would say a flat no to having their wives see what could happen to the wives of sodbusters down the road, that they could go crazy. Mary Bee declared she wasn't concerned what the husbands said. With examples like these set before them, they might take better care of their wives, not use them like slaves and brood sows. And so declaring, she saddled Dorothy and rode off toward the train. She looked back once, and Briggs had started the wagon again. He was not a man to wait upon time, tide, or women with vipers in their mouths.

The ox-drawn wagons were circled now, the cattle herded inside, and a man rode out to meet her. They introduced themselves, and in the custom of the West, exchanged information. His name was Henry Trowbridge, and he had been elected train master by this company of Congregationalist families from Massachusetts. Except for household goods they had outfitted themselves and crossed the Big Muddy at Kanesville. They numbered sixteen adults, twelve children, and two infants. They were twenty-five days out from the river today. The weather had been tolerably good, and praise be to the Lord, there had been no sickness among them, nor had they encountered any Indians. Henry Trowbridge had taken off his hat, and Mary Bee told him it was a pleasure to converse with a gentleman again. There were only six in her party, she said, five women including herself and one man, traveling by frame wagon, and they were eleven days out of the neighborhood around Loup, in the northwest corner of the Territory. They had survived a fierce ice storm but had seen no Indians. Small game had been plentiful. She said she had ridden over on impulse, thinking it might be mutually enjoyable if her party camped this night with his. Had he any objection?

He smiled. "None at all, ma'am. It would be our privilege."

"I should tell you one thing, though," she said. "The other four women have lost their minds."

He stared. "Lost their minds?"

"I'm sorry, yes. There is no asylum in the Territory. Mr. Briggs and I are taking them to a Methodist society in Iowa. From there they'll be escorted to the homes of relatives." Trowbridge put on his hat and pulled down the brim so far that his face was half-hidden. "I thought it might be beneficial for them to mingle with the women in your party."

"The sane women," he said.

"Yes." She bent, peering under his hatbrim, trying to look him in the eye. "Does this alter your position, Mr. Trowbridge?"

He met her look, and his was honest. "Miss Cuddy, I'm afraid it does. At least I should talk it over with the men in my company, the husbands. Will you give me a few minutes to do so?"

"Certainly."

"Thank you." He wheeled his horse, then wheeled again. "Are they harmless?"

She paused. "They are wives and mothers."

His face flushed a deep red. "I regret I asked the

question. I apologize." He wheeled again and rode away toward the train.

Mary Bee dismounted and let her mare graze, and presently a boy and girl, brother and sister by their likeness, wandered out from the wagons to see the stranger. They were followed at intervals by two more, then five, then three youngsters. Some walked out warily, some skipped, some ran. A lady in a rabbit hat materializing out of thin air was an object of considerable curiosity, and she was soon surrounded by boys and girls big and small, dark and fair, boisterous and shy, a dozen of them, and all of them, plus herself, jabbering away at a great rate and swopping whoppers. They told her about fording a river and how they all nearly "drownded." She told them about the ice storm. They told her how tiresome it was to herd cattle after the wagons all day, which was their chore, and how dangerous—they'd seen hundreds of savage Injuns lurking everywhere. She told them how she had shot and killed a rattlesnake in her schoolroom. Their eyes popped. Her schoolroom? Yes, she'd fess up, she had once been a teacher. Oh, they said, shame on her, but they were out of school now for good, they'd never, ever have to go again. Mary Bee begged to differ. The fact was, as soon as their parents settled somewhere, one of the first things they'd do was build a school and hire a teacher. And speaking of that, she teased, they'd played hooky long enough, and this was a perfect opportunity. Why didn't she drill them right now, right here, on their multiplication tables?

They groaned. All right, what about a spelldown? They pretended to be sick at their stomachs. All right, then, what about a game of Pass-the-Shoe? Hooray, they cheered.

The eldest was nine or ten, the youngest four or five. Mary Bee seated them in a circle on the grass, side by side, cross-legged, and had each one remove a shoe or boot. Several didn't know the game. Circling behind them, teacher explained it. Someone would chant a count-out rhyme. On each beat, everyone was to bang his shoe or boot on the ground before him. On the last beat, the shoe or boot was passed to the person on his left. So on and so on, shoes and boots moving around the clrcle. But as soon as a shoe or boot was passed to its rightful owner, the game was over, that person was the winner and received a prize. Did everyone understand? All right, get ready, get set, who'd sing out the first rhyme?

It was a stout boy with a muddy face. "Oneso, twoso, zickasi zam," he declaimed as boots and shoes were banged. "Poptail, vinegar, pickle in the pan/ Ram, scam, birds anam/ Tee, taw, buck!" And on the shouted word "buck," boots and shoes were passed and grabbed and someone else began to chant, a small girl with a runny nose. "Eerie, orie, ickery Ann/ Phylisy, phalisy, Nicholas John/ Queery, quary, English Navy/ Stinkum, stankum, buck/ You're out!" Several passed to the right rather than the left and tangled arms, and the rest fell over backward, laughing. Everyone had a repertoire of count-out rhymes, so there was no lack of volunteers. "Peter Mutrimity Tram," chanted a girl with pigtails, "He is a good water man/ He catches hens/ And puts them in pens/ Some lay eggs and some lay none/ Wire briar limber lock/ Three geese in a flock/ O-U-T spells out!" Then two boys counted out together at the top of their lungs. "Ibbity, bibbity, ibbity sob/ Ibbity, bibbity, vanilla/ Dictionary down the ferry/ Tun, tun, American gun/ Eighteen hundred and fifty-one!"

"Miss Cuddy!"

It was Henry Trowbridge on horseback. She broke up the game by clapping hands and saying she must talk with Mr. Trowbridge, but they'd finish the game and get a winner some other day, the next time they crossed paths on the prairie.

"Shucks," said the boy with the muddy face. "We won't never see you again."

"Ever," she corrected. "Why, of course you will—it's a small world," she assured them. "But until you do, just remember: be good boys and girls, mind your parents, say your prayers, do your homework, don't have bad dreams, be nice to your teachers, wash behind your ears, and Merry Christmas when it comes!"

Two girls hugged her and they all put on boots and shoes and mogged away to the wagons. Mary Bee hated to part with these children, to let them go to the future. How would they fare? What fate awaited them in the West? She wished them God's speed and God's love.

She went to Trowbridge and had only to see his face to know his message. "It's no, isn't it?"

He took off his hat again. He nodded.

She turned away from him and walked to Dorothy and mounted. The afternoon had waned, and it was almost dusk. Lines of cooking smoke rose from the wagons as the women got supper for their families. She rode back to Trowbridge, her eyes full of tears.

"I am more than embarrassed," he said simply. "I am ashamed."

"I am naive," she said. "I didn't realize how cruel we can be to our own kind."

" 'A new commandment I give unto you,' " he quoted. " 'That ye love one another.' "

She nodded at the irony and blinked back the tears. Trowbridge reminded her of Alfred Dowd. An educated man in late middle age, his hair was white, and he wore a well-kept spade beard, also white.

"I take your cause, believe me," he assured her. "But please look at it from the other side, the husbands'. Cruelty is not intended. They only want to protect their womenfolk. As I said, we are more than three weeks out of Kanesville, and all has gone exceeding well. Our wives sing at their work. To put before them poor lunatic women—sisters under the skin—as proof of what they themselves may come to, of how rigorous may be the life they will lead—that would be cruelty indeed. It would cast a pall. Do you not see this, Miss Cuddy?"

"I suppose so."

Trowbridge was cheered. "But all's not lost. I am authorized to offer you whatever supplies you may need. We have ample."

Mary Bee was not cheered. His offer had the contrary effect, and blinking could not stay the tears this time. "No!" she cried. "Tell them no! We don't want food! What we want is simple human kindness!" And she reined her horse around and put it to the trot and left Trowbridge in the lurch.

It took half an hour to find her party. Briggs had kept the wagon moving till almost dark. All he had done was picket the animals. There was no fire, and the women, poor things, were still strapped in the wagon. He leaned against the wagon enjoying the sunset and humming a tune—"Money Musk" she thought it was. Had she been male, Mary Bee would have cursed him to a fare-thee-well. But the worst thing was, he had been right about the emigrant train and she had been wrong. It seemed to her that he was beginning to be right more often than a man had a right to be.

Constance, the baby with the big blue eyes, four months old, the one who laughed so much and whom they loved so much, took sick in early morning and wouldn't nurse or anything.

The little boys, Clinton, three, and Denton, two, were all right, though.

As the day passed Connie got sicker. She cried. She twitched and twisted in the big bed or in her mother's arms as she walked her. Her neck swelled up. She started a dry cough. Her eyelids turned red. Her breathing was noisy, but by evening she had a terrible time drawing a breath at all, and when she exhaled, her breath smelled. Then she began to burn up with fever. They had no patent medicines. Arabella kept cold compresses on her forehead and a milk poultice around her swollen neck, but neither did her an iota of good. Garn walked her and changed Clinton's and Denton's diapers while Arabella got supper. After supper he made her go to the outhouse, and when she came back, he'd made up his mind. He handed her the infant.

"Belle," he said, "I'm goin' for Doc Jessup."

She shook her head.

"I don't get 'im she might die!" Garn burst out. "I might be too late already!"

She shook her head. She'd been silent a lot lately, he didn't know why, and fussed over the children more than natural, like a mother hen with a brood too big. Garn looked at her and made a face as though he might cry like a baby himself. Suddenly he jumped to her and put Connie on the bed and threw his arms around his wife and hugged her tight.

"Belle, I gotta go," he said. "I'm scairt, honey. I'm scairt."

He let her go and got dressed and hugged her again and kissed her. "Don't you fret," he said. "I know the way and I'll stay to the high ground, where there ain't much snow. Be back in two, three hours if the doc's in. You pray to God he is."

He kissed her again and was gone.

Garn Sours was twenty-one.

Arabella Sours was nineteen.

He had eight miles in front of him. Lucky for him, they'd had a three-day thaw, but Garn would have chanced the ride no matter what. He'd ride to Timbuctoo for Belle or the kids. The night was dark and no moon, and it was colding up again, and the wind, he could tell from the whistle in his ears, was fixing to blow hard. He kept to the high ground, avoiding the draws, which would be drifted full. Blunder into one of those and a whole herd of cattle might disappear without a trace till spring, much less a horseman. So they plowed through starlight and snow bellydeep now and then, and after one stretch he stopped to rest his animal, laid his left leg forward, and could feel its heart booming. It was an old horse but a brotherly horse, and up to the task. He rode on until it was past midnight, he reckoned, and soon saw far off south a star low down, which had to be a lantern. Doc Jessup had long ago put up a tall pole and lanyard, and pulled a lantern up every winter night to guide him home. Garn's heart boomed with relief. The last quarter-mile he spurred his horse into a gallop and played like he was a U.S. Dragoon chasing Indians.

Jessup had just come home from delivering a baby ten miles west and was down on his uppers, he said, but when Garn told him what was wrong with Connie he put on his boots again, and a greatcoat and a hat of badger skin with earflaps. In the stable he saddled up a fresh horse and tied his bag on. Then he had a long swig from a whiskey bottle, slipped it into a coat pocket, climbed aboard with a grunt, and they were off, north. After a mile he gave Garn his reins and told him to lead and went sound asleep in the saddle.

Doc Jessup was a blessing. He answered every call. He had no formal medical training, he said so himself, and might be behind the books on contagious diseases, he said so himself when in his cups, but he had a natural gift for fractures, gangrenous infections, gunshot and arrow wounds, and childbirth. He had brought Clinton into the world. Denton and Constance were too fast for him. And he was a crackerjack surgeon. One dark night, after the roof of a sod house caved in, he had successfully removed a ruptured appendix on a wagon bed outdoors by the light of matches struck near the abdomen. Finally, he was reasonable. A dollar a visit plus ten cents a mile, and if you had no cash money and ran up a bill, he would settle for a calf or a pair of shoats. If he tippled on the job, everyone agreed, better a drunk doctor than a dead patient.

Garn shook him awake when they got there and tied both animals in the stable and followed him into the dugout. Jessup was examining Connie, who now lay still on the bed, eyes closed. Belle looked a fright she was so pale and worn.

"Is she dead?" Garn had to ask.

"Coma," Jessup said.

He examined Clinton and Denton, who were both crying and fidgeting now in the wooden box where they slept. Belle seemed unable to say anything.

"What is it, Doc?" Garn asked for her.

"Diphtheria," Jessup said. He opened his bag, rustled around, and handed Belle a small white envelope. "Powders. If you can, Miz Sours, get a pinch down the three of them in water every two hours." He looked directly at her, as he might have another child. "And try to sleep some yourself." He closed the bag and put on his badger hat. "Garn, come along with me."

They left the house and went to the dugout stable a few yards down the ravine. The wind blew harder now, and sharp cold cut the cheeks. The thaw was over. Inside, Doc Jessup tied on his bag, had a long pull on his bottle, and insisted Garn have one, too. A newcomer to whiskey, Garn coughed and spluttered. The physician leaned against his horse as though his legs might give weary way.

"Christ," he said. "I've had seven kids die on me the last month. Diphtheria. Could I, I'd get so drunk I wouldn't come to till summer."

Garn waited.

"No charge for this call, son. Forget it. Because those powders are not worth a tinker's damn. We're going to lose the baby. And prob'ly both boys. In short order. All three. You hear what I'm saying to you?"

Garn heard, but couldn't comprehend.

"All right now, listen. Don't you go back in that house or you'll likely get it and you better not because she'll need you."

Garn just stood there.

"That girl of yours, she's the one worries me. You can have more kids. But in the next day or two your wife's going to get old. All of a sudden. So you be a husband and take care of her. Be a man."

Jessup waited now, and in a minute heard Garn crying. In the dark he moved to him an put his arms around him like a father and groaned into his neck.

"Son, son, you're going to have a bad time. I wish I could bear it for you, but I can't."

He let loose of the boy, shook his head, and said out loud, to himself, "God, God, this is a hell of a place for a girl to grow up."

Then he untied his horse, backed the animal out of the dugout, mounted, and without another word rode off into the night.

After he got hold of himself Garn went to the house and rapped on the door and told Belle he couldn't come in, Doc Jessup said so, and he needed a couple of blankets. She brought them, but when he asked how Connie was, she just closed the door. Back in the stable he wound himself into the blankets, burrowed into the haypile, and tried to sleep.

Though pitch-dark it must have been morning when he heard Belle calling. He ran to the dugout door, and when she handed him Connie, wrapped in her mother's best dress, he burst into tears. Belle wasn't even crying. She just closed the door. He carried the tiny body back to the stable and buried it in the haypile near him. Come another thaw and he could maybe dig a grave, and they would have a proper funeral.

Garn and Arabella Sours, just married, he at eighteen, she at sixteen, had wagoned west from Ohio three springs before with his family, his father, his mother, and two younger brothers. Everyone complained they were too young to marry, but Garn's father was in a fever to start, so the youngsters, who were woefully in love and might pine away if parted, had a hurry-up wedding and spent their wedding night in the bed of the wagon camped out. Arabella left a large, warm family and was homesick for a month. Garn's folks outfitted the newlyweds with wagon, stock, implements, and some furnishings at Glenwood, crossed the Big Muddy there, followed the Platte along with most everyone else, then struck off north into the Territory to look for land. Garn's youngest brother, Bert, age thirteen, drowned in a swollen river they tried to ford, and they never did find his body. They couldn't locate adjacent claims either, Garn and his father, which was what they'd planned, so they had to stake out and register acreages almost thirty miles apart. Garn and Belle built a dugout house and stable because that was the easiest. Picking out a ravine that would have an east outlook, they went to work with shovels on the west bank and in a week had an excavation fourteen feet wide and sixteen deep into the hillside. Garn framed a wood door and a small window beside it, and set them up and filled in and around with dirt, then bored a small hole down from topside and ran the stovepipe up through it above grass level. It was a snug dwelling, warm in winter and cool in summer, and Belle placed her new bed, table, and two chairs where she pleased. She was too young to own a trunk, hiding her trinkets and pink cameo under the bed. Then they dug out a stable some yards down the draw, Garn glassed the window and put up an outhouse, hired a man with oxen and a breaking plow, bought seed, and inside of a month Mr. and Mrs. Sours were homeowners and farmers and happy as mice in a grain mill. Inside of four months she was four months along and showing and he was round-shouldered with responsibility, and they fell into bed every night worn to the nub.

During that day, when Garn was doing chores, he puzzled, and when he wasn't, walked up and down before his house, helpless, or put his nose to the glass of the window and stared inside. He couldn't understand Belle. She had pulled the wooden box over near the bed and sat on the bed staring into it at her little boys. She didn't walk them in her arms or try to get the powders down them. She didn't even cry. It was as though she'd given up, as though she knew they were dying and had locked all her grief and mothering inside her and couldn't or wouldn't let it out. Garn's heart ached for her. And the sight of her shamed him. He had married her too young and brought her to a land too wild and given her a hole in the ground to live in. What a hell of a place, Jessup had said, for a girl to grow up. Oh, he, Garn, was to blame all right. But how could he have known how awful hard she'd have to work? How could he have known she'd have three babies in three years? How could he have known that Arabella Sours, the most beautiful thing he'd ever seen, would come to look sometimes as old as his own mother?

Around noontime he knocked at the door and said he was hungry. She brought him some cold dodgers.

Later he took his nose from the window and knocked again. She opened the door.

"How are they, honey?"

She looked at him as though she had never seen him before.

"Belle, I've got to know!" he cried. "I'm their father! How are they?"

She just stood there.

"Belle, what's wrong with you!"

When she closed the door, Garn burst into tears again and walked round and round in a circle, crying.

Night came down colder than ever, and it began to snow. He was in the stable when he heard her call him. He ran to the house and she handed him another baby, wrapped this time in a feed sack, and closed the door right away. He carried his son to the stable, unwrapped the sack to see which one, and struck a match. It was Denton, the middle child. He had naturally curly hair, fair hair, like his mother. Garn got the dry sobs so bad they seemed to pitchfork his chest. He buried the boy in the haypile beside the girl, Connie.

That night he couldn't sleep, not lying under hay that near to his own flesh and blood, to his own little son and daughter. Belle was quite religious, at least she read the Bible a lot, or had lately, but Garn was not. He believed, he had faith, but he didn't put his mind to religion much. Nevertheless he prayed now. "Oh, Lord," he asked, "why did You kill these children? Why did You cut off my dear wife's tongue? We're good people. We've been true to Your teachings. We've made crops here, where nobody ever did before. We've multiplied ourselves, me and Belle. We helped build a church for You. But now we are bent down and don't know why. Please spare Clinton. He is all we got left. And please save my wife. I love her something terrible. I pray you, Lord, leave us one child and give my dear wife back to me. Thank you. Amen."

He couldn't sleep. He lay shuddering with cold until, maybe around midnight, something made him get up, throw off his blankets, and clump through falling snow to the dugout. There was faint light in the window and frost on the glass, but he put his nose and bare hands to it until enough melted so that he could see. The light came from a candle on the table. Belle sat in a chair. Something small was on the bed, and he knew in his guts it was Clinton. Garn could bear the wait no longer. He opened the door and went inside, damn the diphtheria.

It was Clinton, dead. But it was his wife, Arabella Sours, who crippled him. She sat stiff in the chair, as though she couldn't move her arms or legs either, like an old woman made of wood or stone. In the crook of one arm she held a doll. It was the doll Arabella had brought with her from Ohio. She kept it under the bed, and he thought she had forgotten it. That made him remember the early morning they left home three springs ago, his mother and father up front in the wagon, him and his brothers and Belle in the bed behind, and back down the road, watching them go for good, Belle's big family waving and calling goodbye, and Belle, sixteen years old, a new bride, waving and calling goodbye to them until they were out of sight and sound. The recollection of it caused Garn to cry again, even though he was cried out. He went to his wife, knelt before her, and laid his head in her lap in hopes she would comfort him. But she did not, and suddenly he looked up. She was holding her doll and waving one arm.

"Goodbye!" she called. "Goodbye!"

One morning the Worker refused the harness.

They had breakfasted, the fire was out, bedrolls on top, women in the wagon, they were ready to go, but the Thinker would not stand for the harness. He'd been off his feed, too, Briggs had noticed, and wasn't pulling his share of the load lately. Now he walked around grinding his teeth, long strings of saliva dripping from his mouth, and exhibited every sign of pain. Also he extended his front legs and stretched himself like a cat, shaking his head.

Briggs opined he had botts.

Mary Bee asked what "botts" was.

He said she ought to know. Didn't she doctor her stock?

No, she didn't. A neighbor, Charley Linens, did for her. So what was botts?

Stomach worms.

Oh, she said. What could be done?

Drench, he said.

He took out his plug of Star tobacco, broke it in half, gave her half, and told her to start a new fire, put the tobacco in a half-gallon of water, stir it well, bring the drench to a boil, then let it cool to warm.

She did as bid, and brought the mixture, which stank to high heaven, back to Briggs, who was in the process of casting the animal.

He tied its hind legs together and ran the rope to the left foreleg, which he tied and cinched tight to the hind legs. He told Mary Bee to put down the pan and be ready, when he got the animal down, to fall on her knees on its neck, fast.

Standing in front of the mule, he yanked on the rope. The hind legs were pulled forward, the animal sank on its hind end, and with one jump, Briggs slapped a hand on its right shoulder and gave it a shove, causing it to crash to the ground on its left side.

"Now!" shouted Briggs.

Mary Bee tried to kneel on its neck, a difficult exercise because the mule was rearing its head and thrashing its legs in vain attempts to regain its feet. Briggs soon had all four legs tied, though, and she could plant her knees in place.

"Get off!" shouted Briggs.

She sprang up, and Briggs replaced her instantly, then raised the animal's head and opened its mouth by seizing its upper jaw.

"Pour!" he shouted.

She tried to pour from the pan. The outraged beast lashed its tongue and gagged and let out a roar not unlike that of the King of the Jungle.

"Pour, goddammit!" shouted Briggs.

She poured as best she could. He was deluged with drench, she was deluged, the mule got perhaps half of it down, whereupon Briggs leaped up from its neck, almost bowling Mary Bee over, and untied legs and sprang free as the animal lurched to its feet and began to buck about, coughing and braying.

They watched the Thinker.

"He'll harness now," said Briggs, filling his cheek with a wad of Star.

Mary Bee was ready to retch. "How awful," said she, "to put that vile stuff in your stomach."

Briggs responded with a first, satisfied spit. "Guarantee you one thing, Cuddy," said he. "I'll never have the botts."

*   *   *

Then, that afternoon, while he had the reins, he stopped the wagon suddenly and stared. She followed his gaze and went cold all over. On a ridge, a quarter-mile to the north, a strange band of horsemen had stopped. She stared till her eyes watered. She counted eight men, Indians. Some were mounted on spotted ponies, some saddled, some bareback on blankets.

"What are they?" she asked under her breath, as though they could hear.

"Pawnee, prob'ly. Maybe some Otoe."

They were a ragtag bunch. She could spot several blue coats and caps and rifles.

"Somewhere along the line," said Briggs, "they've killed them some U.S. Cavalry."

He clucked to the mules and the wagon moved on east. Up on the ridgeline the riders walked their horses east. Man and woman behind the span of mules heard a blat sound.

"What's that?" she asked.

"Bugle."

Briggs pulled up the mules again. The horsemen reined up and waited.

"What do they want?" whispered Mary Bee.

"Whatever we've got. Trouble is, they don't know what that is. They've never seen a wagon like this. Could be goods inside, soldiers, anything." He was thinking. "Stand up."

She stood, he with her. From the compartment under their seat he took out her rifle and some shells and gave them to her. They sat down again. He started the wagon. The Indians started with them along the ridge, keeping distance but keeping pace. Briggs reined up. The Indians did likewise.

"They won't turn us loose," said Briggs. "I count four rifles. If they think we're worth it and come on down here, we're dead."

Again the bugle blatted. Mary Bee got goose-flesh. Indians were what she had most feared.

Briggs decided. "All right, I'll try to buy 'em off." He jumped down, fished inside his cowcoat, and handed up to her his heavy Colt's repeater. "If they come, don't fool with the rifle. Get inside the wagon as fast as you can and shoot the women. In the head. Then shoot yourself."

And before she could protest, he was off behind the wagon, and before she could stop him, he had untied Dorothy, led her out facing the Indians, let go of her bridle, and given her a whack, and she, good, obedient mare, was on the run to the Indians.

One hand over her mouth to keep from crying out, the other gripping the pistol, Mary Bee watched her go, and watched as one of the horsemen rode out, caught dear Dorothy by the bridle, and galloped her back up the ridge. When she was surrounded by milling animals and riders, two or three rifles were fired in the air as acknowledgment and the whole band went to the trot off the ridge and disappeared.

Briggs climbed up to the seat, put away rifle and revolver, took up the reins, and got the wagon moving. It was at least a mile before Mary Bee could trust herself to speak.

"I loved that mare," she said.

Briggs was silent.

After another mile, she spoke again. "Oh, if I'd only done that to your horse. When you sat on him with a rope around your neck."

Eventually she brought herself to ask, "What will they do with her?"

He shrugged. "Fine, fat mare like that? My guess is, eat 'er."

She marked the days off in her mind. When they woke the morning of the nineteenth day out, it was sprinkling and Arabella Sours was gone. She had somehow managed in the night to untie her wrist from the wheel spoke. Her rag doll was gone, too.

Mary Bee said it was impossible, the girl hadn't taken a step by herself since she was first carried to the wagon.

Briggs said it was probably a damn waste of time but he'd look for her. He told Mary Bee to feed the women, load the wagon, and leave the mules unpicketed to graze. He saddled his hammerhead horse and rode in a wide circle till he found the girl's bootprints. These he followed away south.

The grass was wet, her prints deep. Rather than making a beeline, she had wandered around in the dark like a child, which she was, the little bitch, wasting his time, holding up the wagon. Even so, she could cover ground. He was by his guess a good

two miles from the wagon when her prints stopped
and bunched and were replaced by hoofprints, which
turned straight south. Somebody had offered her a
ride. She was up on a horse with somebody. Another mile and he made them out ahead through
the sprinkle. He kept going and caught up, and they
stopped and turned toward him.

The horse was a black-and-white calico gelding
showing some rib. The man in the saddle was thirty
or so and short, with a mane of oily hair, and wore
a buckskin shirt and thigh-high Mexican boots. Behind him, one arm around him, the other holding
her doll, was Arabella Sours.

"Morning," said Briggs.

"Mornin'," said the man.

"Where you from, friend?" Briggs asked.

"Off a freight train down south a bit."

"Big one?"

"You bet. Thirty wagons, six yoke. Two weeks
out of Falls City, headin' for Salt Lake."

"You a whacker?"

"That's right. Huntin' meat. You seen any? We
eat one hell of a lot of meat."

Briggs nodded. The freighter had a rifle in a
scabbard. As he spoke, he eased open the front of
his cowcoat. "Well," he said, "I'm out looking for
this young lady. She's lost."

"She ain't now," said the freighter.

"Well, let me tell you," said Briggs. "I've got a
frame wagon back there. Three weeks out of Loup
on the way to the river. I'm carrying four crazy

women. Taking them to Ioway to a church so's they can go home, back east. This young lady's one of 'em. Her name's Sours. She's married and had three little kids. They all took sick and died of the diphtheria in short order, and she lost her mind. She ran away from us last night. I'm her friend."

"So'm I," said the freighter. "Say, she'll have a passel of friends I get 'er back to the train."

Briggs frowned. "You wouldn't want her. Not the way she is."

The freighter grinned. "She can spread 'er legs, we ain't particular." He thumbed backward. "Whyn't we leave it to her?" He turned his head slightly to address his passenger. "See here, you sweet thing—who'd you ruther go with, him or me?"

Arabella Sours rested her chin on his shoulder and stared over it at Briggs.

"There you be," said the freighter. "She cottons to me already."

Briggs regarded him soberly. He had a cast in one eye, which gave him a look of evil, but Briggs had no animus toward the man. On the contrary, he admired freighters. Many the train he and his dragoons had escorted west from Fort Kearney, riding in awe of what a bullwhacker could accomplish with a Wilson wagon and three tons of freight and six yoke of oxen and a fifteen-foot whip with a buckskin cracker. This one, now he had the girl, would be a hard cat to skin. To convince him to do what's right and proper, Briggs thought, I might even have to kill the son of a bitch. With an elbow he eased open still further the front of his coat.

"Friend," he said, "I'm taking her home."

"Not likely. She's mine now. Possession nine points of the law."

"Sorry," said Briggs. "I'll just have to have her."

With one scoop of his arm, down and up, the freighter had his rifle out of its scabbard and pointed at Briggs. Then his good eye narrowed, the reason being that Briggs had materialized a Navy Colt's out of thin air and cocked it and pointed it at him. They recognized a stand-off.

"Goddlemighty," said the freighter.

Both men thought it over.

"Fight you for 'er," offered the freighter. "Best man takes the prize—how's that?"

"I'm agreeable," said Briggs.

"All right, I say pitch and we pitch these guns—how's that?"

"Anytime."

"Pitch."

Each man swung his arm, but neither let go of his weapon, with the result that rifle and revolver ended up in their original positions, pointed.

"Goddlemighty," said the freighter.

"Say it again," said Briggs.

"Pitch!"

Both men tossed guns this time. Briggs swung off his roan and was starting to free himself of his cowcoat when the freighter, unwilling to wait, vaulted out of the saddle and with a shout hurled himself at

Briggs like a cannonball and bore him to the ground. It was rough-and-tumble fighting. They rolled around in rain and wet grass like a dog and a badger in a barrel. They cursed and spit blood and whistled air. They tried to bite ears, gouge eyes, crack skulls, break bones, knock teeth out of jaws, and knee stones. At one point Briggs rammed two fingers of one hand so far up the freighter's nostrils that the man's eyeballs bulged. But he was a bullwhacker, he had more muscle than Briggs, especially in his right arm, his whip arm. He had ten years on him, too, and Briggs was bothered by his coat, and in the end these told. Briggs's heart banged like the bass drum in a dragoon band. On top of him, the freighter finally got a chokehold on Briggs's neck, tight and tighter, and Briggs could not draw breath and was going limp and unconscious when suddenly there was a world-ending detonation, very like gunpower going off in a dugout, and his neck was released and he sucked air and something warm and sticky flooded one side of his face. He opened an eye, only to look directly into another eye. It was sightless. Briggs lay under a dead man. He pushed the buckskin off and away from him and hauled himself up on an elbow.

What was on his face was brains. The whacker's head had exploded.

Arabella Sours stood over them, Colt's in one hand, doll in the other. She had put muzzle to the freighter's temple, pulled trigger, and blown half of his face and head away, a good deal of it onto Briggs.

He sat up and flipped the bone and slop from his physiognomy and cleaned it with a coatsleeve. He struggled to his feet, dizzied, heaved a breath or two, moved to the girl, held out his hand, and she gave him the repeater. He stowed it under his belt and made an effort to smile at her. With her youth and flaxen hair and heart-shaped face, she was quite a looker.

"Missus Sours," he said, "I am very much obliged. I thank you."

"Goodbye," she said.

He went through the freighter's clothing, finding nothing of value except a double-edged bowie knife with a spear point. It was a wonder he, Briggs, hadn't got it in his gizzard. He hung the knife in its sheath on his own belt. Then he mounted the girl up on the calico, which seemed to be a reasonable animal, took her reins, and started off trailing horse and girl but stopped beside the freighter.

"You dumb son of a bitch," he said to the corpse. "I told you she was crazy."

Halfway to the wagon he could have kicked himself. He had forgotten the freighter's rifle, pitched into the grass. So be it.

To see as far over the prairie as possible, Cuddy stood on the wagon seat, shading her eyes against the morning sun. As far as he could see, she had failed to feed the women or load the wagon. When they came up she ran to Arabella Sours, helped her dismount, then flung her arms around the girl as though she were her own flesh and blood.

"Thank God, thank God," she said, and then to Briggs, "Did you have to take an eternity?"

He was dismounting. "Cuddy," he said, "you've lost a horse. Here's another one."

She let go of the runaway and gave the black-and-white gelding a quick look-over. She made a face. "Where did you get this one?"

"Man let us have him."

"I don't believe you. Why?"

"He was dead. Missus Sours shot him."

"I don't believe you."

"What can be done?"

"Why, put in new."

Several nails had sprung from the sideboards of the wagon box. With hammer and nails Briggs had brought from her place, he replaced them, the work of a few minutes. She would never have thought to bring hammer and nails.

"What can we do?"

"Bind it and hope."

This was another day, and he'd found a small crack in the nigh shaft of the wagon. If the shaft broke, they had no means of making a new. With the bowie knife he'd acquired, Briggs cut a long strip of the buffalo hide he'd taken from the Winnebago burial scaffold and bound the shaft as tightly as he could. She might have thought to try that. On the other hand, she might not. But then, she would not have had the buffalo hide.

"What happens if it comes off?"

"Wheel breaks up."

"Mercy."

"We need a blacksmith."

"You can fix it."

Briggs scowled at her. This was still another day, and the iron tire on the left rear wheel of the wagon had loosened. If it came off, and the wooden wheel disintegrated, they were helpless, high and dry. Buster Shaver would have wedged the tire or heated it red-hot and let it cool to a snug fit, but Briggs lacked a forge and tools. For the next hour he drove very slowly, sparing the tire and listening to it ring over stones, going out of his way to drive down into every draw.

"What're we looking for?"

"Water."

At length he located a stream wide and deep enough. When the wagon was unloaded and the women out, with the mules he backed it into the water so that a good portion of the rear wheels was underwater.

"What'll that do?"

"Wood's dried and shrunk away from the tire. Soak those fellows good and they'll swell and we'll have us a tight fit again."

During the night he waked her, and she put a shoulder to the wagon with him until they pushed it far enough into the stream to soak another section of the wheel. She was sleepy and surly.

"This is ridiculous."

"Ride or walk."

In the morning, when the wagon was on dry land and they headed out again, tire and wheel fit perfectly, without a wobble. Briggs hummed "Money Musk" on the seat beside her, but Mary Bee was darned if she would thank or congratulate him. She might not have brought hammer and nails, she conceded that, and probably couldn't have repaired the cracked shaft, but a tire, tightened to fit by whatever means, was scarcely one of the Seven Wonders of the World.

They edged into the eastern half of the Territory. The lay of the land was the same, flat as a tabletop for the most part, with now and again a ridge or a draw or wooded river bottom. Sod houses were more frequent, even a few log cabins, and fields that had been cultivated, and Briggs complained of the effort required to avoid them. Hunting was spotty, there was less game, and having used up the pork and potatoes, Mary Bee relied increasingly on the sacked provisions, the cornmeal and beans, which made for a monotonous diet. Then, for three days in a row, they headed into a careening wind of such force that the wagon swayed and Mary Bee believed she might be blown from the seat. It scoured the skin. It dried eyes. It blocked nostrils with dust. It made ears ache. It howled under the wagon at night and robbed sleep of rest. After three days the whole party was exhausted—save the mules. They set an example. Briggs said he was getting fifteen to twenty miles a day out of them, wind or no wind. They were troopers.

There were signs of travel, too, along their route now, boxes and farm implements and pieces of prized furniture left behind by emigrants to lighten their loads, and signs of tragedy as well. They passed several graves one day, weather-worn mounds of earth with handmade headboards or crosses. In the late afternoon they rolled within ten feet of another, but here the mound had been torn open. Mary Bee, who had the reins, stopped the wagon and asked Briggs why.

"Indians. For the clothes."

She handed him the reins and climbed down and went to see more closely. Bones were scattered about the grave, small bones. She asked Briggs why.

"Wolves."

She shuddered, and spied a headboard facedown in the grass. She turned it over and read the chiseled inscription:

CISSY HAHN 11 YRS 2 MOS 9 DAYS
GOD LOVED HER AND TOOK HER
UNTO HIM

Mary Bee felt her eyes fill. Eleven years old. A fifth-grader? She picked up the headboard, took it to the wagon, showed the inscription to Briggs, and then, remembering, read it aloud. "Give me the shovel, please."

"Why?"

"I want to tidy up this grave."

He sat like a bump on a log.

"The shovel, please."

"Getting late."

"I don't care."

"Suit yourself. I'm going on. You'll have to ride the gelding."

He would not lift a finger. He let her haul down her saddle from the wagon top and cinch it on and tie the freighter's horse to a bush before he rose and got the shovel from the seat compartment and handed it to her. No sooner done than he clucked to the mules and away they went, leaving her just as he had the afternoon she visited the emigrant train.

To tidy up the grave turned out to be a much longer and more arduous job than she had expected. She toiled in twilight, digging down into it until she struck something and what seemed an unholy stench sickened her. She collected the scattered bones and placed them in the earth and dug extra shovelsful of thawed ground from around the grave with which to rebuild the mound, higher and wider, invulnerable to animals. After smoothing it she set the headboard and hammered it into an end of the mound with the flat of the shovel, then stood for a minute in silence, sweating and saying a prayer for the soul of Cissy Hahn. When she opened her eyes it was dark.

The calico was snuffy. When she untied him, he backed off and stamped a two-step, describing a circle, tossing his head and tugging her around with him by the reins. She dropped the shovel and held on with both hands. Finally, after a last whuff and a sashay left, he stood, eyeing her with suspicion, and she came close and talked into his ear, softly, saying she would call him "Shaver" and they'd be friends because they both needed a friend. He attended her, but when she eased into the saddle he dashed off in a fast trot in what she was sure was the wrong direction, and not until she had almost bent the bit in his mouth did he have the courtesy to stop. She stood in the stirrups. The moonlight was meager. She couldn't find a fire anywhere. He should have started a fire for her. As it sank in how alone she was, even her horse a stranger, and how lost, truly lost, she began to go void. Darkness was in her, a darkness deeper than the night, and she felt ice forming. She shivered, then with a shake of the reins wheeled the horse and set him trotting in the opposite direction. She gave him his head a mile one way, then a mile another, she wore out her eyes for a pinpoint of light somewhere, anywhere, on the prairie. Her self was solid fear, it blocked her breathing, her mind trotted this way and that in panic, and finally she threw away the reins and set the animal under her free to wander the world west of the Missouri. Whether she saw the groundstar first or Shaver did was immaterial. All at once they were speeding to light and into light and she was tumbling off the horse aware only of a man and women seated by a fire as she stumbled, sobbing for breath, up a step into the wagon box and closed the doors behind her. There, sealed, safe, she struggled for breath with sounds that were like wails. The ice in her melted, streaming down her cheeks in the form of tears. After listening to her cry long enough, Briggs got up and approached a wagon window.

"What about supper?"

"Why didn't—you light a fire for—me?"

"I did."

He waited till she cried another quart. "Where's the shovel?"

That brought her up short.

"You're trying to—drive me—crazy, too!"

She was having one of her spells. Nothing he could do except not let her rile him. "Cuddy, the hell I am," he said. "I'm trying to move a load to the river. As quick as I can. And draw that three hundred. That's all there is, there ain't no more."

He walked back to the fire. He'd skin out in the early morning and get the damn shovel. He'd never come across such a flighty damn female as this one. Of course, she was an old maid, that accounted for the majority of it, and what she probably needed, to settle her down, was a good man and a good bedding and some brats. Still, he couldn't shake what she'd said: that he was trying to drive her crazy, too. No such a thing. He didn't have to. She was driving herself, and doing a first-rate job of it. Fits and tears and wheezes, snapping at him one time, the women another, till you wanted to take a stick to her. Briggs was hungry. Supper was going to be late if ever. He climbed up on the wagon, opened his bedroll, got out his jug, and had a snort. He could hear her boo-hooing in the box under him. As far as he was concerned, she could cry till the cows came home.

Hedda Petzke was taken sick just before a sunrise, shaking with cold and calling out. Mary Bee covered her with her own blankets and sat up with her till light and time to start the fire. When she could return to her, the poor woman was burning up with fever. It must be the ague, Mary Bee decided, because these were the symptoms, intermittent chills and fever, and she had along none of the proper specifics—Dr. Easterly's Ague Killer or Dr. Christie's Ague Balsam, both widely used and praised. Nor had she quinine or mustard for poultices or Jamaica Ginger for tea, the standard home remedies. She asked Briggs if they might stay the day there, or until Mrs. Petzke turned for the better, but he said no, they weren't lollygagging around over somebody sick, she'd get well or she wouldn't, so beds were rolled, wagon loaded, trailing horses tied, mules hitched, and off they rattled, Hedda Petzke on blankets on the floor of the wagon between the benches, Mary Bee in with her and the other women, using a wet rag in a bucket for cold compresses on her patient's forehead.

But she was mistaken. It was not the ague, because Hedda Petzke stayed feverish all the long, miserable day in the wagon, and that night after supper, after Briggs and the other women were bedded down, Mary Bee sat up with her by the fire wetting the rag, wringing it out, replacing it on her forehead, herself as miserable as the day had been. The night was starry and still except for the sounds of the sick woman, prostrate by the fire under blankets, and the snuff and click of the animals out in the dark, picketed and grazing. In the middle of it, Briggs came to the fire from his bed by the wagon.

"Can't you quiet her down?"

"No, I can't."   "What's wrong with her?"

"I don't know. It can't be the ague. Oh, dear, oh, dear, I'd never forgive myseff if I lost her."

Briggs went back to his bed, rustled about, and returned with his buffalo robe, a blanket, and his precious jug. He laid the robe over Mrs. Petzke, pulled the blanket around his shoulders, sat down, and treated himself.

"She needs to sweat," he said.

"She's already on fire."

"Never mind."

Mary Bee took off her rabbit hat. "How long now to the river?"

"Two weeks. Less. Depends."

"On what?"

"On how much more time you fritter away."

He was cross. He was losing sleep.

"I can't wait," she said. "I want to see a real town, with streets, and trees."

"A real saloon," he said.

"And houses made of wood."

"With lamps."

"And people."

"And a fiddler."

"A hot bath."

"Corn for the mules."

"In a big tub." She sighed. "Hebron. Hebron, Iowa. I dream of it."

The fire was low. Mary Bee got up, poked at it, added wood, sat down again. "Where do you plan to cross?"

"Kanesville maybe. I dunno yet."

"How far is that from Hebron?"

"Mile or so."

The blanketed woman groaned, a series of groans that carried far from the fire. Mary Bee came to her knees, rewet the rag, and bathed her face with it, then lowered her covers and bathed her throat and hands.

"Oh, I feel so helpless. I pray God for her. When her husband came home, and her boys, they found four dead wolves—I told you. She'd killed four wolves. She's been through so much already, and now this. To come this far and lose her would be sinful. It would break my heart."

Briggs commented with his jug. "You mailed that money?"

"You saw me, in Loup. I'm sure Mrs. Carter has it by now. As soon as we meet her you'll have it and be free to go." Mary Bee covered her patient again and sat for a time staring into the fire. At length she said, "I wish you'd treat me decently the rest of the way."

He was silent.

"I have said some things that I regret. I apologize. I've been under a great strain."

The new wood blazed, and she looked into his face and found nothing.

"If it will make you more kindly to me, Mr. Briggs, I'll confess something. I'll confess I couldn't have done this without you."

"Well, well," he said.

"Saving you from hanging—you've repaid that ten times over. I wouldn't have made it a week from Loup by myself. You've been right more often than wrong. Mrs. Svendsen, for example. I had no idea how dangerous she could be. You were wise to strap them in. And then the Indians."

"I hadn't swapped 'em your horse, we'd be dead, the lot of us."

"I know. You were right about the wagon train, too. I couldn't imagine they would turn us away."

"The wagon," he said. In case she forgot, he was glad to remind her.

"I could never have repaired it."

"The botts."

"I simply don't know how to doctor stock. Charley Linens has always done it for me. I could never have tracked Arabella Sours either."

"She saved my bacon. Freighter had her. She hadn't shot him, he'd have killed me."

"Mercy. And when the mules wouldn't go, and you tricked them into it. Well, it's a very long list, and I'm truly grateful."

Briggs hawked and spat into the fire. The cool night air affected his catarrh. Then she said something she shouldn't have but couldn't resist.

"And you dance very well."

He scowled. She bit her tongue. But she was spared his response, whatever it might have been, because Hedda Petzke twisted and turned and groaned again, loudly.

"Hell," said Briggs. "Get me a cup."

She did as bade, searching in the grub box nearby until she found a cup. He poured whiskey into it from his jug, sloshed the jug, listened, poured a bit more, and set the cup in the coals of the fire. The higher fire and the lack of his hat let Mary Bee have a sharp look at him. His cheeks and chin were stubbled. He shaved only now and then. His hair had considerable gray in it. If eyes were the windows of the soul, he was short a soul, for in them there was nothing she could discern or guess, nothing. His was an ordinary face. He was an ordinary man. Neither the ripped sleeve of his coat nor the ragged red scarf always about his neck set him apart. Except for the charred grip of the revolver under his belt, and the special bowie knife, he was nondescript. In a crowd you could lose him and never care. For that matter his name was probably not "Briggs," he had intimated as much himself. Summed up, he was a cipher, and just as it made no sense to witch for water in a place where none was ever found, so it was absurd to plumb for depths in him there couldn't possibly be. His age stumped her. He had to be on the shady side of forty, that was certain, but a difference of ten years between them made no difference. The balding widower Clara Marsh had married was at least fifteen years her senior, but so far as Mary Bee knew, she was content as a cow in clover.

Briggs poked the cup out of the coals to let the liquor cool a trifle. He tilted his jug again and discovered it empty.

"Goddammit," he said.

He stood up in a temper, held the jug at arm's length with a finger through the handle, and taking two steps whirled and hurled it into the darkness. Next he picked up the cup, knelt beside Mrs. Petzke, put an arm under her shoulders, raised her, and forcing the rim between her lips, poured the warm whiskey into her with the same solicitude he had shown the off mule while getting tobacco tea down its gullet. She spluttered, choked. When she had somehow got it down, he laid her back, pitched the cup, and seated himself in his blanket.

"There," he said. "That'll do. She'll sweat or she'll croak."

They waited.

"You have no use for women," asserted Mary Bee after a spell.

"So you think," said Briggs.

"Yes, I do."

"I lived with one once."

"Oh?"

He didn't take the bait, but could not have anyway because Hedda Petzke groaned suddenly and lifted herself on her elbows and Mary Bee crawled to her and found her gushing sweat.

"The fever's broken!" She uncovered the woman again and washed her face and throat and hands with the rag. "She's wringing wet, oh, I'm so glad!" And when she had finished, let her down and watched over her as she fell into an exhausted sleep.

After a few minutes, on his own initiative Briggs lifted Mrs. Petzke in his arms, blankets and robe, carried her to the wagon, laid her underneath, tied her wrist to a wheel spoke, and rolled himself into his bed, leaving Mary Bee alone by the fire. Soon she heard him snore.

Before she bedded down herself, on her knees, hands clasped, eyes open to the stars, she thanked God for the deliverance and asked Him to bless George Briggs, thief and cull and dancer, for the sacrifice of his whiskey.

She found a second reason, in the ensuing days, to be thankful. It seemed to her the condition of the four women was much improved, at least physically. The bondage of their lives to the frontier, to husbands and children and weather and pain and solitude, was behind them now. Someone else fed them now, washed hands and faces, combed and brushed hair, attended them in every way with constancy and affection. They had color. Their tireless hands were now at rest. And they were more at ease with each other. In the beginning, each one had claimed her own space in the wagon, her own isolation; now they impinged upon each other daily, shoulders, elbows, hips, and did not appear to dread or resent it. Mrs. Sours could walk now—indeed, could run away if she wished, as she had done. There was nothing hostile in Gro Svendsen's manner or movements. Time and kindness and absence from the marriage bed had washed away her hatred as surely as lye soap. Hedda Petzke had regained mobility of arms and legs. The size and shape of her eyes were normal. She no longer whimpered. The wolves she had slain were slain forever now, and forgotten. Theoline Belknap, who only weeks ago had bitten through the radial artery of her wrist, was a different person altogether. Her wrist had healed. She did not cast her eyes this way and that. She ate heartily, slept well. But though Mary Bee tried often to speak to her friend, her replies, as they had been, were only monosyllables. "Dear Line," she would say, "how are you today?" "Dar, dar," was the response, or "Im, im, im," or something equally meaningless. Communication with the others was no more possible. She could address them directly, looking directly into their empty eyes, to no avail. They had simply lost the power of speech. That was the sadness. There was no mental improvement whatever. She likened them in a small way to herself. They, too, were void inside, but whereas she was filled on occasion with fear or fury, in their case neither love nor memory nor light would ever suffuse that total darkness. Mary Bee was of divided opinion about them. If they had been defeated, in defeat they were also victorious. If they were free now, that freedom had been won at awful cost. She wondered sometimes—in which state were they better off, sane or insane? Suppose, she mused, suppose she were to wake one morning and find these women restored in mind and body by a miracle. Would she turn the wagon round and take them back to drudgery and hardship, to babies and loneliness, to disease and the demands of men who would ask of them more than they had power to give? Perhaps not, perhaps she would stay the course. They were going home, after all, ghosts of what they had been, yes, but going home, to their roots, freedwomen, to the arms of their kin and the mercy of their Maker.

Arabella Sours's recovery most pleased Mary Bee. Nineteen! By that age the girl had lived a lifetime. Wed at sixteen, toted all the weary way out west from Ohio with a doll for a child and a boy for a mate, keeping house in a dugout, mothering three babies in three years to stand by, helpless, while they perished one by one in less than three days— only someone as young and strong as Arabella would survive such dire events and bloom as she was blooming now. Her step was light again, her cheeks rosy. Though she was speechless, she smiled sometimes, particularly at Briggs. This vexed Mary Bee until she could construct a logical explanation. The girl was grateful to him. She had lost her children, and lost her mind because she was unable to save them, hence blamed herself for their deaths. On the other hand, she had indeed killed the freighter during her runaway, and in so doing saved Briggs's life. To the extent that this deed redeemed her, and reduced the burden of her guilt, she was therefore grateful to him. She smiled at him during meals. Mary Bee was touched. Arabella then began to look long at him in the evenings by the fire. Mary Bee was alerted. The next evening young Mrs. Sours offered the man food from her plate. Mary Bee was alarmed.

Matters came to a head that very night. She woke, soon after falling asleep, to hear a voice, a man's voice, speaking in low tones. She raised herself on her elbows. She had bedded down as usual on one side of the wagon, Briggs on the other. There was yet light enough from the fire to let her look under it. She could see only three sleeping, blanketed forms. One of the women had untied her wrist from the wheel spoke and risen. Mary Bee got up and in bare feet slipped around the rear end of the wagon. What she saw shocked the breath from her body.

Arabella Sours had freed herself and come to Briggs's bed. She knelt beside him, bending over him, his face in her hands. She was kissing him passionately, his cheeks, his forehead, his lips.

Mary Bee went void. In the dark deep inside her a light flared, and instantly she was full of flame, which was fury.

She ran to them.

"In the name of God!" she cried.

She seized one of the girl's arms and pulled her to her feet, then hauled her round the front end of the wagon and over the shafts, and pushed her roughly down and over onto her bed, crawled in after her, and tied her wrist tightly to a wheel spoke. Arabella Sours did not struggle. The other women were awake now, and watching.

Mary Bee then crawled out from under the wagon, and standing, bending, glared beneath.

"Shame on you, Arabella Sours," she said. "Shame on all of you. I've seen you look at this man."

She waved a finger like a switch.

"You stay shy of him. You don't know what you're doing. You don't know anything."

Briggs didn't trust his ears.

"I warn you, mind your p's and q's or you'll be sorry!" she threatened. "I'll leave you to shift for yourselves! D'you hear me? I'll leave you!"

She was beside herself. She strode to Briggs to loom over him, gasping for breath, hands clenched into fists.

"You beast!" she cried. "How dare you!"

Briggs propped his elbows, looking up at her.

"To take advantage! Of a girl lost her mind! The lowest thing! A man can do!"

Her words came in bursts as her lungs labored.

"None of my doing," Briggs objected, his face poker. " She came to me."

"Did I bring you along? For a bull? To service us all?"

"Shit," said Briggs.

"Damn you! None of us safe! Damn, damn, damn you, Devil!"

This outburst used her up, her breath and strength. And this time, for the first time ever, she was entirely consumed by the flames within the void. Mary Bee fainted dead away, falling heavily over the man on the ground as a tree falls in fire.

She was shocked again, into consciousness, minutes later. He had carried her back to her bed, covered her against the damp, found a cup in the grub box, filled it, and slapped her face with cold water, after which he went back to his own bed.

She did not utter a word to him the next day, early morning to evening, did not address him with so much as a look. Briggs knew she was madder than a wet hen, but this was more than one of her fits. She had been het up before at him, but today was different. She seemed to drive the wagon, to cook, to see to the women as though she were alone, separate and remote, as though she had left the party and gone off by herself somewhere. And that was exactly what she did that evening after supper. She washed the dishes in a red sunset and walked away into a twilight hush, and when she was gone too long, he went out on the prairie in search of her. He had strolled perhaps a hundred yards when he heard a woman singing. He moved silently in the direction of the song until he could understand the words.

> If thou should hasten
> To lands wild and wide,

> Take thee this token,
> My heart from my side.

> Take thee this token,
> My love with thee bide.

He moved closer. A middle moon was rising, and that, with the last of the twilight, enabled him to tell that she was seated on the grass, her back to him, and spread out before her was a long strip of cloth with dark and white markings which looked to him—he squinted to be sure—like a keyboard. Her hands moved over it, her fingers touched it. Dammed if she wasn't playing a piano keyboard made of cloth, and accompanying herself as she sang. It was a fact. Make-believe music, sort of. He'd heard everything out here—wolves howling and buffalo bellowing and Indians whooping and bugles blowing and the roar of a prairie fire—but never anything like this. He shivered. The woman's song hunted the dark plain like a hawk.

> If thou should prosper,
> Hear my heart pray,
> Send me a summons
> To wed thee one day.

> Take thee this token,
> And love me alway.

> But if I should perish,

Thy promises keep,
Take thee our two hearts
And bury them deep.

Take thee our tokens,
In love let us sleep.

Briggs backed away, slowly, turned, and headed for camp. Well, hell, he thought. If she's ready, there's room for five in the wagon.

And when, during the night, someone or something touched him, he was instantly awake with a hand on his Colt's, and when he saw her seated beside him, he shivered again. This was batty, too, her being here, just like singing and playing a cloth piano. Not a word out of her to him all day yesterday and here she was. Look out, he said to himself. She might have a knife. She could harm you or, just as likely, harm herself.

"I couldn't sleep," she said.

"I could," he said.

She sat between him and the remains of the fire so that she was outlined, and he noted the breadth of her shoulders. Cuddy was a big woman. In bed she could break a man's back.

"How long now?" she asked.

"Week. Thereabouts."

"We haven't had meat for three days. I'll use the last of the beans today. We can't live on corn. If we come near a shebang, please stop so we can buy something. I have a little money."

Once a woman wanted to chew the rag, night or day, he'd learned, there was no stopping her. Combs removed, her long hair hung down her back. Hands behind, she divided it and pulled it around and over her shoulders like a shawl.

He yawned, uselessly.

"I wish there were some way we could give them a bath. I'll be ashamed for them, coming into a minister's house."

"We might come on a crick."

"Ice cold. They'd catch their death."

She drew up her knees and rested her chin on them and brooded. "I'm homesick. I miss my house and so many people. Alfred Dowd. Charley and Harriet Linens. Buster Shaver. Even that miserable Vester Belknap. By the way, I'm getting along famously with the freighter's horse. I call him 'Shaver.'"

Briggs let go of his weapon under the blanket and began to wonder where in hell she was taking him besides around the barn.

"Well," she said, "it's almost over. What will you do afterward?"

"I dunno."

"I mean, will you stay in Iowa or come back to the Territory."

"I dunno yet."

"You're not much for making plans."

"Not much."

Mary Bee would have liked to poke him with a stick. But this was the time. Now or never. "Mr. Briggs," she said, "I have a proposition to make to you. You're an intelligent man, and if you'll think on it, I'm sure you'll see the wisdom in it." She drew a deep breath. "After we've turned them over to Mrs. Carter, why don't we marry and come back together?"

He sat up, suddenly, and as though overcome by catarrh, coughed, hawked, and spat as far as the fire. She waited. She supposed he was surprised. Let him be. She'd give him time, then logic. Men's minds were like wooden axles. Now and then they needed grease.

She waited in vain. He sat staring at her as though she'd just asked him to run for office.

"Think it through," she said. " I am thirty-one years old. If I'm ever to marry, it had better be soon. And you're not getting any younger. Think of what you'd be returning to. You've seen my house and stock. I have two fine claims and money in the bank. I'm in good health and capable of child-bearing. I'll have sixty acres into wheat this summer, and I'll buy shoats this spring and fatten them on corn. I plan to put in pumpkins, too. I'm convinced we'd make a good team, you and I, and if we pull together, we're bound to prosper. Don't you agree?"

Briggs was dumbfounded. He had to say something, but whatever it was, he had to be sure not to throw her into another of her fits. She was too close to the edge already.

"I'm no farmer," he said.

"You could be."

"No, I tried it once."

"When?"

"I told you, I lived with a woman once. North of Wamego. She was a widow woman, with two kids. She'd married a city man and they came out here and he couldn't make a go of it. One day he stuck a shotgun in his mouth and blew his head off."

"No."

"Well, he did. In the stable, and she found him. Anyway, a year later I moved in with her and tried farming her claim. Up and down those damn fields from morning to night. There's prettier sights to look at than the hind end of an ox."

"What happened?"

"One sweet day I just walked away."

"Oh." Mary Bee folded hands in her lap, tightly. "Why?"

Briggs scowled. "Because I'm no farmer. I figured we were fair and square. She'd worked me for two years, I got my keep. She was a good cook and kept a clean house."

"You deserted her."

"Look at it however you want."

"Probably she wanted a husband."

"Yes, she did. And I wouldn't. When I rode away I was sorry, but I never looked back."

"I see. So you won't marry me."

"Nope."

"Will you think about it? From here to Hebron? And talk with me about it again?"

"Sure. Talk's cheap."

There was long silence between them. Beyond

the wagon, in the vast dark, the animals moved and snuffled, grazing. Under the wagon, one of the women stirred in her sleep and muttered an unintelligible word or two. It was almost impossible for Mary Bee to comprehend that he had refused her. Proposing to him had not been planned. She had done it on impulse, just as she had slipped out alone into the twilight to play and sing. She didn't know what different tack to take, but she wouldn't give up on him, not yet. She heard a buzzing in her ears.

"I want to say something else," she said.

He yawned.

"Perhaps you don't realize what a grand thing you're doing, Mr. Briggs. Taking these poor, helpless women home. If you don't, I assure you the good Lord does. And I do. This may be the finest, most generous act of your whole life."

"May be three hundred dollars."

"No. It's more than that. You won't admit your own worth. You've made mistakes, I grant, but underneath you're a decent, honest—"

"Hold on, Cuddy," he interrupted. "You sure have reformed me. A few weeks back I was a man of low character. Now I'm a decent, honest—"

"I was wrong."

"Truth is, you don't know me from Adam."

"I didn't. I do now."

"I deserted from the Dragoons."

Once, the spring she taught subscription school, she had walked after school through a grove of trees and been attacked by a swarm of bees. She ran. They followed and stung her repeatedly on the face and neck before she thought to pull up her skirt and shield her head. Now, at this instant, as she heard the buzzing, she was stung again, sharply, painfully, but inside her head. It was as though her brain had been stung.

"Deserted!" she exclaimed.

"That's right," said Briggs. "Comp'ny C, First U.S. Fort Kearney. I put in two years, signed up for another hitch, served half of it, and stole a horse and away I went. I'd had a bellyful by then. Sneaked on up to the Territory."

"Deserted," she said, thoughtful. "That's why you don't tell your name."

"Right as rain."

"And why we took this route. And why you avoid people."

"Army's got a long arm. They'll look for me as long as I live. They catch me and it's the stockade, hard labor." He had been sitting. Now he adjusted his black-and-white cowcoat, which he rolled up for a pillow nightly, lay back, and joined hands behind his head. "So I won't settle down. Anyhow, steady goes against my grain."

She was stung again.

"And you won't marry me."

He closed his eyes as though to sleep. "Nope. I'm married to myself."

"I am plain as an old tin pail."

He would not respond.

"I have a viper in my mouth."

He yawned.

She was stung again by a bee. Pain spread from one side of her skull to the other, and the savage buzzing in her ears was so loud she couldn't hear herself think.

"You're the second man I've asked to marry me. He said no, too."

Briggs opened his eyes, then opened them wider. Her big hands were pressed tight against the sides of her head as though she were in pain.

"Then if I was you," he said, "I'd sure as hell quit asking."

That started tears, which dribbled down her cheeks. Tears were women's guns, to be shed when no other weapon would work. He couldn't judge what she was up to unless it was to shame him, which she had no cause to.

"Oh, oh," she whimpered. "How I wish you'd say one kind word to me."

"Such as what?"

"That I am a good woman. That I've helped you."

"Fair enough," he said. "Cuddy, you're a damn good woman and you've helped me."

With that she let out a groan that sounded like the woman who was burning up with fever, staggered to her feet, and left him. Briggs was powerfully relieved. He burrowed into his blankets. Any day now the river, he thought, any day. She may make it, she may not. She's hollow in the head, all right. No telling what she'll do, one minute to the next. I better bow low to her and do-si-do. I better handle her like a cracked egg, because she's about to bust. Or has already. And I better push those mules.

He woke and went rigid.
A light rain fell, almost a mist.
She stood beside him, stark naked.
"No," he said.
"Yes," she said.
"No," he said.
Plain-faced she might be, but she had a shapely body. Her skin was pure white, her breasts were large and uplifted, the nipples sharp as arrowheads. She had a flat belly and a belly button deep and dark. Her legs were long and strong-thighed, and the black V of hair above them looked to be firm as a pincushion. Despite himself he felt desire.
"I want to, to lie with you," she said.
"No," he said.
"You must," she said. "I saved your life."
"No," he said.
She knelt beside him and put her face beside his so that their cheeks touched. Her long hair tented his head. He did not move. She made no attempt to kiss him. She did not know how to arouse a man, any more than he knew, for the life of him, what to do with her.
"Don't make me beg you," she murmured.
It griped him hard to be stuck in such a position.

Bedding down with a woman out of her mind or almost was about as low as you could go. It might damage her more. On the other hand, it might help get her on an even female keel. Maybe, maybe. Damned if he did, damned if he didn't.

After a time he pushed her away, turned back his blankets, stood, and stripped. She lay down on his bed staring at him, at what she had never before seen. Hair surprised her, how much of it, mats of it, mist wet, on his chest, legs, shoulders. She stared at the member of a man. Distended, straight as though aimed, it looked to her like the barrel of his big repeating pistol, and the hair at its base like the burned black of its grip. Then he came down over her on hands and knees.

"Raise your knees," he ordered.

She raised them.

"Take me in your hand."

She did.

"Just you remember, Cuddy," he said hoarsely. "I didn't force you."

"I will."

"If I hurt you I can't help it."

"I know."

"I didn't ask you, you asked me."

"I know."

"Now put me in you."

"Yes," she said, and began to tremble throughout her whole body as though with cold and fear and the mist falling.

When, later, it was done, and she went back to

her bed on the far side of the wagon, Mary Bee Cuddy knew in her soul that the women were awake, and had seen it, and so had He.

Briggs fell out of sleep. It was the mules. Every morning they brayed reveille. This morning they had not.

He opened his blankets, stood, and peering into the gray could count two mules by the ears and one horse by the tail, his own, but couldn't locate the freighter's calico she had taken a liking to.

Without pausing to yawn, stretch, cough, spit, or scratch himself, he put on his boots and stepped around the wagon. The women slept. Her blankets were where they should be. She was not.

He climbed up to the wagon seat. Her saddle was gone. She had saddled up the gelding and ridden off somewhere for some dammfool female reason.

He stepped up on the seat itself. The plains were rosy now, and he turned a slow circle searching them, but there was nothing but rose and empty plain and one tree, a dark smudge a mile away to the north and east. He recollected how she had hugged a black walnut tree and talked his ear off about the trees she had doted on back home in York State. Standing all by its lonesome, this one looked to be an old cottonwood.

And just as he studied the tree, the meaning of it kicked Briggs in the pit of the stomach. Years ago he'd had a scrap with an Irishman from back east in the Company C barracks, a big, dumb, drunk recruit who kicked him in the stomach, took the fight out of him, then knocked him cold. For days afterward bile rose up in him sometimes and he was ready to puke, and when it receded left a green, maggoty taste in his mouth. Now the meaning of the tree got the bile going again and made him want to puke over the side of the wagon.

Instead, he hauled down his own saddle, went out and unpicketed his horse, and saddled him and mounted up and started off for the cottonwood tree at a walk. But halfway to the tree he couldn't wait, he needed to get it over with, so booted the roan into a gallop.

There was her horse, Shaver.

Briggs pulled up and left his animal and walked around the tree.

Sure enough.

She had done it to herself just the way she had seen it done to him.

She had ridden under a long limb and dismounted. She had slung the coil of rope up over the limb, yanked it into a fork, then walked one end to the tree trunk and looped it around the trunk and tied it. Returning to her horse, she had removed her black melton coat and rabbit hat, taken the free end of the rope, mounted, taken up as much slack in the line as she could, tied the noose, worked it over her head and under her chin, let loose of the free end, and kicked the gelding out from under her. Since she had not had any help, it was not a tidy job. There had been too much slack in the line, so she hung with her boots no more than a foot off the ground, and the free end of the rope dragged. The drop had been too short to break her neck, and she had strangled. In her fits, he recalled, she had always been short of wind, and now that was what she had died of, lack of wind.

She loved trees.

Briggs's instinct was to go cut her down. He pulled his bowie, stepped around, and saw her face. Her face did him in.

The rope had made red marks on her neck. Her cheeks were a bluish color, almost purple. Her eyes were closed. Her viper tongue stuck out an inch or more from her mouth.

Briggs swung away from the sight and fell to his hands and knees, trying to vomit and being unable to. There was nothing in his stomach. He had the dry heaves. He heaved until he thought his guts were ripped. Then he sat back with sweat pouring out of him and his mouth full of maggots.

What got him on his feet again was rage. He faced her and yelled.

"Goddam you, Cuddy!"

He sheathed his knife and waited as though he expected her to answer.

"God didn't care what we did! I tell you! God didn't give a damn!"

But she hung lifeless and blue in the face and stuck out her tongue at him.

"Why, goddammit?" he yelled. "Why?"

When he couldn't get a word out of her, Briggs

left her hanging and turned, marched around the
cottonwood to his horse, mounted, caught hers, and
trailing him, rode on back to the wagon. Here he
broke camp. He moved in a deliberate manner. He
felt like a trigger being squeezed. He tied horses to
the wagon. The women were awake now. He put
their boots on and one by one took them out on the
prairie to relieve themselves, then stowed and
strapped them in the wagon. Washing up and comb-
ing hair and breakfast be damned. He rolled beds,
loaded and lashed the wagon top, harnessed and
hitched the mules, climbed to the seat, got the
wagon going, and drove the mile to the cottonwood
tree. He stopped by the tree and rousted the women
out of the wagon like a schoolmaster with pupils.

"All right now," Briggs said to them, "see there.
See what you've done."

They looked at him, and at the tree, and at the
trailing horses, and at the ground underfoot.

"Goddammit!" he cried. "Look at her! You look
at her!"

He took them roughly by the waists and turned
them to face the corpse. They looked at the hanging
woman with no more and no less interest than they
might have a line of laundry. His rage returned and
got the better of him.

"See what you've done!" He pointed. "Killed
her, that's what! You've killed her!"

They stared at him.

"It hadn't been for you," he snarled, "Cuddy
wouldn't be dead. She wouldn't even be out here

God knows where. You hadn't gone cuckoo, she wouldn't have made this trip. It was too much for her—too damn far, too many chores, taking care of you night and day." He shook a finger at them. "If you'd been like a wife should be, strong and steady, she'd be alive and home in her own house and so would you. But no, you went crazy and drove her crazy and killed her. Killed her! Well, what've you got to say?"

He didn't expect them to burst into tears, but they might at least have shown some shame or sympathy instead of standing like a row of fenceposts.

"The hell with you!" he roared. "Not worth a pinch of dried owl shit! Not even human anymore!"

He spat his contempt.

"A fine bunch," he said, subsiding. "You should be locked up. If we had a bughouse out here, that's where you'd be. And stay there."

Briggs turned his back on them, went to the corpse, and with one arm around it cut it down with his knife. He laid it on the ground, stepped to the tree trunk, untied the rope, pulled it over the limb, coiled it, slung it on top of the wagon, then got the shovel from the underseat compartment and picked a place farther under the tree for better shelter and began to dig a grave. Recollecting how fussy she had been about the little emigrant girl's grave a few days back, staying behind to rebury the bones and thwart the wolves, he dug this grave a full three feet down; but then, when he rolled her into his buffalo hide, which he had no need of in warmer weather, the hole was deep enough but inches short. She was a long woman. So he cut it inches longer and found it, when he lowered her in again, a perfect fit.

He stood up sweating, back aching. She weighed a ton. And now he had to think what to put in with her. From on top of the wagon he brought down her bedroll, untied it, and found a green velvet sewing bag he hadn't heeded earlier. He sat down on the grass to open it, and as soon as he did, the four women did likewise. He scowled at them. All they had between the ears was air. He opened the bag.

The first thing, rolled up, was the long strip of white cloth she'd marked out to be a piano keyboard, the one she'd played the other evening to sing to. Next were a comb and brush and a sliver of soap and two handtowels wrapped in what he supposed were undergarments. Also wrapped was ten dollars in greenbacks. She must have brought these to buy for herself in Hebron. He shoved the money down deep into the inside pocket of his suitcoat. Then there was a stack of paper consisting of a folded sheet with names and addresses on it, a packet of letters and another folded sheet, and sticking out of the sheet, the end of a greenback. He unfolded it and found eight dollars in greenbacks. These he added to the ten dollars in his suitcoat. Then he found a small square of cardboard to which was pinned a pink cameo pin carved with the face of a young girl with a crown on her head. Briggs calculated the pin would fetch several dollars anywhere, and so put it in a side pocket with the tin of sardines he'd salvaged from the Giffen dugout. Next was another folded sheet with names and addresses. And finally, there were three envelopes, two un-sealed and one sealed, and these he opened. The first contained only a sheet with names and ad-dresses. He replaced it. In the second was a letter to Cuddy signed "Dorothy," he guessed, her sister, which he couldn't read and didn't care. He put it back in its envelope and set it aside. The writing on the last envelope he had seen before, and remem-bered: "Mr. George Briggs, c/o Mrs. Altha Carter, Ladies Aid Society, Methodist Church, Hebron, Iowa." It was sealed. With a finger he slit it open. It held six fifty-dollar notes on the Bank of Loup. Briggs was astounded. He frowned at the notes until it came to him—she hadn't mailed them at all, that day in Loup. She'd kept them, brought them along, and he knew why. She didn't trust him. He was a man of low character. He might desert the party any day, leave her and the women high and dry and ride on by himself, to Hebron, collect the envelope—it was addressed to him—and be on his way flush with cash. And so she told him a white lie, that she had mailed the money at the general store, when instead she'd hidden it in the sewing bag all the long miles and days. Maybe, too, she wanted the satisfaction of paying him off in person, when he had finished the job. He glanced at the grave. Some satisfaction. And he had eighteen dol-lars in greenbacks to boot. He counted the notes again. He had never set eyes on three hundred dollars in a lump sum. He let himself anticipate a few of the things it would buy him: a bath, a soft bed, stove-cooked victuals, a river of whiskey, a woman, a game of cards, etc.

Briggs folded the banknotes into the envelope and stuffed it down deep with the greenbacks inside his suitcoat. The letters, except the one from her sister back east, and sheets of paper he put back in the bag, then got to his feet. Sure enough, so did the women. Monkey see, monkey do. He picked up her coat and hat and personal items, rolled them up in her bedroll, tied it, and stepping up on a wheel hub pushed it under the tarp on the wagon. He went then to the grave and, kneeling by it, placed her sister's letter inside a fold of the buffalo hide and draped the cloth keyboard, stretching it to full length, from one end of her to the other. He sat back on his haunches.

"Cuddy," he said, lowering his voice so that the women couldn't hear, "you listen. Don't you haunt me. It won't work. I'm not to blame. You were already a gone goose. Out of your mind, I mean. I know that for a fact, because last evening I missed you and went out and there you were, singing and playing all to yourself. Playing a cloth piano." He paused. "Anyway, goodbye, and thanks for the money. You were a damn good woman and you helped me a lot." He was embarrassing himself. "Goodbye."

He stood, took up the shovel, and began to fill.

When the hole was half full, he stepped in and tromped on the earth to tamp it down, then filled to the top and tromped, and when finished, smoothed the excess dirt into a neat mound and stepped back satisfied. Some satisfaction.

It was time to make ready. Briggs brought his horse and tied it to the wagon. From the grub box he got a cup and spoon and cupped a small sack of cornmeal from the larger—he could make gruel in the cup—and from the compartment under the wagon seat he got her rifle and ample cartridges. The rifle he stuck in his saddle scabbard, and the other truck in his saddlebag. He tied his bedroll and cowcoat on behind. He moved in a deliberate manner, the women watching.

The last thing was what to do with the sewing bag with its letters and relatives' names. Where to stow it where someone would be sure to find it. He settled on the underseat box and put it there and dropped the lid.

He led his horse around in front of the four women and mounted up and gave each of them a long, disgusted look. God but he was sick and tired of tied tongues and faces like walls and eyes like broken windows. "All right," he said, "we are parting company. I'm going on by myself. I have worn my ass to the bone for you on that wagon, and a good woman has died for you, and that's enough. You can just get to Ioway under your own steam. The woman you have to see there is named Mrs. Altha Carter. Altha Carter. You set out from here

236

straight east till you come to the river, then go south to the ferry at Kanesville, cross, and go south to Hebron." He raised a finger. "Now what's the name of that woman?"

He waited. They looked at him as though he'd been reading from the damn Bible—"And Ner begat Kish, and Kish begat Saul," so on and so forth.

"What's the name of the town?"

They were women made of straw. Fussing over them accomplished nothing. What they needed was a few whacks on the backside.

"Shit," he said. "All right, you are on your own. You've got cornmeal and four wheels and a riding horse and a crackerjack span of mules and you ought to get there. If you don't, it'll be no loss to the U.S. of America." With his free hand he touched the brim of his slouch hat. "So this is goodbye, ladies. Goodbye and good luck."

He twitched the reins and the roan walked him away forever from the tree and fresh grave and wagon and the giddyup girls. He had felt all morning like a trigger being squeezed, and now the hammer had gone home. He hadn't ridden ten rods when he heard someone calling after him: "Goodbye! Goodbye!" Waving one arm, he supposed, and holding her doll with the other. The hell with her. The hell with the whole millstone, crack-brain bunch. This was a free country. George Briggs was finally by God a free man.

The first thing he did was reassure himself.

He made comfortable the sheath of his knife and the barrel of the repeater under his belt.

Then he laid a hand on his saddlebag and the rifle butt and his bedroll and cowcoat behind.

He made certain of the cameo pin in a side pocket and the riches of greenbacks and banknotes deep in the inside pocket.

Peaceful of mind he rode on. He had an inclination to glance back over his shoulder to see if there was any sign of life around the wagon, but that would be borrowing trouble.

April.

Sunshine a-plenty. The sky was lake blue, the clouds feathers, and the songs of birds on high pierced the blue like pins.

The prairie reminded him of a big boardinghouse platter. On it a feed of spring was served, green and brown, new buffalo grass supplanting old. And any day now there'd be more wildflowers, blue and yellow and orange and white, than the eye could eat.

He almost looked back but caught himself.

He was a man who never looked back. That was what he told Cuddy after he told her about the woman he lived with, who wanted to marry: "I rode away from her and never looked back."

If they had any brains and gumption they'd get along fine. They were farmers' wives. They could handle a horse and mules and a wagon and cook and do for themselves, and with their dumb luck they'd stumble onto somebody who'd take pity and peek under the wagon seat and see they got where they were supposed to go.

The need to look back was powerful.

He hoped Hebron was more than one of those small, Sunday-go-to-meeting towns. Even so, with the Kanesville crossings nearby, there must be some places where a man could raise some hell.

He pretended to be a dragoon on parade. He squared his shoulders and stiffened his neck.

Even if they didn't make it, if they milled around and starved or killed each other, it would be a blessing. They were no earthly good to anyone. They would just be a burden to their kinfolk.

Briggs looked back.

"Godamighty," he groaned.

Here they came, following him. They were strewn out in single file like sheep coming to a fold, Sours first, then Petzke, then Svendsen, then Belknap. They trudged along as though, if he were in the lead, they'd follow him through fire and flood, up mountain and down, to the grave or to everlasting life; as though, if he would be their guide, they'd walk around the whole, monstrous world.

He stopped. He sat his horse, waiting. He was unable to look back again.

The girl reached him first, put an arm around his leg, and held him tight as she might have a dying child. The wolf woman stretched arms over both his legs, strapping him to the saddle. The barren woman and the woman who had murdered her infant came up on the other side and laid hands on him, one his thigh, one his hip. And there on the prairie, under the lake sky, the five were joined in a kind of communion. The horse did not move, just as he had not moved under the taut rope that long night of life or death by the river. There was no sound but the songs of birds on high. The man looked down at the women, at the tangled hair and dirty faces, into the empty eyes. He was not free after all. He had replaced Cuddy. Likely they did not understand her ending, but whatever she had meant to them, he meant to them in her stead. Briggs had been a solitary man, and staying shy of others, riding away from love or friend or any sort of tether, had never found what lay inside him unfulfilled. Now it seemed to him that, as blood tunnels silently within the veins, something like a common prayer passed upward from their bodies into his, a plea to which his undiscovered self said yes.

He moved his animal away from the women and turned around and headed for the wagon at a walk. After a few rods he looked back.

The four were following.

Half an hour later he had everything in its rightful place and the women back in the box and the wagon rolling, again trailing the horses, and George Briggs up on the seat, driving and cussing George Briggs. If he'd been somebody else, he'd have beaten the tar out of George Briggs. Just because a woman who'd called him a "man of low character" had strung herself up to a tree. Just because four cuckoo clocks had hung on to him like a husband or brother or side-of-the-road savior. The man who never looked back had now, just once, and made maybe the biggest mistake of his life. If he'd had tobacco, he could have chewed. If he'd had whiskey, he could have got drunk. But all he had was a hollow gut and a sunk sensation and a set of reins in his hands, so he struck a bargain with himself: three more days, counting this one. He'd haul these half-wit hens three more days, and if he hadn't got them on the ferry by then, so long, sisters. Starting now he'd slant south and east, and after three days could leave them with a clear conscience. The farther south, down toward the Platte, the more travelers. Some outfit heading west would be sure to run into them and find the papers and Mrs. Carter's name in the sewing bag and put two and two together.

That afternoon he spotted two wagon trains in the distance, and sod houses, he noted, were giving way to log cabins. Game was clean gone. He took stock. The mules were skin and bones. They pulled heads-down. What they needed was some corn and a couple days off to laze around and fatten up, but he could give them neither grain nor time. Stay upright long enough to pull the wagon to the river and they could fall dead for all he gave a damn. His horse was in good shape, as was hers, the gelding, Shaver. The frame wagon had aches and pains and the iron tire on the left rear wheel had loosened again and rang as it rolled. He looked for a creek but could find none, so made a dry camp that evening and cut wood and wedged the tire, hoping it would last two more days. Maybe it would, but the cornmeal wouldn't.

He had to do everything now. He fried up the remaining cornmeal into dodgers and apportioned them carefully. After supper's, the rest would make two cold meals tomorrow, not a crumb more. They'd be bound sooner or later to come onto a road ranch or a shebang and he could buy food. He had money. You bet he had money.

He made a discovery in the morning. He could take the women out to the bushes two by two rather than singly, and they wouldn't fuss or fight. Not only that, they'd beeline right back to the wagon on their own hook. Wherever he went they went, following him like pups even when he went to take a leak unless he thought to lock them in the box first.

That day, the second, the weather wouldn't settle down. It would rain cats and dogs, then stop, then drip awhile, then stop while it made up its mind what to do next. Briggs kept a sharp eye out through the gloom. He much preferred a shebang to a road ranch. There might be a crowd at a ranch, with several trains stopped at once, blacksmithing and repairing wagons and trading footsore animals for fresh and drinking whiskey while the womenfolk bought bread and cheese and molasses and hominy and dried apples for pies and sundries from a general line of merchandise. There might be teamsters, too, and worse, some Army. It had been five years since he had flown the coop at Fort Kearney. Enlisted men did not fret him, they were common ruck and would come and go; but where there was Army there might be officers, career men, some of whom were confounded smart and had memories like steel traps. No, he wanted a shebang.

He almost passed one by in the middle of the morning. It edged a grove of willow trees and was a sorry sight. Two crotched stakes supported a ridge-pole over which was drawn a big sagging square of sail-cloth pegged out on four sides to form a poor kind of tent, with a flap door for light. There would unlikely be Army here, or any customer by choice.

Briggs climbed down and stretched a cramp out of a leg and opened his cowcoat to have easy access to his belt and walked on in through the flap door. The tent was as cloudy inside as the weather was out. Two seedy men, one long as a ladder, one as sawed-off as a stool, both skinny, both big-eared, brothers maybe, or cousins, sat on a plank over sawhorses. They had a proprietorial air.

"How do," they said.

Briggs nodded, and while they took inventory of him, he took it of their establishment. They had not invested much capital. He observed two barrels of whiskey up on cordwood, a table with a few canned goods, a glass jar of pickles that made his mouth water, and an open barrel beside it that apparently contained salt hog.

"Where from?" asked Ladder.

"North and west."

"Where to?" asked Stool.

"Kanesville."

"What for?"

"To cross. Where's Hebron?"

"Ioway?"

"That's it."

"Well, on the far bank."

"I know that."

"Mile downriver from the Bellevue crossing."

"What you freightin'?" asked Ladder.

"Goods."

Stool got up and went to the door.

"Kanesville, y'say," Ladder said to Briggs, scratching an ear. "Well, hold yer horses."

"Mules. Why?"

"River's up southa here. Y'can't cross."

"Yes, I can."

"Cheese Creek? Not this high, y'can't."

"Which is it?" asked Briggs. "A creek or a river?"

"Dry it's a creek. Rains it's a river."

Stool was staring out the door. "Ain't never seen a rig like that. What is it?"

"Frame wagon."

"Frame wagon? Mind if I look 'er over?"

"I mind."

Ladder elongated himself off the plank. "What can we do for you, Mister?"

"That salt hog." Briggs indicated. "How much?"

"Dollar a pound."

"A dollar?"

"They got some cheaper over t'Tolliver's."

"Where's that?"

"Other side the creek."

Briggs scowled. "I'll have three pounds."

Ladder got a small meal sack and began to paw meat from the barrel with his bare hands. Briggs missed Stool, strode to the door, and found that individual standing on tiptoe gaping into a wagon window. He swung round to Ladder.

"I told him to stay shy of that wagon. Get him in here."

Ladder finished pawing and tied the sack. "He's my cousin. He's set in his ways."

Briggs stepped to one of the whiskey barrels and drew the bowie knife from its sheath. Swinging side-arm, he stabbed the barrel like a belly, then stepped around, drove the blade into the other side up to the guard, and withdrew. Whiskey peed from both holes. Ladder looked as though he'd been stabbed instead of the barrel.

"Whud you do that for?" he cried in anguish. He swiped up some rags and made for the barrel.

"Hold your horses," said Briggs calmly, waggling the knife at him. "You can plug the barrel when you get 'im."

Ladder reached the door in two steps. "Jesus Christ, Cousin, get back here!" he bellowed. "He's a knifer!"

Stool jumped a foot in the air and came on a three-legged tear into the tent.

"Goods my pud!" he yelped at Ladder, who was

on his knees plugging the near split. "He's got him four wimmen in there!"

Briggs turned sideways so neither of the cousins could see, fished in his inside pocket for the greenbacks, sorted out three singles, returned the wad, and laid them on the table.

"Wimmen!" yelped Stool.

"Shut up y'dumb sonofabitch and plug t'other hole!" Ladder hollered at him.

Stool jumped for the barrel. Briggs took off the top of the jar, speared himself a big pickle with his bowie, had a bite, liked it, sheathed his knife, picked up his meat, and walked out the flap door with the pickle between his teeth like a cigar. The commercial cousins hollered after him.

"Pay up! Pickle's a dime!"

Briggs belched. The pickle had given him gas. The money-grubbing bastards had been right, all right. Cheese Creek was a river now, roiled and swollen with rains and runoff and close to ten rods across by his reckoning. That afternoon he had driven the wagon down into its bottom, which was timbered with hackberry and green ash trees, and studied the river, deciding whether to try a ford here or look for a better. There was only one way to find out for sure. He climbed down, took off all his clothing, emptied the water keg lashed to the rear step, plugged it again, and, lugging it, stepped down to the water and nakedly, cautiously, inched into the river and headed for the far side, feeling forward with each foot for bushes or tree limbs or boulders. The water was cold as hell. Briggs had never learned to swim. Even in the Dragoons he stayed aboard his mount in the water, and since then used ferries. He kept a tight hold on the keg, and it was well he did for halfway across, in water up to his armpits, he ran smack out of bottom, there was nothing underfoot. He had come onto a deep hole. With his left arm he hugged the keg for dear life and with his right flailed at the stream, and by this crude means found bottom eventually and waded at length to the far bank. Here he stood the keg on its end and sat down on it, shivering and puffing like a good fellow.

Down in this timber, the day was more murky than ever. The trees dripped. Off to the far north, thunder rumbled.

Briggs cogitated. If he unloaded, women and all, could he float an old frame wagon over the hole? How would the mules behave? If he managed the float, and swam the mules back, could he trust the women to stay up on them crossing? Mightn't they have a fright and fall off? And suppose he got them over on the animals, what about the rest of the load? Grub box and bedrolls and so forth? He had to do something. He was damned if he'd sit here fishing for crackers and waiting on the Cheese. After today, there was only one day left of his deal. Of course, if the wagon sank and they drowned like a litter of cats, no deal.

With the aid of the keg he splashed back across

the stream, then dried himself with a blanket, dressed, saddled his roan, and looked into a wagon window. There they sat, bless their hearts.

He rode down the riverbank east, winding among the trees in search of a more likely ford. He hadn't gone a hundred yards before he came into a clearing from which every tree had been cut, and in the center of it, a split-log shed which stumped him till he rode near enough to see the wooden rollers and an evaporator under roof. These identified the rig at once: this was a molasses mill, abandoned. Someone had given up on it despite ample wood for fuel and running water to keep the utensils clean. Sugar was dear lately, and the processing of molasses from sorghum had become a robust business in the Territory. The mills were simple contraptions. One man fed the sorghum between two rollers geared to turn by horse or mule power; the rollers pressed out the juice, which ran down an incline trough into the evaporator. The latter was a large pan with high wooden sides and an iron bottom in which the juice was boiled to syrup. A one-horse mill, Briggs understood, would press twenty to thirty gallons of sweetener every hour.

He stared at the pan. It was about five feet long and a hair over two wide. He snapped his fingers. Swinging down from the saddle, in three minutes flat he was mounted again and towing the molasses pan by a rope out of the shed, through the trees, and back to the bank of the Cheese by the wagon.

He got the women out and seated them in a row

on the bank. He unloaded everything, from top to interior to underseat. For added buoyancy, he lashed the empty water keg in its place at the rear. Then he stripped again. The women paid his anatomy no more mind than they would have a frog in a well. Up on his roan, gelding tied to the wagon, he led the mules into the river. When they ran out of footing they swam, and Briggs talked to them and encouraged them and the frame wagon floated and the mariner mules traversed the hole and found bottom and walked out of the water with their load as though they forded rivers every Sunday in the week. Briggs looked across.

"No!" he yelled.

On the far side his four cases were wading into the water, following him like good little girls.

"Oh, my God, no!" he yelled.

They'd drown. They were crazy. They'd never let him go. He'd never be shet of them.

"Go back!"

He was off his mount and lunging toward the hole and thrashing river, over it before he remembered he couldn't swim.

Arms wide he swept them onto the bank and sat down and worked his gills for a while like a fish out of water. It occurred to him he was naked as a jaybird again, and it made no never mind.

After a time he stood the women around the trunk of a big green ash and tied them to it with rope, which he wound round and round. He chopped down a sapling, trimmed it of branches, and fashioned himself a ten-foot pole. He then made two round trips to the far side of the Cheese in the molasses pan, propelling and navigating himself with the pole. On the first he carried across the grub box, bedrolls, and tools; on the second, Shaver's saddle and the underseat gear and the green sewing bag. Now he had everything over the river but the women.

Briggs rested. He was tuckered. The day darkened. The thunder ceased, but a breeze blew down the river bottom and tossed tree branches and caused small rains.

He began with Sours, thinking she would be the least trouble, seating her in front of him in the pan, and they made the crossing easily. But on the return, he looked over his shoulder.

"No!" he yelled. "Goddammit, go back!"

It was his fault, he'd forgotten. They'd stay as close to him as a flea a dog. Sours was in water up to her waist, following him, nearing the hole. He dropped the pole, jumped out of the pan, splashed water till he reached her, and arm about her waist guided her to the bank from which she'd come. He opened the rear doors of the box. What he ached to do was give her such a crack on the rump she'd practically fly inside. Instead, he assisted her up the step like a gentleman, then slammed the doors, bolted them, and turned to the stream. His pole was gone. Turning end for end in the current, the molasses pan disappeared around a bend. He trotted after it, waded out, tangled one leg in a submerged bush, untangled it, caught the pan, pulled it near shore and down the bank back to the wagon. Here, using the ax, he made another pole and set out again.

He untied Petzke from the tree and ferried her across without a snag, and stuck her in the wagon box with Sours, then did the same with Svendsen. He watched Svendsen closely, though, until he had her locked in the box. That left Belknap, the last.

But he was too tired and too cold. He was turning blue, and he shook with chills. He wrapped himself in a blanket and was immediately doubled up with coughing, hawking, spitting—the catarrh. This whole stunt, he decided, blowing his nose with a finger, was too much for any one man. If she'd been there, Cuddy, she could have handled one side of the river, him the other, and they'd have pulled it off slick as a whistle. And how, afterward, would she herself have crossed the Cheese? Simple. She'd have walked on the water.

He dropped the blanket and pushed off in the pan for the far side. Once there, he let Belknap loose of the tree, sat her down in the pan, coiled the rope, and pushed off again. Suddenly, over the deep hole, so suddenly he couldn't prevent her, the woman leaped up and stepped out with such force and cussedness that she tipped the pan over and Briggs with it.

He swallowed water and churned with arms and legs and got a grab on her, whereupon she flung arms around him and together they sank like a stone. Going down into dark he recalled what Cuddy had once said about Belknap: that she had to stay insane, for if she ever got sane, for even a minute, she would realize she had killed her baby and would try to kill herself. She was trying to drown the both of them now, no doubt about it, which enraged Briggs. Kill herself if she wanted, but leave him be. He hit bottom with his feet and crouched and used his legs like springs to shoot up through the water to the surface, carrying her with him, but couldn't prize himself from her embrace and went down a second time with her dead weight, lungs like full bladders. Again when he hit bottom he sprang up, wrestling her with him, and on sucking in sweet air got free enough of her to let fly with his right fist to her jaw. He knocked her unconscious. Theoline Belknap went limp, and Briggs reached and seized her by the hair and with the dregs of his strength splashed her and himself off the hole and found bottom and horsed her to the bank by the wagon and fell on his face beside her in the mud trying to breathe and, scared because he had come so close to death, crying like a boy.

That night he fed his passengers half the salt hog and half the dodgers, and in the morning the other half. That ran them entirely out of food, which was all right with Briggs because this was his third and last day wet-nursing. They had to be nigh on to the Missouri by now. Wagon trains heading west were thick as flies, having bunched up to cross the river at Kanesville, then spread out on this side as they entered the Territory. He avoided them like the plague. One was a long line of six-mule rigs freighting goods, so near he could almost hear the crack of whips and the oaths of the whackers. Another, consisting of only four covered schooners, had a big herd of cattle for a hindrance, and children, trudging along with sticks, for drovers. Indians, he figured, would run off half that herd in a week. He saw men on foot pushing carts, a swarm of them, Mormons probably, on their weary way to Salt Lake. It looked to him like the whole U.S.A. was playing pilgrim. Well, when he left the women tonight they wouldn't starve. He'd bed them down near the main trail and slip away and be in Kanesville by morning.

The storms had passed, and there was sun that day, and late in it Briggs came upon a sight so surprising that he stopped the wagon. A long, flat stretch of prairie lay ahead, and far off, in the center of the flat, stood a two-storey structure of large proportions. A westering sun flashed from two rows of real glass windows, above and below, and glared the color of the structure: a loud, strutty blue. A building like this had no business here. And just as unbelievable were the hundreds, no, the thousands of white stakes in the ground in even rows on all sides of it. He moved the wagon on and discovered that the placement of the stakes, white with new paint, was neat and regular, some rows far enough apart to drive along between, which he was doing. Then it came to him. This was a street. This was a paper town. And sure enough, he reached a sign, stopped, and worked the big letters in his mind until they made sense:

TOWN OF FAIRFIELD WELCOME.

If there was one paper town in the Territory, there were, or had been, or would be, a hundred. Briggs admired the brass and vision of the promoters. A gang of them got together, put up some money, bribed the legislature to pass an Act of Incorporation, hired ne'er-do-wells to perjure themselves and claim up to a thousand acres of land, and staked the acreage into streets and building lots a hundred twenty-five feet by twenty-five. Next they put up a hotel to accommodate themselves and any tinhorn investors they could lure off the trail. Then they high-tailed it to the nearest newspaper or print shop and rolled out fliers touting the new town. To buy "shares" in it now, these proclaimed, ten lots at a crack, was a guarantee of riches later, for this was a town singularly blessed by location and the Supreme Being. It was based upon a prosperous agriculture; it was well watered and timbered; it possessed fine indications of lead, iron, coal, and salt. A railroad line was on its way. Lithographs pictured broad avenues, elegant residences, an opera house, churches, a college, and a river with wharfs to which swarms of steamboats were tied. Fliers and lithographs were mailed east by the thousands, while salesmen were employed at a dollar a day and commission to work the adjacent states of Iowa and Missouri. The drumbeating done, the trap baited, the promoters then sat back, rubbed their hands, and awaited the bonanza. When it arrived, and with it thousands of innocent dollars, they decamped to seek opportunity elsewhere, not even troubling themselves to tear down the hotel or pull up stakes.

Sure enough, the blue paint on the hotel was new and the lettering on its front said FAIRFIELD HOTEL. And just as Briggs pulled the wagon up before it, he had a notion. This was the night to leave them and this was the pluperfect place. He'd take two rooms, one for them, one for himself. They could sleep four to a bed. He'd order supper for all and see they got a hot bath. Then during the night he'd be gone, depositing the sewing bag and their papers on the hotel desk. Bless them, he'd leave them clean and sound asleep in a real bed with their stomachs full—what more could they ask? Let the owners take care of them where he left off. For their troubles they could keep wagon, mules, and the gelding. Fair exchange.

He climbed down, mounted the steps to the hotel door, and entered. The inside, thanks to the windows and the sinking sun, was as light as the out. His first feeling was one of impermanence. It was a paper hotel for a paper town, nailed together in a hurry, furnished to be habitable and respectable for a short period, then stripped of its glass and whiskey and left with ghosts for guests until it fell down of rot or was blown away by the wind. Facing him, some feet away, a broad staircase ran up to the second floor. To his right, before the row of bare, uncurtained windows, was an assortment of old chairs and sofas. To his left was a long bar in front of shelves stocked with bottles, and between the bottles and the bar, leaning on the latter looking at him, was a great big belly of a man, presumably the barkeep. He was no spring chicken. He had a bald head, gray chop whiskers, and owl eyes with fat under them. Briggs moved slowly toward him.

"How do," he said.

The barkeep nodded.

"Nice place you've got here."

This was not a talkative barkeep.

"You open for business?"

Owl Eyes nodded.

"Well," said Briggs, "you've got some. I'm carrying four women outside. I'll need a room tonight for them and one for me. We can use a bath now and supper later."

"We're full up."

Briggs cocked his head. "With who?"

"Take my word."

Briggs moved to the bar and laid palms down on it. "It says hotel out front. Now we've come a hell of a long ways. We need two rooms and so on."

"Sorry."

Briggs scowled. Easing back from the bar, he opened his suitcoat to show off his cannon. He had a hunch the sight of that black, burned handle might make an owl blink. "Mister," he said, "I didn't stop here for a ruckus. But I am damn tired, and when I'm tired I get temperish. This is a hotel. I've got money. I want two rooms and the rest or the reason why not. Right now."

The barkeep blinked. "Just a minute." And he was out from behind the bar and following his belly to the stairs. Light as a feather on his feet, he was. "Mr. Duffy!" he called up the stairs. "Somebody here! Can you come down?" He looked at Briggs and levitated back behind the bar.

A man tripped down the stairs in a stovepipe hat. He stepped briskly to Briggs.

"My name is Aloysius Duffy," said he, offering a hand. "And yours, sir?"

"Briggs."

"What can we do for you?"

Briggs listed his requirements: two rooms, five hot baths, five suppers. Duffy listened politely. A gent in his forties, of average height, Duffy was a ruddy-faced fellow and wore, besides the stovepipe, a boiled shirt and red cravat and black trousers and snappy yellow oxfords and what passed for a diamond stickpin. The hand he had offered was soft, and it had surely signed a worthless certificate more often than it had swung a scythe. His movements and manner bespoke business before pleasure.

"I see." Duffy did not. "But why two rooms?"

"Well, I'm not by myself. I'm driving a frame wagon with four passengers. Women."

"Women?" Duffy's eyes were brighter than his stickpin. "Ah. An unusual cargo, I must say." He sobered. "In any case, Mr. Briggs, I regret I can't oblige you."

"I'd like to know why not. This is a hotel, ain't it? Open for business?"

"Let me explain." Duffy held up two fingers to the barkeep. "Come along," he invited. "Pleasure before business. Have a drink on the house."

They went to the bar and watched as two shots were poured. The promoter gestured with his glass. "To your health, sir." He fired his off and waited on Briggs. "Now, then. My partners are upstairs. The four of us are heavily invested in Fairfield, which will one day, I have no doubt whatever, be a city envied far and wide for its thriving trade and commerce and the natural beauty of its situation. In the meantime, sir, in order to recover our outlay, we are selling shares in it." He licked his lips, held up two fingers, and the barkeep poured. Duffy tipped and downed and Briggs did likewise. "Mr. Briggs, you couldn't have shown up at a more inauspicious time. It so happens we are bringing up from St. Louis a party of potential investors, sixteen of them, by steamboat. Some may be accompanied by their wives. They are to debark at Upper Mormon, and we have spring wagons waiting there to carry them overland here. We expected them last night, but they failed to appear. However, they will certainly arrive tonight, and their numbers will strain the resources of this hotel." Duffy put a consoling hand on Briggs's arm. "That's it in a nutshell, sir. I trust you recognize we cannot accommodate anyone else. These are gentlemen of means, and we hope and expect to convey to them a very considerable wad of shares in Fairfield. In fact, the fate of our entire venture may very well depend—"

"They've lost their minds."

"Who?"

"The women."

Briggs heard his words. Had it not been for the whiskey, he would not have uttered them. He must have been worn to the bone. Two drinks had never had such sudden effect. It had been like having gunpowder go off in his guts.

Duffy's mouth was open. "Are you, are you saying they're insane?"

"They're crazy."

The promoter stared. "You expect me to believe—"

"This winter. One murdered her baby. Wolves scared one cuckoo. One tried to kill her old man. The youngest lost three kids in two days. Diphtheria."

Duffy continued to stare. Even the barkeep's eyes were wide.

Briggs went on. "We set out from up near Wamego four, five weeks ago. I'm taking them home. That is, I'm taking them to Hebron, to some church-women who'll carry them on to their kinfolk back east on the cars. They're in sad condition. Dirty and tired and hungry. That's why I need—"

"That's enough!" Duffy snapped. "More than enough. Let me see them."

Briggs started for the door. Duffy turned back and said something under his voice to the barkeep, then joined Briggs, who led the way out the door and down the steps. Duffy stopped.

"I've never seen a wagon like that."

"Or what's inside."

The promoter gave him a glance and, approaching the vehicle, chose one of the windows. He attempted to peer in, but in the process knocked off his stovepipe. He picked it up and handed the hat to Briggs. Then he hooked fingers over the lower edge of the window and stuck his head inside. A minute must have passed. He withdrew his head.

"Lord God," said Aloysius Duffy.

Briggs returned his stovepipe. Duffy stood with it in his hands, on his face the expression he would use at a funeral or a bankruptcy.

"A tragedy," he said.

"I told you," Briggs said.

"I apologize."

"They were fine women."

"From the heart."

"How can you turn 'em away?"

"I can't."

Duffy shook his head and, carrying his hat, started for the hotel door, Briggs after him thinking he'd pulled it off, that the women had been their own best witness, and that he'd even buy Duffy a couple of drinks once the new guests were bathed and fed and tucked in their trundle bed.

But the instant they entered the hotel the promoter jumped aside, and three men faced Briggs, two with rifles, one with a pistol, obviously Duffy's partners from upstairs. No one pointed anything at him, the rifles cradled, the pistol hanging, but there they were, two men bearded, one clean-shaven, all in boiled shirts and all three looking a hole through Briggs, and there were the weapons, loaded and ready.

And then Duffy stepped over beside them and there were four, though Duffy wasn't armed.

"Mr. Briggs, I've apologized to you, but that's as far as I'm prepared to go," he said, his contrition gone. "That's my limit. Those women are pitiful, I concede, but we can't have them here tonight. The milk of human kindness be damned. My partners and I have put our souls and bankrolls into this project, and we won't lose out under any circumstances." He donned his stovepipe and gave the top a tap. "Now just you turn around and be out the door and take that wagon away and Godspeed to you."

Briggs did it without thinking. His snake of a right arm had the repeater out of his belt and leveled so rapidly none of them had time to draw breath.

"Shoe's on the other foot," he said. "You just let those guns down on the floor—be real careful—and open up those rooms and heat water." With his thumb he cocked the Colt's. "Do it, goddam you. Do it right now."

Then something was pressed into the small of his back, hard and round. He knew what it was. The barkeep was indeed light as a feather on his feet.

"Shoe's back where it belongs, Mr. Briggs," said Aloysius Duffy. "Behind you is Mr. Jacobus, our host and barkeep, with his trusty shotgun. Either you put your weapon away or he will blow you to Kingdom Come. Do it. Right now."

Briggs belted the gun.

"Well done," said Duffy. "On your way, my friend, and be grateful for the whiskey."

Briggs stood where he was. "All right. But I'll tell you what I think. You are the worst bunch of pissant reprobates I've ever run into."

The shotgun pressed him. He turned and began to move very slowly toward the door, hands at his sides, the tread of his boots heavy on the wooden floor.

"You shut your door to these poor women," he said so they could hear him, "and you'll answer for it the rest of your lives. You won't sleep. You'll choke on drinks. The food you eat'll block up your bowels and you'll die of your own shit."

This time the shotgun hurt.

Nevertheless he stopped. "I'll be back this way," he said, and searched for a word he'd never used before until he found it. "You have insulted me," he said, "so I'll be back. You wait."

The bastard barkeep shotgunned him out the door and down the steps and kept the weapon on him while he climbed to the seat and took the reins and moved the mules away at a trot.

Briggs was sick. Briggs was blood-mad. He took care to direct the span over as many white stakes as he could, trampling them under hoof, crushing them with wheels. Past the last of them, gone for good from the paper town, he drove in a straight line over the prairie in gathering darkness. He was sick because the bottom had fallen out of his plan. How and where was he to dump them now? He was furious with himself because he'd let four boiled shirts who scarcely knew one end of a gun from the other get the drop on him. How, going back into the hotel with Duffy, could he have missed the barkeep's absence? How, in the name of Christ, could he ever settle the score? Sooner or later, he had to.

He spotted a small stand of trees and pulled into it and sat smoldering and thinking until a round, consoling moon came up and he had worked up a scheme as good as the first one and a damnsight more gratifying. Jumping down, wishing he had some corn for them, he tied the mules to a tree and went to the rear of the wagon, unbolted the doors, and opened them.

"Hullo, ladies," he said.

Moonlight let him see, and what he saw was that they were loose, he'd forgotten that morning to strap them in. Well, they hadn't harmed one another, so the hell with the straps from now on. He opened the grub box, found a tin cup, and gave them each some water from the keg.

"Now I'll be gone a spell," he told them. "You be good girls and go to sleep and I'll be back, all right? Wait for me."

Bolting the doors, he patted Shaver on the rump and untied and saddled his roan. Then, making sure of Cuddy's rifle in its scabbard, he got several boxes of cartridges for it and for his Colt's and slipped them into a side pocket. He mounted, leaned forward, blew a breath in the animal's ear, and headed him for Fairfield.

It was no more than a mile. He kept to one of the staked streets until the hotel loomed, its windows, eight above, eight below, like mirrors in the moonlight. A lamp glowed in one on the second storey and in two on the first, one by the bar and one at the back. When he was a few rods off the building he walked his animal entirely around it and dismounted at the rear, where, as he expected, there was a stable, a lean-to. He counted five horses. One by one he led them out and whacked them away into the night. Mounted up again, he drew rifle from scabbard and said to himself: do it awful fast. Do it faster than you ever did anything or you will get yourself killed.

Briggs kicked the roan into a canter and rode around the hotel in a wide circle, reins in left hand, rifle in right. He fired deliberately, round after round, reloaded, rode on, and fired. He blew out every window on the first floor.

During the second circle he blew out every window on the second floor. The light up there went out and he was fired on. He saw muzzle flash and heard lead whine. He had driven them upstairs now, four partners and the barkeep, where he wanted them. He'd broken thirty-two windows, every one in the hotel.

He hauled up by the back door, shoved rifle into scabbard, swung down, pulled the repeater, and slamming wide the door, barged in.

It was the kitchen.

He took in a stove and a coal-oil lamp and a long table, under it a woman on her hands and knees yowling like a scared cat and on it a stack of towels and two loaves of white bread.

"Get out of here!"

Yelling at the woman he plunged through a door to confront the rear stairway and fired a pistol round up the well.

Past a lighted lamp on the bar he ran to the front stairs and to keep them honest upstairs fired two rounds up the well.

Belting the Colt's he broke back into the kitchen. The woman was gone. He seized the lamp and with the other arm swooped up the towels and lunged back into the bar area and let go half of the towels on the lower steps and ran around to the front stairwell and let go of the other half. Pulling the wick from the lamp, he poured the oil over the towels, dropped the lamp, struck a match, and threw it into the wet towels, which blazed up in excellent fashion.

Opening the front door for a draft he dashed back to the rear, stopping for the lamp on the bar, and using the oil and a match in the same manner got himself a fine fire going on that end.

He heard shouting overhead.

"We'll kill you, Briggs!"

"This way, for Christ's sake!"

"You murdering sonofabitch!"

Drawing the pistol he emptied it up the stairwell, three rounds, to keep them trapped, then heard running in the other direction, down what must have been a hall. He ran himself, reloading, caps and cartridges, to the front stairs, and as they reached the well, stuck his forearm around the edge and fired three rounds upstairs. This time they answered, rifles and a pistol down the well, but Briggs was over behind the bar.

Stacking bottles in the crook of an arm, he ran to the front stairs and began to hurl them one by one up the well. As they hit the risers of the upper steps, they smashed, and whiskey flowed down to flare up as it met the rising flames.

He collected more bottles, ran them to the rear stairs, and by the same means hurried the fire upward to the second floor.

Briggs could do no more. He was full of smoke and his legs were shaky and he backed off and stood in the kitchen door to see what he had wrought. The two fires, rear and front, ate up the stairs with such a sound that he could no longer hear anything above. And even as he watched, eyes watering, flames licked across the ceiling. He'd better go while the going was good.

He passed through the kitchen, pausing to tuck the two loaves of white bread under an arm. Out back, his roan stood exactly where he was left. That hammerhead would stand till Judgment Day if necessary, fire or flood or a man on his back with a rope around his neck. Briggs mounted him and walked them away amongst the white stakes until, at a safe distance, they turned, horse and man, and had the pleasure of a long look.

It was a hotel in Hell. It was a paper hotel in a paper town and blazing like paper, both floors and roof, and roaring like a thing alive. Every bone of it traced red, and smoke lofted in a pink pillar straight up to the stars. Set on miles and miles of stark plain, it seemed a fire capable of being seen from the Atlantic to the Pacific. Briggs was proud of his night's work. Wasn't he a Christian, though? One man against five and hadn't shot a soul! So bright was the fire now that he could make out dark figures jumping from second-storey windows, and if he'd had a mind to, he could have picked them off with the rifle like big birds, one at a time. They ran to the rear, probably to saddle horses that weren't there and chase after him, and this gave him much satisfaction. You insulted me, you bastards, he said to them. You insulted the women, who are in my care. Let this be a lesson to you. Lend a hand. Out here in this country that's what we do for each other. We lend a hand.

Just then the Fairfield Hotel fell in on itself. The walls caved in and the roof dropped on the walls, sending up fireworks of sparks and a huge dying sigh to the sky along with the last green-lumber smoke. The show was over. Briggs turned his horse for home. Under his belt, against his stomach, the steel of his Navy Colt's was still warm.

Once arrived at the trees, he let the ladies out of the box, took them around a tree to relieve themselves, and used the opportunity himself. "Listen, ladies," he said to them, "I put on a big party tonight. Word gets around. And the next time you want to stop at a hotel, I'll bet they treat you right."

Then while they watched he picketed the animals, laid and started a small fire, hauled out the grub box, and placed it near the fire. Finally he stepped again to the wagon, returned with something behind his back, and sat down at the box. The women sat down around it.

From behind his back he brought a loaf of white bread, set it ceremoniously on top of the box, pulled his Barlow, and sliced the loaf into five slabs. Then, from his coat pocket, he produced the tin of sardines he'd carried all the way from the day Cuddy spared him hanging. He peeled it open and lifted the sardines out by their tails onto the bread, portioning them equally. Pitching the can over his shoulder, he picked up the slab before him and began to eat. So did the women, immediately.

Briggs had never tasted anything as delicious. He paused and glanced around the grub box at the giddyup girls. There in the moonlight, Mesdames Petzke, Belknap, Sours, and Svendsen were having the time of their lives, chewing and licking their lips and letting sardine oil run down their chins. Happily he loaded up again.

"Ain't this good, girls?" he enthused, his mouth full. "Oh, ain't this grand?"

*   *   *

But he couldn't sleep. He was too full of bread
and the roar of flames and men shouting and walls
falling down and the crack of guns working and
succulent sardines. He'd shown them a thing or
two, the shit-brindle bastards. He laid back a blanket, got up, and had a look at the women sawing
wood under the wagon. He'd forgotten to tie their
wrists to wheel spokes, just as he had to strap them
in the box today. No harm in it. He'd have them
over the river tomorrow or the day after. He built
up the fire a bit, brought the green sewing bag from
under the wagon seat, and sitting down by the fire
went once more through the contents. The first
thing he noticed, though, was his right hand. So
desperately had he gripped the handle of his pistol,
firing, that the palm of the hand was black as the
ace of spades. He looked over the women's papers:
Belknap's sister's name and address on a sheet; the
name and address of Petzke's brother, plus a packet
of letters; the many names and addresses of Sours's
relations; the envelope with name and address of
Svendsen's cousins. These would presently be important, and the right papers must go with the right
woman—in Hebron he'd be the only one who knew
which one was which. He counted the greenbacks
from an inside pocket. After paying three dollars
for salt hog, he had fifteen dollars left—not much,
but better than a poke in the eye with a bull thistle.
Then he reappraised the pink cameo with girl's face
and crowned head and judged again it would fetch

enough to make up the three dollars. Finally he counted again, twice, the six fifty-dollar notes on the Bank of Loup, before stuffing them down deep with the greenbacks and cameo. The corners of his mouth stretched into a wide grin. Three hundred dollars. He was rich. Replacing the papers in the sewing bag, rising, putting the bag back in the underseat compartment, he stepped a few paces away, unbuttoned, took a leak, and eased again between his blankets. He lay on his back, folded his arms under his head on the bedroll, and looked up through an opening in tree branches at the faraway stars.

Cuddy.

He had refused to think about her, but now, using her bedroll for a pillow, and this close to the end of everything, he allowed himself.

I hope you are satisfied, he said to her. I gave my word I would see this business through and I am. We will reach the ferry tomorrow or the day after. They have been bothersome, too. They run after me like chicks after a hen. I can scarcely take a piss in private. I had to spend some of the money to buy meat. I hadn't knocked her cold, your dear friend Belknap would have drowned me. And when they were turned away, insulted by a gang of no-good grifters, I had to get shot at and burn a damn hotel to the ground to pay 'em back. If you don't know these things, you'd better. Also, I take back what I said. That you're plain as an old tin pail and have a viper in your mouth. Cuddy, I apologize. Anyway, your women are as good as home. I have earned your three hundred dollars. So I hope you're satisfied and will think kindly of me hereafter.

He let his thinking roam over the entire journey, from the day she had found him with a rope around his neck to the morning she had tied one around hers. It seemed to him he could now see the whole of what had happened, and the why, clear as crystal. When they set out from Loup, she was as much man as she was woman. She could ride and shoot and handle a span of mules and give orders. Day by day, though, on the trail, there were more and more things she couldn't do, that only he could, and did, and that rubbed her the wrong way. Gradually all she could manage was to cook and care for the passengers and take his orders and be a woman. That broke her spirit and her mind. Then she asked him to marry her and he said no, for one reason because marriage wouldn't have sufficed her. She'd have expected him to love her, too, and he didn't know what love was. He'd never had any. Lucky for her, he'd said no. She deserved a better catch. And begging him to lie with her—that he couldn't understand, unless she simply didn't care to die a virgin. And of course it went against the grain of her religion. Well, when he thought it over, her death was none of his doing. It had to happen. He had to be a man and she had to be a woman, made from his rib. He could be at peace. In the end she wasn't pushed, she jumped. It was just like those paper-town promoters. When they were trapped upstairs by fire, no way down, they jumped out the windows. The difference was, they made it and she didn't. She had too far to fall.

Still he couldn't sleep. A little wind soughed through the trees, lifting the branches, and over it he swore he heard her singing:

> But if I should perish,
> Thy promises keep,
> Take thee our two hearts
> And bury them deep.

Briggs stuck fingers in his ears. Wouldn't it be a caution if he went, too? Crazy? That would be everybody. One hundred percent. He couldn't stop his ears.

> Take thee our tokens,
> In love let us sleep.

Neither could he close his eyes. He had asked her not to haunt him, but in death as in life she did as she pleased. He listened to the song and stared at the stars.

They breakfasted on the other loaf of bread and Briggs shaved, just in case. He cut his neck in two places and stanched the flow of blood with spit and oaths. Then he harnessed and hitched, and tied and seated the ladies, and got the old gray mare of a wagon going. There were about a dozen crossings of the Missouri River along this middle reach, but Briggs had used only one, at St. Joe, when he enlisted and came west as a dragoon recruit. He had heard of Kanesville, which people had begun to call Council Bluffs, that it was not one but two widely separated crossings, Upper Mormon to the north and Bellevue to the south, and he aimed, if possible, to hit the lower, the Bellevue, which would take him across only a mile or so above Hebron.

It happened so unexpectedly, in a late hour of that afternoon, that he thought his eyes misled him, and had to stop the wagon. He had topped a rise, and there before him and below, there at long, long last, was the Big Muddy. It had to be the Missouri, one of the most meandering and contrary of rivers in the U.S.A. Sparkling in the sun through lowland on either side, it twisted and turned upon itself, running north, south, east, and west, take your pick, in different places. Here it was wide and deep, there narrow and shallow; here its bottom was firm underfoot, there quicksand would make a meal of a wagon or a yoke of oxen in less time than it took to tell it; here it ran free, there it was choked with towheads. That any steamboat, no matter how slight its draft, could navigate it was a wonder. Briggs supposed he should stand on the seat and wave his hat and yell "Yahoo!" but had no inclination. The way had been too long and hard and sad, and he was tired in every inch. What would Cuddy do if she were here now? He knew at once. Climbing down he stepped back to a window in the wagon and putting his face to it said, "Girls, we're there. The river. We've done it. We'll be over it soon and you'll be in better hands. So cheer yourselves and rest easy. D'you understand?" He expected no answer and had none and took the seat and clucked to the mules.

During the downslope to the river he observed several things. On this side of the Bellevue there was nothing in view but an emigrant train plodding west, the covered wagons so heavy-laden with household truck that half of it would have to be left by the wayside. After every crossing it took every train a week or two to learn and start shedding. A small cabin on the west bank might house the ferryman and his helpers and might not. On the east bank was a stand of tall trees, in and around which was a bustling encampment of tents and wagons and animals and humans, the pile-up of trains waiting their turn to cross. The ferry itself was a side-railed, flat-bottomed, flat-topped scow which used the strong current of the river as motive power. This was accomplished by means of a large hawser fastened to a tree on the bank upstream, and block and tackle playing freely on the rope attached to both ends of the scow. Just now the ferry was in transit from east to west, and Briggs figured he would make the west landing by the time the scow was unloaded of two wagons and teams of horses and some milch cows and he could therefore cross without delay. The span stepped out at a fine clip. Even the off mule, the one she'd called "the Thinker," leaned into his collar and shared the chore with the nigh, "the Worker." But then, all at once, they must have put on the smell of the Big Muddy like a nosebag—and away they went. Together they took up such a fast trot that the wagon bounced and swayed like a buggy. Briggs hauled on the reins and hollered, but he could no more slow those crazy jacks than he could have a herd of buffalo on the prod. Their ears were down and their tails up. "Whoa, goddammit!" he yelled. "Whoa!"

They knew better than he. They timed it like a clock. They covered the flat like scared cats, and just as they slowed themselves at the landing, the last of the milch cows was cursed off the scow and he was able to drive the wagon and trailing horses aboard directly. Getting down, he was approached by the ferryman, a Kaw Indian. For some reason, no one knew why, most of the ferry owners and operators along this reach of the river were Kaws. This one, who wore an assortment of attire including a once-white shirt and a plug hat with an eagle feather, spoke in grunts, indicating the passage price would be a dollar for the wagon and fifty cents apiece for the animals. Briggs said he had no money. No money, no go, the Indian replied. Briggs took him to the rear of the wagon, unbolted and opened the doors. The Indian peered inside, then looked impassively at Briggs, who, trying sign language, tapped a finger on his temple and rolled his eyes. The man stared at the four women, curious, then said something unintelligible in some tongue and, turning away, waved at his helpers. They laid to, working the rope, and the scow eased slowly from the bank. Briggs bolted the door and enjoyed the free ride, which required only a few minutes. He enjoyed skinning any Indian anywhere anytime, even a Kaw. He recollected occasions when Indians would have skinned him alive if they could. As the scow nosed to the east landing, he was up on the seat, and in a moment more shook the reins and the wagon rumbled off the ferry onto the solid, civilized soil of the State of Iowa.

Briggs was bewildered. Sights and sounds and hurly-burly overwhelmed him. For days his place had been the prairie, his company that of members of the opposite sex who could neither speak nor respond when spoken to. He had been in charge. Today he had stumbled upon the Missouri, been rushed to the river and crossed it, and now he was surrounded by human kind—a current of events was bearing him along too swiftly to resist or navigate. He was like the blind man brought suddenly to an elephant and asked to make sense of it.

He threaded the wagon through the commotion and inquired of a man the way to Hebron. It was down the bank half a mile south, just follow the road.

He put the mules to a brisk walk, the river on his right and on his left a line of establishments sprung up to outfit those emigrants who had come west with little more than cash and the clothes on their backs. There were wagon yards and smithies and pens for cattle and oxen and corrals for horses and mules, all of them doing a land-office business.

Then, as abruptly as everything else that day, he entered Hebron. Briggs recognized it at once as the small town Cuddy had imagined one night by the fire. Its main street was lined by shade trees already leafing out in April green. The houses were humble and clapboard, with neat and grassy yards in front and beds of many-colored flowers. Most were painted, even to the privy in the rear. Briggs was returned to his boyhood back east. He came upon the business center and noted two general stores, a hotel called "Hutchinson House," a blacksmith's, a bank, a barber pole, a doctor's shingle and a lawyer's, and a livery stable, but not a single, solitary saloon. Hebron was dry as a bone.

He stopped and, tipping his hat to a matron emerging from a general store, asked for the home of a lady named Altha Carter. That would be the minister's wife, was the reply. Just travel on to the white Methodist church and the white house beside it, the parsonage.

It was a small frame church with a steeple. The parsonage sat next to it, also white, behind a row of bleeding-heart bushes. There was a two-track drive past a stoop on the church side of the house, which led back to a barn, unpainted, where the parson probably stabled his horse and buggy.

Briggs turned into the drive and pulled the wagon

up even with the side door. Hanging the reins he slid down, got the green sewing bag, and moving slowly to the stoop, mounted the steps. He buttoned the collar of his shirt. He knocked at the door. The late-afternoon sun lingered. The air was still, and there were smells of mud and spring and river in it. His legs went weak. He had to get hold of himself. To do so, he spat over the stoop into a bed of lilies of the valley.

"Sir?"

"Afternoon, ma'am." He removed his hat. "Are you Missus Altha Carter, wife of the minister?"

"I am."

"Well, ma'am, my name is Briggs," he said. "I've come from the Territory, from Loup, and brought you those four women."

"Women? Oh! For goodness sakes, yes!"

She switched through the door so suddenly that Briggs had to hop out of the way of her hoop skirt. If he'd expected Altha Carter to be wearing wings or bigger than life, she surely wasn't. She was short and sturdy as a stump and getting on in years, in her fifties probably. Her hair was gray and there were lines in her cheeks and crinkles at her eyes. Half-spectacles, which she looked over or through, rode the bridge of her nose, and she looked him up and down. There was warmth in her, and iron. She made him think of a small steam engine. All she lacked was a whistle and a bell.

She smiled her first impression of him. "You've

been a long time coming, Mr. Briggs. I am relieved you're here. I'm sorry Reverend Carter isn't—he's out somewhere burying someone."

She bustled past him to see his rig. Her dress and starched white collar were satisfactory, but the hoop skirt he disapproved, especially on a parson's wife. He had seen only one other, on a filly in Wamego last year, and wondered then, as he did now, what in hell women would think of next. Of course, an Altha Carter would wear what she pleased, and devil take the hindmost.

She turned. "Just a minute. I thought a woman was bringing them, named Cuddy. That's what Reverend Dowd wrote me."

He frowned. "Ma'am, I'm sorry to have to tell you. Mary Bee Cuddy, her name was. She was with us up to a week ago, worked like a trooper. Then a fever took her." Her face fell. "Ma'am, I feel bad about it, but I did everything I could, and it was no use. I buried her and we moved on."

Mrs. Carter shook her head. "Oh, what a loss. I'm sorry for her and for you. She must have been a fine, intrepid human being."

Briggs nodded. "She surely was."

"How cruel—to come so far, on such a mission, then fall. I'm sure the Lord has taken her to His bosom." She turned again. "What is that? I've never set eyes on a wagon like that."

"It's called a frame wagon."

"Exactly like a big box, with windows. And

they're—they're inside? They've ridden in that box all this way? Mercy!"

"Yes, ma'am."

"It's time to meet them." She stepped down from the stoop and approached the rear of the wagon. "I'm not sure I'm ready," she murmured, almost to herself.

Briggs put on his hat and strode past her. "Ready, ma'am?"

"Yes, please."

He unlocked, then opened wide the doors. Mrs. Carter moved close and looked inside, into each of the four faces. Then she turned away, to Briggs, put a hand on his arm as though to steady herself, and bowed her head. He'd been mistaken. Behind her beans and mettle was a soft side. She'd take in any strays, from cats to persons, and find good homes for them. He waited. In a tree nearby, a mockingbird sang about love and insects and chivalry. Mrs. Carter raised her face, and her eyes were full.

"You must have had an awful winter," she said.

"Ma'am, we did."

"Let us take them in the house."

"All right. Will you please hold this bag?"

She took the sewing bag from him, retreated a pace, and watched as he helped each woman down the step. Then, when they were on their feet, she was uncertain. "How shall we do it?"

"I'll go first and they'll follow me," Briggs assured her.

"They will? Through that door, then, the one I came out of, and turn right into the parlor."

He nodded. "Let's go, girls," he said to his group. "Come along now."

He led the way, and they followed him single file across the stoop and into the house, turning right into the parlor. Here they bunched up behind him as he hesitated.

"Put them on the sofa, Mr. Briggs," said Mrs. Carter coming after. "I'm sure there's room."

He was unsure how to do it, but taking the first woman's arm, he guided her to a long black horsehair sofa, sat her down successfully, then returned to the second, and so on, until all four were seated in a row.

"There," said Altha Carter. She handed him the sewing bag. "Give me just a minute."

She stepped back through the door and he heard her raise her voice, perhaps to a servant girl in the kitchen. "Hallie, will you run an errand? Please go to Mrs. Conner's house, and Mrs. Offutt's, and Mrs. Vaughn's, and Mrs. Campbell's. Tell them the women are here from the Territory, and please come over when it's convenient."

Briggs helped himself to the parlor. Cluttered it might be, but he couldn't recall ever being in a room as fancy. Walls and ceiling were pure white plaster. Rep drapes bordered two glass windows. The floor was finished plank, most of it covered by manufactured carpeting with a pattern of pink roses in full bloom. Besides the sofa there were several small tables, one of them marble-topped, supporting a lamp with a brass reflector, and another which looked to be distant cousin to a table. Its legs were iron, attached beneath it was a kind of metal treadle, its top was like a hood made of tin with a lift handle in its center, and before it was a straightbacked chair. In one corner stood a melodeon, its stop knobs and keyboard uncovered, which implied it was regularly played. But most interesting to him was the large flag framed and hung on the wall over the sofa. It was just a corker of a flag. The field was of white bunting, edged all round with a wide band of gold thread. The centerpiece, incredibly, was a great big green silk alligator. Its tail thrashed, its head reared, its red eyes raged, while around its gaping jaws marched ranks of savage teeth. The flag was streaked gray by powder smoke, torn at one corner, and pocked with small holes, probably grapeshot.

Altha Carter returned to Briggs, who was fascinated by the alligator. "Isn't it colorful?" she asked. "It captures everyone. It was a regimental flag—have you ever served your country, Mr. Briggs?"

"No, ma'am."

"Well, that was the flag of Beale's City Rifles. In 1815, after New Orleans, it was presented by Old Hickory himself to my husband's father, Gershom, who fought with Beale, in recognition of his bravery. We're very proud of it." She gave her attention to the four women, saying softly to Briggs, "Do they speak?"

"No."

"Do they—understand anything?"

"Ma'am, I don't know."

"I notice their eyes move around the room. What does that mean?"

"It's hard to tell."

"Perhaps each remembers a parlor," she guessed. "From her own past, I mean. Oh, poor dears, poor dears. Have you observed any, any improvement in their condition?"

"Not much, ma'am. Well, they don't scrap with each other anymore, or try to run away."

"I see. That's a good sign." The minister's wife drew a long breath. "We'd better get down to brass tacks. Tell me their names—otherwise I won't know one from another. And don't you have some papers for them?"

"Yes, ma'am. Here." Briggs opened the sewing bag, removed the sheaf, and placed the bag on a table. "What I'll do, I'll put the proper papers on each one's lap." He started on the left. "Now this here's Belknap." He could read out the name and address on the sheet because he was familiar with them by now. "Theoline Belknap. She's from Kentucky, and here's her sister's name and address."

"Theoline Belknap," repeated Mrs. Carter.

"She killed her baby."

"Oh, no, no, don't tell me." She clutched his arm. "Please, I don't care to know, it isn't important."

"All right." Briggs laid the sheet in Belknap's lap and read from the top letter of a packet. "This is Petzke. Hedda Petzke. Her brother lives in Illinois."

"Hedda Petzke."

He placed the letters. "This is Svendsen." He read from an envelope. "Gro Svendsen. Norskie, I reckon. She's got two cousins in Minnesota."

"Gro Svendsen. Very well."

He put the envelope in Svendsen's hands. "And last is Sours."

"But she's only a girl. Why, she even has a doll!"

"Yes, ma'am, and never lets go of it. She had three children. Lost 'em all to diphtheria."

Altha Carter closed her eyes. "Dear Lord. Don't say any more. What is her full name?"

"Arabella Sours."

"Arabella Sours."

He laid the sheet in the girl's lap. "She's got a lot of family in Ohio. There's their names and where they're located."

Briggs stood with empty hands and queer, whipsawed sensations. Once the sheets and envelopes had passed from him, the names and addresses on paper, written out, something was severed. His care, his keeping of the persons represented by the names, was at an end. He was lightened of a burden, but with relief came a sense of loss which was almost physical. He stared at the table with iron legs and a lift hood, yet did not see it. He appeared to be listening to Mrs. Carter, who wanted to tell him what would transpire now. After what he'd been through, she said, he had every right to know. She would proceed just as she had last year, when a fine man named McAllister brought three women to her. Each of his four would have a sponsor. She had just sent for them, members of the Ladies Aid. Each of this four would be taken into her sponsor's home, bathed, rested, and provided with proper clothing. In a few days they'd be carried down to St. Joe, to leave there with their sponsors on the cars. She predicted they'd be home again, with loved ones, in less than two weeks. The funds were available, too. In winter her Society appealed to congregations back east, and their generosity had never failed. Altha Carter stopped. He was not the kind of man who listened long to women. She'd lost his attention, and she found its subject.

"You're curious about that table."

"Yes, ma'am."

"It isn't a table at all—let me show you." She went to it and lifted the hood. "It's a sewing machine!"

"Sewing machine?"

"A very recent invention. This is a Wilcox & Gibbs. Reverend Carter gave it to me last Christmas. It will stitch, hem, tuck, cord, bind, braid, quilt, and embroider. Just thread the bobbin and away you go—so they say." She sent a glance at the women on her sofa, to see if the machine interested them. It did not. They had eyes only for Briggs, or other furnishings, or the distance. She replaced the hood. "I'm learning to use it as fast as I can—I give classes for my friends. But it's very complicated."

Her words were only words. She stood by the sewing machine, Briggs in the center of the room.

He realized he'd been standing around her parlor with his hat on. He took it off. And then it dawned on him it was time to go, that Altha Carter wanted him to go, needed to tend to her own business. She didn't blow a whistle, but there was such a head of steam in the woman that, when she was stopped up, he could almost feel the pressure.

"I'd better get a move on," he said.

Her silence agreed.

"I sure hope they stay," he said. "They might just up and follow me."

"I don't think so, not now. I think this room will hold them."

He turned for the last time to the giddyup girls as they sat in a row, papers in their laps: Belknap, Petzke, Svendsen, Sours. He looked into each worn face, three of them old beyond their years, at each dirty coat or wampus, at each pair of cut and run-own boots.

"Well, well," he said to them.

If there had been a clock in the parlor, it would have been heard to tick.

"Oh, say, I forgot." He dug into a coat pocket and brought out the square of cardboard and the pink cameo pinned to it. "I found this along the way." He showed it to Mrs. Carter.

"It's lovely." She smiled.

"I thought I'd give it to one of you girls," he said to them. "And I guess it'll be Missus Sours. She's the youngest and will have the most use of it."

He leaned and placed it in the girl's lap on top of

her kinfolk sheet, then straightened and stood hat in hands, turning it by the brim as though he didn't for the life of him know what to say. He was confused again, not by a kaleidoscope of events in the present but by those in the past. He recalled how they had located the women one by one, he and Cuddy; how Petzke's husband, Otto, had cried and carried on; how he and young Sours had chaired the girl and her rag doll up the side of the ravine to the wagon; how the husband Svendsen had put a rifle on him and Cuddy had countered with her own rifle so that they could get away; how he'd had to tap Vester Belknap on the noggin to teach him not to rankle a man with a gun; how Cuddy sat up high and spunky on the seat and talked his arm off between stops; and finally, after they had gathered the four and set out east, how the women had all of a sudden set to wailing.

"This is goodbye, ladies," he said. "You take good care of yourselves and do what Missus Carter tells you. You're about home now." He inclined from the waist as though trying to bow, then clapped on his hat. "Well, goodbye, ladies. God bless you."

He turned, awkwardly, and strode from the parlor and blundered through the doorway.

On the stoop there were footsteps after him. It was Altha Carter.

"They'll be all right," she assured him. "I want to say goodbye to you."

But he was moving. He climbed to the wagon seat, got hold of a bedroll, brought it down, and presented it to her. It was her bedroll, he said, Miz Cuddy's, and there were some things in it she could maybe use, soap and clothes and so on. She said of course, and thanked him and laid it on the stoop. Then he said he'd been thinking. He had no use for the other bedrolls, or the wagon for that matter, or the mules, so he'd give them to her and the Methodist ladies to sell and use the money for railroad fares and whatever else. Was she agreeable?

"Oh, Mr. Briggs!" Tears glittered again even though she smiled. "Am I agreeable? I'm delighted! How generous of you!"

He was embarrassed. He unbuttoned his shirt collar. He said all he asked in return was that the Reverend Carter feed the mules some corn before he sold them. They'd earned it.

"I'm sure he can, and will," she promised. "How I wish he were here to meet you. Now you'll be gone. Where, Mr. Briggs? Will you stay in Iowa or go back to the Territory?"

"I don't know."

"If you do go back, please thank Reverend Dowd for me and wish him well. And tell him, please, to stick a pin in your Territorial Legislature. They simply must build an asylum. We can't go on this way, depending on a few brave souls like you and Miss Cuddy and Mr. McAllister last year."

"I will, ma'am."

She moved to him. "Then this is our goodbye. But I'm not here to say goodbye. I'm here to thank you. Give me your hands, please."

He gave them, and she clasped both and looked directly into his eyes over the tops of her specs. She said she would say to him what she had to Mr. McAllister. That he had done a splendid deed. He could be, and should be, proud of it as long as he lived. That most men were good, she believed, and decent, and honorable if given the chance to be, but men who did for others what he had done of his own free will were few and far between. In his own time and place and way, he, too, had been a savior.

"I shall pray for you," she said, gently and bowed her head.

Briggs did not bow his. He stood on one foot, then the other while she composed her thoughts. He fixed his eyes on the stoop in case his four friends followed him outdoors. The mockingbird still sang, and would sing the night through since it was spring. Evening lay over the small town and the river like a benediction.

"God our Father," she prayed, "bless this good man wherever he may go. Keep watch over him, cause Thy face to shine upon him, and bring him home to Thee one day. If he has done this for Thy daughters, do as much for him, for he has been Thy true and faithful servant. Father, I ask it in the name of Thy son, who also did Thy work on earth, died for us all, and lived again in glory. Amen."

Briggs's stomach added a loud amen, and he turned red. He was starving hungry.

Altha Carter raised her head, disregarded her hoop skirt, stood on tiptoe, gave him a smack on the cheek, hustled away and up onto the stoop, and spoke to him a last time. "I'll go to them now," she said, smiling. "I hope we meet again, Mr. Briggs, and soon. Goodbye."

So startled by the kiss was Briggs that he was struck dumb, and when he could have said goodbye she was inside the house.

It was done.

He was free.

He stirred his stumps. First he saddled the roan, tugged his bedroll from under the tarp on top, and tied it on behind the saddle with his cowcoat. Then he went up front to the mules, sidled between them, and hung a friendly arm over the Thinker's neck and one over the Worker's. "Goodbye, you old pluggers," he said to them. "You are the best damn mules ever came down the pike. May the Lord bless you with corn because you are His true and faithful servants." He then untied Shaver, the gelding, led him alongside the roan, mounted up, untied his own animal, and leaned forward. "How about some corn yourself, Handsome?" he inquired into the horse's ear, then wheeled him and kicked him into a trot. So glad was the hammerhead to hear the word "corn," and to be loose at last of the wagon, that he let a long, joyous fart. Out the drive to the street they trotted, rider, roan, and gelding, out of the world of women and into the company of men, where they belonged. Briggs did not look back.

THE
HOMESMAN

But they had no corn at the livery, so he ordered both animals a big feed of oats and a damn good currying and then, leaving his cowcoat and slinging saddlebags over a shoulder, stepped down the darkening street. He was worn to a fare-thee-well. He entered the Hutchinson House. There seemed to be nobody about. He noted one counter and six cubbyholes and six keys in them and no furniture. After a wait, he brought a fist down on the counter hard enough to wake the dead, and immediately a girl of fifteen or so gawked through a door from out back somewhere. Briggs was disgusted. The company of men, hell.

"I need a room," he growled.

"Yes, sir."

"Best one in the house."

"That'll be No. 5, sir, upstairs."

"Well aired."

"Yes, sir. Two windows."

"No ticks."

"Oh, no, sir. And how long'll you be with us, sir?"

"As long as may be. How much'll you soak me for the room."

"Dollar a night, sir."

"I'll want meals."

"Yes, sir."

"Who'll cook?"

"My mother."

"She don't seem to draw much trade."

"She's a very good cook."

"I'll be the judge, young lady. Let's go."

The girl lit a candle, took the key, and led the way upstairs. Briggs observed she was barefoot. The room was decent enough, supplied with a small table and chair, a whiteware pitcher and washbowl and soap and towels and mirror, a high-post bed, a peepot under it, and lace curtains at the windows. Briggs dropped saddlebags on the bed, threw up both windows as far as they would go, and sat down on the bed to test it. With her candle, the girl lit one on the table.

"Bed'll do," said Briggs. "I want a hot bath. Where is it?"

"Down the hall. Fifty cents for the bath, sir."

"Start heating water. After that, serve me supper in here. I'll have a side of beef, a hill of fried potatoes, half a loaf of white bread and butter, and some coffee. Real coffee."

"That'll be seventy-five cents, sir."

Briggs gave her a sergeant's scowl and, in so doing, actually saw the girl for the first time. He was shocked. His eyes began to sting as though there were tears in them. Double her age, darken her hair from auburn to black, put shoes on her to get a couple inches of height, and add forty pounds of flesh, and Jesus—Mary Bee Cuddy alive and breathing. Right now she was thin as a rail, all knees and elbows and backbone, but her shoulders were wide and her face plain as an old tin pail and her eyes looked through you to your shady side. He could see her someday riding a horse and teaching school and good with a rifle and living alone, no man man enough to marry her, and yes, God help her, one day broken-hearted and hanging from a tree.

"What's your name?" he asked.

"Tabitha Hutchinson."

She wore a faded muslin dress with short puffed sleeves, clean enough but frayed at the neck and two sizes too small.

"Hutchinson. Tabitha. All right, Miss Hutchinson, you have your marching orders. A bath and supper, the sooner the better."

"Yes, sir." A spark of fire in her eye and she was gone.

Briggs lay on the bed listening to Tabitha Hutchinson stumble ustairs with full buckets and downstairs with empty and looking around at the room, his room. It was magical to be in a real room again, with four walls and ceiling and windows. He would never again root-hog as he had the past few weeks, damn the pay or the reason. He had given enough. It was his turn to take. For a while at least, he intended to live off the fat of the land.

A knock at the door, and he went down the hall, stripped, and washed his body and hair in a tin tub with hot water and soap and groans of pleasure, and dried himself with a thick towel. He thought it absolutely the best bath he had ever had.

When he returned to the room, the table was set with his supper, and he lit into it. After he had sopped the plates with a crust of bread and got rid of some gas and picked his teeth with a matchstick, he thought it undoubtedly the best meal he had ever eaten.

He locked the door then, blew out the candle, took off his longjohns, opened the bed and lay down on it on his back with his legs spread and his head on a pillow, let fresh air waft over him, pulled a clean cotton sheet up to his hips, and closed his eyes.

For twelve hours he slept the sleep of one who has done a splendid deed.

In the morning he thought it surely the best sleep of his life.

He banged a boot on the floor till Miss Hutchinson, the go-ahead girl, stampeded up the stairs and took his order for breakfast.

By the time he had snorted and dressed and spat his catarrh out a window it was on the table: four eggs, more potatoes, a stack of rind bacon, some fried bread, a piece of dried-apple pie, and a pot of coffee. He ate with appetite. The only thing lacking was one shot of whiskey for digestive purposes and a second for the well-being of his soul. Whiskey could wait, however. He had a busy day ahead of him, and a busier night.

Going downstairs, he used a fist on the counter. "Tell me, Miss Hutchinson, where I can buy myself some new duds."

"Duds?"

"Clothes."

"Oh. We have two general stores. I guess I'd go to Keppler's first."

She had quit sirring him and started looking him over—the gun under his belt for one thing. He wondered if she would snoop in his saddlebags.

"Fair enough," he said. "And is there a stone-cutter hereabouts?"

"A stone-cutter?"

"Man who makes gravestones, markers, and such."

"Oh. I'll ask my mother."

Briggs waited.

She reappeared. "She says to see a man named Janz. He's down the street south, not too far. There's gravestones in front of his place."

"Janz," repeated Briggs. "Thank you."

He took his leave and walked first to the barbershop, where he got a shave and a haircut and some information for two bits. According to the barber, one Thomas Hutchinson had started the Hutchinson House but wasn't doing very well with it and so, being a carpenter, had hired out to work upriver on a building at the Upper Mormon crossing, and came home when he could. Meantime his wife ran the hotel, their daughter helping out. Tabitha, Briggs said. The barber thought that was her name.

Briggs then strolled the street south. There was next to nothing to see. The principal activities in Hebron, he speculated, must be quilting, swatting flies, singing hymns, twiddling thumbs, and thumping the Bible. Why, there was a hell of a lot more going on in Loup, and compared to this jerkwater town, Wamego was practically Philadelphia.

The stone-cutter advertised his trade with a few unmarked stones in front of his place, a kind of shed attached to a small house, and Janz himself was a small, elderly man with a beard that would make a fine broom. Briggs told him he wanted a headboard. Oak or walnut? Briggs asked the difference. Two dollars more for walnut, Janz said, because it looked nicer. Walnut then, Briggs decided. And what did he want on it? Ten cents a letter. Briggs told him. Janz wrote out name and inscription and did some figuring and said the job would come to fourteen dollars and ten cents, make it fourteen even. Briggs said that was mighty steep. Janz stroked his beard. Briggs said all right, dammit, get to work, he'd be by for the board that evening. Janz said he'd have five dollars on account. Briggs tried to stare him down, but Janz played with his beard and in the end had his money.

Briggs meandered back to the livery, saddled both

horses, and trailing Shaver, rode north on the river road toward the ferry crossing. He'd no sooner trotted out of town than he met the U.S. Cavalry riding south, three of them, two officers and a noncom. The Dragoons were no more, he'd heard, having been cut down by Washington into ordinary cavalry. At the sight of the detail he broke into a cold sweat but slumped in the saddle and pretended to be woolgathering, and the military passed by without incident. Even if they had suspected, and taken him in, they'd have had no "Briggs, George" in their records. Turning in to the first stockdealer's he came to, he jawed away an hour selling the gelding. The trader wanted to swap him a snide for his sound animal, a mare with worn molars, a sweeneyed shoulder, and a blind left eye, but Briggs wasn't swapping, he was selling, and eventually made that clear and eventually got twenty dollars for Shaver, saddle thrown in.

He returned to town then, stabled his roan, and went straightaway to Keppler's, a general store. Here he advised them he wanted new attire, skin out, top to bottom. They were pleased to oblige. In the course of the afternoon he tried on, in the back room amid bolts and sacks and barrels and boxes, and selected a black suit identical to the rusty one he had lived in all winter, plus a shirt, longjohns, a hat in the same style as his old slouch, and two pairs of rugged socks. A new pair of boots he balked at, claiming them too damn dear. Furtively, while the clerk was totting up his bill, he transferred his greenbacks and the banknotes to the inner pocket of his new coat, stuffing the extra socks into a side. After he had paid, and was asked what he wanted done with his old clothing, he said to give it away to someone in need and deserving. On the way out, in his new raiment, he bought several boxes of cartridges for his repeater and for Cuddy's rifle. He then left the store, about-faced, and went back in to buy some Star tobacco. He then left the store again, about-faced, went back in again, and consulted with the clerk. How much for a fancy pair of young lady's shoes? High-button or high-laced? Which was the fanciest? High-button, and what color? Color? White, black, or brown? Which was the fanciest? White. Three dollars. Three dollars! For a pair of shoes? That was right. Briggs scowled and considered. Did he, the clerk, know a young lady named Hutchinson, folks ran the hotel? Yes, she came in to Keppler's now and then. Briggs handed over one, two, three dollars. All right, the next time she showed up, fit her a pair of white, high-button shoes. The clerk said he would. Briggs said he had the money, he had damn well better.

Then it was back to the hotel, where he ordered a light late dinner from Miss Hutchinson: a whole chicken, hominy, a slab of corn bread and butter, stewed fruit of some kind, and plenty of coffee. After it was served and he had eaten it, he was drowsy and so stretched out on the bed in his longjohns to rest up for the big night ahead. The bliss of the bed, the load of food in his belly, and the evening's prospect made his final decision for him: he'd be damned if he'd go back to the Territory. What was there for him? A frozen ass? A hungry gut? A rope around his neck? The chance to freight poor cuckoo creatures all over hell's half acre? No, sir, he'd settle down in Ioway. Tonight would be his start. He'd invest some capital and double or triple it. Then before long he'd move on out of Hebron, which was too tame for his taste, change his name again, and meet somebody who'd put him into a new kind of roust, profitable and surefire. But wait a minute. If he was staying on this side of the river, what was the use of buying Cuddy a headboard? No use. And goddammit, he'd already given Janz five dollars down. Oh, well, might as well pay the balance and have the thing. He'd probably stray along that way again sometime, and would put it up for her. If he'd earned his three hundred dollars, and the mules some corn, Cuddy was sure due something to mark her grave.

Briggs slept on that and, when he woke, surged off the bed with excitement. It was already dark. He dressed in a hurry and betook himself downstairs and fisted the counter. She appeared with a candle, tall and skinny and bony and Cuddy as ever.

"Miss Hutchinson," he said, "I've had a hard day. Where does a man get a drink and play cards and have a good time around here?"

She looked down her nose. "I'm sure I don't know," she said.

"The hell you don't."

She had placed the candle on the counter, her big hands were at her sides, and he saw them turn into fists. "I'll thank you not to curse in my presence," she said, sounding so much like somebody else it gave him gooseflesh. "And if you're going to gamble, I'd like you to pay your bill now."

She had raised her voice, he was sure for the benefit of her mother, out back with ears flapping.

"I'll pay up when I'm ready," he gruffed.

She wasn't cowed. She looked his new duds up and down and set her chin. "If you can buy new clothes, you can pay my mother. You're eating her out of every penny she has. I wish you'd act like a gentleman, even if you're not, and pay what you owe."

"Come along."

Briggs reached across the counter, took her by an arm, and started her around the counter.

"No," she said, resisting.

"Come with me."

If he knew little about women, he knew even less about girls, but something, the touch of his hand, the urgency of his manner perhaps, persuaded her, and she allowed herself to be escorted out the door into the quiet street, away from her mother, out of candlelight into moonlight.

He got hold of her by both bare elbows, as a father might, or a big brother, looking close into her homely face. She trembled. The likeness still shook him. Cuddy's young sis. Or the child Cuddy never had. To recognize her dried his mouth and constricted his throat.

"Miss Tabby," he said, "I'll trade you. You tell me where I can have a good time, I'll give you a piece of good advice."

"You first," she said.

"Fair enough. When you grow up and marry, stay here. Don't fall for some dumb kid going west to farm it. Don't do that."

"Why not?"

Briggs shook his head. "Just don't."

At fifteen she didn't, couldn't, understand. He wanted to say for God's sake, girl, don't ride a wagon out there and live in a sod house and have a litter of brats and grow old before your time and go queer in the head and have somebody strap you in another wagon and carry you back here to your ma and pa who'll be dead and gone by then, but he didn't, he couldn't.

"Your turn," he said.

She pulled free of him. Her face twisted, and for a moment he feared she might cry on him.

"Candletown," she said, and rushed herself back into the hotel.

Candletown?

He stepped it off down the street and inquired of the man at the livery. Candletown was two places, the man said, a sort of saloon and a dance house, with women, take your pick. Where was it? Up the river road north, turn off east between two outfitters, take a lane into trees. So Briggs saddled up, left his cowcoat there as the night was warm, rode away north, turned around and rode south because he recalled Cuddy's headboard, reached the stone-cutter's, looked the board over, pronounced it satisfactory, and paid Janz, noticing as he did that after buying clothes and cartridges and tobacco and high-button shoes and paying Janz nine dollars his wad was much diminished. No matter—in an hour or two he'd have greenbacks coming out his ears. He tied the marker onto the bedroll behind his saddle, mounted up again and heeled the roan into a canter up north again, thinking, as he passed the Hutchinson House, he should maybe drop the board off, then thinking the hell with it, he didn't care to see that stick of a girl again, he was on the prowl.

Candletown.

There were indeed two places down a lane into trees and set in a clearing of stumps. One was ramshackle, part tent, part lean-to of poles, the tent with one side ripped open to the night and letting out yells and howls and the crash of shattering glassware. Its patrons were probably freighters and no-accounts and plain drunks out of the line of wagons waiting for the ferry at the Bellevue crossing, and to pass the time they were putting on a fight. Briggs had heard such a racket many a time. It was usually caused by stabs in the belly or kicks in the stones or bottles broken over heads. Fights were free entertainment, but he had money, and so gave his attention to the dance house. It was actually two houses, a small one to the right, from which wafted the scratchy strains of a fiddle. That was where they danced, must be, where the women were. But the small house was connected to a large one of two storeys by what they called in these parts a "dogtrot," which was a covered walkway. The open windows of the large house beckoned with light. Home sweet home.

Briggs dismounted, tied his animal to a stump near some others and several buggies, walked first to the dance house, and stood in the doorway. In a corner, a fiddler sawed out "Devil's Dream." At length Briggs could discern a half-dozen sweaty couples, men and women, shuffling round and round a wooden floor, silent and serious, and in the far wall doors to several cribs. He could wait on a woman. He turned and walked the twenty feet of dogtrot and opened a door and stepped in and thought he was in Heaven. The company of men at last. Every person in the place could stand up to piss.

This house was a single room, two storeys high, well-lit by hanging coal-oil lamps. It boasted a handsome oaken bar and glassware, a chuck-a-luck layout, and at least fourteen tables of cards at which sat a smatter of the solid citizens of Hebron and the area thereabouts. It wasn't noisy. Poker here was bread-and-butter. The players were fairly well-dressed and sober, and even the house gamblers, whom he could spot by their fancy hats and white shirts and ruffled cuffs, looked to be gents. The last thing he searched for was firearms, and couldn't locate a one. What was under his belt was more than an equalizer then; if necessary, it was an ace in the hole.

Briggs strolled to the bar and had two whiskeys in short order, poured from a bottle. The man pouring was middle-aged and rigged out like a deacon—shirt, cravat, vest, gold watchchain, and a gold ring. Briggs judged it the best whiskey he had ever imbibed, and it should have been at fifty cents a crack. It warmed all the way to the crotch. He leaned on the bar until he selected a likely table, then moved casually to it, pulled out a chair, and sat down. There were three players, two town men and a gambler with a waxed mustache. The three nodded. They were between hands.

"Evening," said the gambler, riffling the deck. "We're playing higher stakes, sir. Can you show fifty dollars?"

Briggs looked him dead in the eye. It seemed to him he'd waited half a lifetime for this moment.

"I sure can," he said.

From the inner breast pocket of his new suit he brought out his pile. Unfolding it, he laid a fifty-dollar note on the Bank of Loup in the center of the table and proceeded to lay the other five, one by one, on top of it.

"That enough?" he asked.

The gambler reached for the topmost note. "Mind if I have a look?"

"Help yourself."

The gambler inspected it, then raised an arm and

waved at the man behind the bar, who worked his way through the tables.

The gambler handed him the note. "Will you have a look at this, Mr. Carmody?"

Carmody glanced at Briggs. "I own this place," he said. He, too, studied the note, then placed it on the table beside the others. "Bank of Loup," he said to Briggs. "Up near Wamego, I hear. How long since you were there, sir?"

"Five, six weeks," Briggs said.

"Well, the Bank of Loup's gone bust," said Carmody. "Man was through here from the Territory last week and said so. That's what happens with these sodbuster banks. I've been stuck with a lot of their paper." He nodded at Briggs. "I'm sorry, sir, I can't accept those notes. For that matter, I don't know anybody around here will."

Briggs sat his chair. Carmody, the gambler, the other two players, all watched him. But he thought he'd been hurled from the chair to the floor. He thought a thunderclap had deafened him. He thought a lightning bolt had riven him, had split him apart. He thought he was stone dead.

"I'm sorry, sir," Carmody said to him again, and went back to the bar.

Pushing the banknotes over to Briggs, the gambler shuffled his deck and dealt hands to the two town men and himself. They played the hand, discarding and drawing and betting. The gambler won it with two pairs, jacks and treys. He riffled the deck and looked curiously at Briggs.

"I'm sorry, sir," he said, "but it's a policy of this house that you can't claim a seat at a table unless you play. I have to ask you to leave."

"What," Briggs mumbled.

"I must ask you to leave the table."

Briggs looked around it. Suddenly he tried to rise, failed, then struggled to his feet, knocking over his chair in the process. From his belt he pulled the Colt's repeater, slowly, raised it at arm's length, and fired a round into the ceiling.

The effect was miraculous. Play ceased, and conversation. Not a man in the room moved a muscle. Briggs let the pistol down to his side.

"Now everybody listen," he said.

He was hoarse. They had to strain to hear him.

"My name is Jack Martin. I've just had six weeks on the trail, down from Loup. I carried four women in a wagon. Wives and mothers. They were crazy. That's right, crazy. Lost their minds last winter. They couldn't stay home. No asylum in the Territory. So I brought 'em here for the Reverend Carter's wife, the Methodist minister. Her and some church ladies will take 'em on home, to their folks. If you won't take my word, ask Missus Carter." He spoke in bursts. "Well, I had a hell of a time getting 'em here. I was paid three hundred dollars for the job, at the start—that's the money right there." He pointed down at the table. "I could've taken it and left 'em out there high and dry, but I didn't, I stuck it out. Missus Carter says I did a splendid deed— that's what she said. And I should be proud of it."

He paused to run a hand over his face. "But I bought new clothes and came here tonight to have a good time and my money's no good. Bank of Loup's gone bust. I'm dead broke. I need to get drunk. I need a bottle bad. After all I did, won't somebody buy me a bottle?"

He waited. The only response was the scratch of a fiddle down the dogtrot.

"I'm no beggar," Briggs insisted. "I've got my pride, same as anybody."

Someone coughed.

Briggs glared around the room. "You goddam cheapskate heartless bunch," he said. "After what I did for those poor women."

Again he waited.

"This is a Christian town!" he cried. "What the hell's the matter with you!"

Carmody, the owner, spoke up from behind the bar. "Martin, come over here. Put that gun away and come here."

Briggs stared at him.

"Come on," Carmody urged.

Briggs stuffed the weapon under his belt and, leaving the banknotes on the table, started slowly for the bar in the wrong direction. He bumped into a table, turned, and walked the wrong way again. While the crowd watched, silent, curious, it took him several starts in several directions to shuffle where he intended to go in the first place. As soon as he reached the bar, the room came alive with voices and the scrape of chairs.

Carmody took a bottle from a row, eased around one end of the bar, and put a friendly hand on Briggs's arm. "Let's go outside," he said. "Where we can talk private. What say?"

They went outside, to the dogtrot, and the owner closed the door behind them.

"You all right, Martin?" he asked.

"I dunno."

"Well, I don't want you taking this personally. I have to watch the wildcat paper from out your way. I've had to eat some of it."

Briggs nodded.

"Anyway, that was quite a story, about the women," Carmody continued. "I get a lot of poor devils through here out of the Territory. Down and out, they claim. Foreclosed, wives died, I've heard everything. And all they want is a drink or a drunk. Do I believe 'em? I better not. I supplied 'em all, I'd have to shut up shop. But I've never heard a yarn like yours. Crazy women." He looked at his bottle, shaking his head. "So damn farfetched it just might be true."

"Goddammit," Briggs mumbled.

"All right, all right. I know Altha Carter and I'll ask her. But I half-believe you. So here's half a bottle of my best." He offered it. "You can get half-drunk. Fair enough?"

Briggs took it.

"Just do it somewhere else, will you?"

Briggs nodded. Carmody clapped him on the shoulder. "Goodnight then, Martin. And better luck to you."

He went back inside, and Briggs at once uncorked the bottle. He had never known a thirst as mighty. He hoisted, had a long pull, and almost choked. Corking it, he stood in the dogtrot until the whiskey hit bottom. At the other place, the tent lean-to, the fight was over. In the dance house, the fiddler played "We'll All Go Down to Rouser's." Presently he started out to find his horse and had the same difficulty he'd had trying to find the bar. He started through the tree stumps in several different directions. He wandered around amongst the animals and bumped into a buggy. He had once met a farmer who'd been struck by lightning while running from his stable to his house during a storm. It had knocked him down, and he lay on the ground under the thunder and thought he was dead. When he discovered he wasn't, and got up, he couldn't figure how to get to his house. His head was on backward. He started this way and that way and had a hell of a time covering the fifty feet to his target. It took that farmer, in the end, a day or two to locate himself. George Briggs could scarcely comprehend the size and the significance of what had happened to him. He had lost his capital without playing a hand. Six fifty-dollar banknotes had turned into ass-wipes. It wasn't his fault or Cuddy's or the gambler's or Carmody's. It was the banker's, up in Loup, and maybe not even his, and maybe not even the big bastard bankers back east. It was nobody's. Splendid deed! It was even splendider than Altha Carter thought because he'd done it for nothing! Half a bottle of whiskey! Shit! Now, finally, Briggs found his horse and, thankful, got some more good out of the bottle. After he untied, however, he had trouble mounting up and holding the bottle. It might have been the whiskey as well as the lightning. He shoved the bottle into a side pocket and tried again. This time his boot rising kicked the headboard out of the rope that bound it to his bedroll. He cursed and found it by grubbing around on the ground in the moonlight, then vised it under his left arm, and this time, the third, managed to clamber up and hang on to reins and marker and settle into the stirrups.

Farewell, Candledamntown. He trotted to the river road intending to turn left, south, toward Hebron, but his head was still on backward and he turned right, north, toward the crossing.

To be ready for business at break of day, the ferry was tied up to the east bank of the river. Fires burned low in the stand of tall trees where the freight and emigrant trains were camped and asleep, waiting for that daybreak. Under a moon like a great goldpiece the Missouri lay, a long molten line between the known and the unknown.

Briggs rode down the bank and on board, hooves echoing off the hollow scow. Halfway he hauled up and slid down and dropped the headboard with a thump and tied his horse to a downstream side-rail.

312

Shoving the board to the rail with a boot, he sat down heavily beside it with his back against a stanchion, slipped bottle from pocket, and had a slow, melancholy swallow.

It occurred to him he had left his cowcoat at the livery stable and his saddlebags in the room at the hotel.

It occurred to him that most of his worldly goods he now had with him on the ferry: a hard-mouth horse, new suit and hat, saddle, rifle, repeater, cartridges for both, a bowie knife, a grave marker, and a few greenbacks, how few he was too drunk to care or count.

One night and one day in Ioway and he had been stitched, hemmed, tucked, corded, and embroidered. Of course, some of it was his own damn fault.

He never should have given Altha Carter the mules and wagon. Goddammit, he could have got at least fifty dollars for them.

He should have brought his cowcoat and saddlebags with him.

He wished he had a pickle.

He should never have splurged three dollars on high-button shoes for Tabitha Hutchinson.

He wished he had let Cuddy teach him to read. Maybe he should have cozied up to her and married her after all. She had been one hell of a woman.

He should have kept and sold the cameo.

Even without thinking, he'd decided to cross the river and return to the Territory. It was home to him now. He'd hitch on to an emigrant train and guide and hunt for his keep and a bedroll, then cut loose and make tracks for Wamego.

Once there, he might set himself up as a lightning-rod agent, which he'd heard was a slick play. You sold a set to some dumb sodbuster, took his money, gave him a receipt, and told him your partner and the wagon would be along the next day with his rods. All you needed was a set of rods to show, and you could make a pile in no time provided you kept moving.

Briggs drained the bottle and set it down beside him. He was splendidly drunk now. There was the headboard. Fourteen dollars. Walnut looked a lot nicer. Pulling it into his lap, he studied the letters of the inscription:

MARY B. CUDY
GOD LOVED HER AND
TOOK HER UNTO HIM

He thought it just right. Then it occurred to him he had wasted fourteen dollars. He could never spot that lone cottonwood, he could never in a thousand years find her grave. The damn board would be a hindrance to him, and pester him, and haunt him. He had an idea.

He put the board down, lay down himself, turned over, stuck his head over the side of the scow, and his new hat fell off and floated away.

"Son of a bitch," he said.

He saw stars in the water. The river back-sucked, then boiled up from below, freed of the ferry.

"Christ!" he exclaimed, and withdrew his head like a turtle. The head of a great big green alligator had broken the surface, its eyes red, its gaping jaws terrible with teeth. Briggs closed his eyes and broke into a sweat. After a spell he dared look again, and the gator was gone.

With his left hand he found the headboard and lowered it to the water. With his right he grasped the bottle and stood it upright on the inscription, then let the marker go. Away they rafted, board and bottle and haunt, and he followed them with his gaze as they drifted downstream in the golden moonlight, followed them until they sank in shadow.

He pulled back then, and lying there on his belly beside his roan, cheek against the planking, closed his eyes again. It seemed to him he heard the grind and rattle of the frame wagon, and the women wailing. He tried, but couldn't recall their names right then.

He slept.

When he woke the moon was down, the stars were dying, and the night was late and dark.

Beside him, on sentry duty, stood his horse.

With a grunt he hauled himself by the rail to his feet, yawned, stretched, and spat over the side.

The river rolled, dredging and drowning and doing

as it damn well pleased. In the stand of trees on the bank there were no fires now, no sounds.

A wind blew softly from the west, from the long plains. He sniffed. It had a clean, open smell, as though borne over lands where a man might still be his own master. In the dawn of the new day he would be the first across the river, the first to set foot again on free soil.

Briggs felt fine. The drunk had done him good. He began to hum "Weevily Wheat," and presently, moving to the center of the ferry, started to dance a kind of jig, or hoe-down, throwing himself into it like a bear into berries. His boots beat on the drum of the deck, he clapped hands, he flapped his arms as though they were wings, and soon he commenced to sing at the top of his voice:

> Take her by her lily-white hand
> And lead her like a pigeon,
> Make her dance the weevily wheat
> And scatter her religion.
>
> Charley here and Charley there
> And Charley over the ocean,
> Charley, he'll come back some day
> If he don't change his notion.

Suddenly he was brought up short by angry shouts from the trees cursing him, and some dogs barked at him. He snaked the repeater from his belt, cocked it, and fired a shot into the trees. That muzzled 'em, by God, men and curs. Briggs was tickled. He liked to run a bluff. The truth was, he'd never shot anybody, but scared a-plenty, and he'd sure as hell learned how to make men sit up and take notice. He belted the pistol, wiped black burn off his gun hand on his new pants, and began to jig and sing again:

> O Charley, he's a nice young man,
> An' Charley he's a dandy,
> Every time he goes to town
> He brings the girls some candy.

The song ended, the night drowsed, but the homesman went on dancing. Dancing.

ABOUT THE AUTHOR

Over the last thirty years GLENDON SWARTHOUT has written fourteen novels, among them *They Came to Cordura, Where The Boys Are, The Shootist,* and with his wife, Kathryn, six books for children. They live in Scottsdale, Arizona.

LIFE ON THE FRONTIER

☐ **THE OCTOPUS by Frank Norris.** Rippling miles of grain in the San Joaquin Valley in California are the prize in a titanic struggle between the powerful farmers who grow the wheat and the railroad monopoly that controls its transportation. As the struggle flourishes it yields a grim harvest of death and disillusion, financial and moral ruin. "One of the few American novels to bring a significant episode from our history to life."—Robert Spiller (524527—$4.95)

☐ **THE OUTCASTS OF POKER FLAT and Other Tales by Bret Harte.** Stories of 19th century Far West and the glorious fringe-inhabitants of Gold Rush California. Introduction by Wallace Stegner, Stanford University. (523466—$4.50)

☐ **THE CALL OF THE WILD and Selected Stories by Jack London.** Foreword by Franklin Walker. The American author's vivid picture of the wild life of a dog and a man in the Alaska gold fields. (523903—$2.50)

☐ **LAUGHING BOY by Oliver LaFarge.** The greatest novel yet written about the American Indian, this Pulitzer-prize winner has not been available in paperback for many years. It is, quite simply, the love story of Laughing Boy and Slim Girl—a beautifully written, poignant, moving account of an Indian marriage. (522443—$3.50)

☐ **THE DEERSLAYER by James Fenimore Cooper.** The classic frontier saga of an idealistic youth, raised among the Indians, who emerges to face life with a nobility as pure and proud as the wilderness whose fierce beauty and freedom have claimed his heart. (516451—$2.95)

☐ **THE OX-BOW INCIDENT by Walter Van Tilburg Clark.** A relentlessly honest novel of violence and quick justice in the Old West. Afterword by Walter Prescott Webb. (523865—$3.95)

Prices slightly higher in Canada.

Buy them at your local

bookstore or use coupon

on next page for ordering.

⊘ SIGNET   (0451)

HOW THE WEST WAS WON

☐ **THE OUTSIDER by Frank Roderus.** Winner of the Spur Award! Leon Moses' life hung on his trigger finger. The odds were against him, but nobody was going to stop Leon from settling his well-earned spread. He was a black man who had to show a lot of folks that courage knew no color—that they'd have to stop his bullets before they stopped him.   (156102—$2.95)

☐ **FAST HAND by Karl Lassiter.** Judge Sebastian Hand sentences the Thornberry gang to the gallows for rape. But when they escape and slaughter Hand's kin, the judge trades in his gavel for a gun, and suddenly he's judge, jury, and executioner all in one.   (161106—$2.95)

☐ **THE BLOODY SANDS by E.Z. Woods.** Jess McClaren's dad owed his life to Joe Whitley, and now Whitley was at the end of his rope. Jess's dad was dead, and the father's debt was now the son's. So Jess arrived on a range where he could trust no one that wasn't dead to pay a dead man's debt with flaming guns. . . .   (152921—$2.95)

☐ **GAMBLER'S GOLD by Doyle Trent.** J.B. Watts liked no-limit poker and no-nonsense women, and now he was primed for both. He had come across a cache of gold in the New Mexico desert, and he figured his luck had turned. His luck had turned, all right—for the worse: J.B. had bucked a lot of odds, but never odds like these . . . with nobody drawing cards . . . and everybody drawing guns. . . .   (157206—$2.95)

☐ **GUNFIGHTER JORY by Milton Bass.** Jory draws fast and shoots straight when a crooked lawman stirs up a twister of terror. When Jory took on the job of cleaning up the town of Leesville, he didn't know it was split between a maverick marshal and a bribing banker. Jory was right in the middle— and the only way to lay down the law was to spell it in bullets. . . .   (150538—$2.75)

Prices slightly higher in Canada

Buy them at your local bookstore or use this convenient coupon for ordering.

NEW AMERICAN LIBRARY
P.O. Box 999, Bergenfield, New Jersey 07621

Please send me the books I have checked above. I am enclosing $_____
(please add $1.00 to this order to cover postage and handling). Send check or money order—no cash or C.O.D.'s. Prices and numbers are subject to change without notice.

Name_____

Address_____

City _____ State _____ Zip Code _____

Allow 4-6 weeks for delivery.

This offer, prices and numbers are subject to change without notice.